PEACH
CLOBBERED

PEACH CLOBBERED

ANNA GERARD

W🌐RLDWIDE

TORONTO • NEW YORK • LONDON
AMSTERDAM • PARIS • SYDNEY • HAMBURG
STOCKHOLM • ATHENS • TOKYO • MILAN
MADRID • WARSAW • BUDAPEST • AUCKLAND

W🌐RLDWIDE™

Recycling programs for this product may not exist in your area.

ISBN-13: 978-1-335-58954-5

Peach Clobbered

First published in 2019 by Crooked Lane Books,
an imprint of The Quick Brown Fox & Company LLC.
This edition published in 2023.

For questions and comments about the quality of this book, please contact us at CustomerService@Harlequin.com.

Harlequin Enterprises ULC
22 Adelaide St. West, 41st Floor
Toronto, Ontario M5H 4E3, Canada
www.ReaderService.com

Printed in U.S.A.

For my friends, Carol and Kathryn,
who remember the original.

ONE

IF THE INCIDENTS of the past few weeks are ever turned into one of those Hallmark Channel murder mysteries, I'll suggest the producers call it *Summer of the Penguins*. Which would be all the more ironic because I live in the small Georgia town of Cymbeline. Here, June temperatures climb well into the nineties, with the humidity equally off the scale. Not exactly a place conducive to our little friends from Antarctica.

And yet, when I answered the door of my three-story Queen Anne home that Saturday morning following Memorial Day, one of those black-and-white flightless birds was camped out on my doorstep. Unfortunately, the penguin in question proved to be but the first of several that I'd be encountering in the space of a few days.

At half past ten in the am, the temperature was already hot enough to drop you if you didn't stay properly hydrated. And that didn't count the humidity, which was thick enough to swim in. That was why I was dressed in ragged cutoff blue jeans and a faded I ♥ AUSTRALIAN SHEPHERDS T-shirt, with my brown hair rubber-banded into a messy ponytail and bangs held back with a sweaty red bandana.

After an hour spent prying errant crabgrass, chickweed, and the occasional nettle from the jade-colored St. Augustine grass that neatly blanketed my quarter-acre front lawn, I was dangerously close to "drop me" territory. I'd just gone inside to grab a tall, restorative glass of homemade lemonade when, from my kitchen, I heard a muffled pounding on my front door.

Matilda, my Australian shepherd and the reason for my doggy T-shirt, immediately scrambled to her fuzzy feet and let out a warning woof.

"It's okay, Mattie," I told her as, glass in hand, I headed to the front of the house again. "Probably more tourists. Don't worry, I'll run them off."

I wasn't kidding about the tourists. I had discovered within the first week of moving from my old condo in Atlanta to my new digs in Cymbeline that owning a historic home in a touristy town came with certain drawbacks. Not the least of which was random strangers knocking on one's door demanding a peek inside. It was probably time to get those rusty front gate hinges oiled so I could actually close said gate and keep out the riffraff. Because sometimes *riffraff* was code for really bad people coming to rob you and murder you in your sleep. Which was why, following my divorce a year earlier, I'd taken up my mother's habit of keeping a weapon by my bedside.

Hers was a Louisville Slugger, the hefty wooden kind that could send a kneecap flying over the left-field fence. Since my ex was a pro golfer, I'd opted for the more appropriate steel-shafted putter...lighter, and not quite so in-your-face until it actually was.

Not that I thought I was going to need my dark-alley equalizer on a bright weekend morning. Instead, I readied my rehearsed "Sorry, go away" speech, opened my paneled front door, and peered through the screen to the wraparound porch beyond. Uh-huh, definitely a penguin, though it stood close to six feet tall, a good six inches taller than me, and was big even for an emperor penguin. He would have been taller except that his head was missing. I located it a moment later tucked beneath one large flipper.

No, he had not been decapitated.

The displaced cranium was part of a costume, one of those big, goofy fleece outfits worn by theme park characters and sports team mascots. The costume-wearer's actual head poked out from between the penguin's oversized shoulders. Even though his black hair was plastered to his smooth forehead by a small river's worth of sweat, he was good-looking enough to pose for one of those "hunk of the month" calendars. You know the type: faintly tanned, a hint of five o'clock shadow, long-lashed blue eyes, neatly chiseled features that were neither too sensitive nor too craggy.

Unfortunately, his scowl as he gave me the once-over was dark enough to forestall any appreciation of said hunkiness. I met his sour expression with a cool look of my own. Obviously not a nosy tourist.

"Yes?" I inquired, even as a possible explanation occurred to me. *Maybe the high school cheer squad is getting a jump on candy sales for the fall semester?* Though, given the penguin's foul—or should I say, fowl?—attitude, I doubted he was selling many chocolate bars.

Then I recalled that the local football team was known as the Bards, one of the many Shakespearean references I'd seen in Cymbeline. Apparently, the town's founder had been smitten by a staging of Shakespeare's *Cymbeline* while in London a whole lot of seasons ago—as in, the 1890s—and had impulsively decided to name his new town after that play. Over the years, the locals had carried on the tradition by naming buildings and landmarks after Shakespeare's works. Penguins didn't factor into it. Besides, a closer look told me this guy was somewhere near my age of forty-one, meaning he was at least twenty years too old to be a high school senior.

The penguin, meanwhile, held out the flipper that wasn't clutching his spare head and waved a pale-purple envelope in my direction. The faintest scent of lilac from the perfumed stationery wafted toward me. In clipped tones overlaid with a hint of a soft Georgia accent, he said, "I have…the…letter."

Forget candy sales. This guy must have gone AWOL from the mental health wing of Cymbeline's small hospital. Though where in the heck he'd found a penguin costume to wear in the sweltering Georgia heat, I couldn't guess. As for the letter, I had no clue about that, either.

"The letter. Uh, yes. You have it. Uh, yes, you do," I stammered, trying for a conciliatory tone. Wasn't that how you were supposed to deal with crazy folks on the brink of snapping?

The attempt at appeasement apparently wasn't the right tactic, however, for the man's scowl deepened.

"The letter," he repeated through clenched teeth. "The one I told you about in the emails I sent you, and the voice mails I left you. If you'd bothered to answer any of my messages, we could have sorted this out weeks ago. You *are* Nina Fleet, aren't you?"

He'd pronounced it *Nee-nah*.

"Actually, it's *Nine-ah*, like the number *nine*," I reflexively corrected him. I always like to get that explanation out of the way immediately when I meet someone new. Not that I have anything against the Nee-nahs of the world. It's just that I've listened to my name regularly being mangled since kindergarten, so I've gotten rather snappish about it over the years.

Then realization hit with the impact of hailstones let loose from a midsummer thunderstorm. Now it was my turn to give *him* the hairy eyeball.

"That was you? You're Harry Westcott? The same guy who's been claiming I stole this house from you?" I sputtered. "Didn't you get that cease-and-desist from my attorney?"

I heard a growl behind me, and forty pounds of shaggy, tricolored canine pushed against the screen. Mattie had wisely deduced that I wasn't capable of running off intruders and had come to lend moral support. I shot her a grateful look. I'd always heard that dogs rescued from animal shelters were especially eager to defend their new families. Mattie was proving that rumor true.

On the other hand, it might not hurt to call the cops, just in case.

Westcott, meanwhile, had managed to pull the letter from its envelope, sending another wave of floral scent wafting skyward.

"Feel free to call the cops," he said, reading my mind, "but you might want to know that the sheriff and I went to high school together. And, just so we're on the same page, *my* attorney is reviewing the situation. He says I have a good case to contest the sale."

Before I could reply to that unsettling revelation, he

went on, "The proceeds of the house sale won't be distributed until we determine if my great-aunt's executor was authorized to sell the place. Auntie's letter"—he waved the lavender paper at me—"very specifically stated that she was going to leave her house to me. Believe me, you'll be saving us all a lot of time and trouble if you just agree to resell the place back to the estate at the same price you paid."

Sell back my house?

I shook my head. I might have lived in the house for only a couple of months, but the three-story Queen Anne was already like a family member to me.

I'd first stumbled across the place during an impulsive antiquing jaunt one weekend right as winter was wrapping up. I'd needed a change of pace from the Atlanta rat race, and a Saturday spent searching for vintage whatevers had sounded like fun. I'd yet to visit Cymbeline, despite the fact that it was one of the state's primo antiquing destinations, located as it was an hour outside Savannah. Thus, I'd decided to make a day of it there.

I never did get to do my planned antiquing. Instead, after taking a wrong turn into Cymbeline's historic district while trying to find the town square, I'd stopped my forest-green Mini Cooper on a quiet side street for a quick replotting of my GPS. That accomplished, I had put the Mini back into gear when I glanced over at the house I'd parked in front of.

In the movie version, that would have been the moment when an angelic choir gave a bell-like *aaahhhh*.

The home sat on a half-acre lot and was separated from the street by a head-high wrought-iron fence. A sprawling magnolia that had to be a good century old held sway over the far side of the lawn, looking like something out of *Gone With the Wind*. On the opposite side of the yard was the requisite peach tree, the variety known as Belle of Georgia Peach. A partially screened in wraparound porch reminded me of summers at my grandparents' place. And the snazzy green-and-yellow paint job on the place was straight from the pages of *Historic Home Digest*. Like the other tourists, I had gaped and sighed and pictured myself in a flowing white gown sitting in its porch swing. Then I'd noticed the For Sale sign on the gate.

Let me explain that this wasn't just a whim, buying a place in small-town Georgia. Atlanta held too many unhappy memories, and I wanted out of there. At my age, I was too old to return to Dallas and live with good old Mom (who would have greeted me with open arms and a chorus of "Told you so!"). And since I did like Georgia's slower pace, I'd been contemplating a move to one of its smaller touristy/historic towns.

Cymbeline fit the bill.

Shopping forgotten, I had whipped out my cell phone and called the real estate agent whose number was listed on the fence. Within five minutes, her baby-blue BMW had screeched to a halt behind the Mini. A bleached blonde pushing retirement age and sporting stiletto heels higher and white shorts shorter than I'd ever dare wear came striding toward me, manicured hand outstretched. We exchanged introductions—she was Debbie Jo MacAfee, Cymbeline's top-selling real estate agent for ten years running, according to her business card—and then she ushered me inside the place.

You know how when something seems too good to be true, it is? Well, for once, that wasn't the case. The inside was as spectacular as the outside, with plenty of fretwork around the doors, funky pink-and-green tile in the baths, and a formal Victorian staircase straight out of a movie. She'd explained to me that the previous owner had been an octogenarian who'd lived there her entire life; hence the time capsule look to many of the rooms. And it had gone on the market only the day before. Fearful that someone would snatch this beauty out from under me, I'd made an offer right there. The acceptance call had come before I left town that afternoon. Even better still, the sales price included whatever furnishings would be left from the upcoming estate sale.

Though my attorney (aka my cousin Kit) had read me the riot act for making such an impulsive buy, all had gone surprisingly smoothly. The required home inspection revealed the place to be in tip-top shape for its age, with no major issues beyond some minor cosmetic fixes. I'd signed the papers and moved in right after Easter, and had been living happily ever after since.

Bottom line, no way was I giving up my house. It would be like returning Mattie to the animal shelter.

"Look here, Mr. Westcott," I said aloud, struggling for an even tone. "I don't know what's going on with your great-aunt's estate, but it's not my problem. I bought this house fair and square. If you think I'm going to give it up just because you're in a snit about how the sale went down, then—oh, no!"

As I watched in dismay, the color abruptly drained from the man's face. He staggered into the door frame and then slid in a black-and-white heap onto the whitewashed boards of the porch. The penguin head, meanwhile, slipped from his grasp. Like an execution scene straight out of *Les Misérables*, the fake fur cranium went bouncing down the front porch steps and gently rolled to a stop in the cool St. Augustine grass. As for The Letter—I'd begun to think of it with capital letters—it flew from his other hand, flitting about like a startled purple butterfly before landing safely a few feet away.

It momentarily occurred to me that the man was faking a faint, just to get me outside so he could bludgeon me with a penguin flipper. Another look at his pale, sweating face told me differently. Forgetting that, ten seconds earlier, I'd been ready to call the cops on the guy, I shoved open the screen door.

"Great," I muttered a bit desperately as, setting down my lemonade, I knelt beside the fallen man. "Mr. Westcott, can you hear me?"

As best I could tell through the bulk of his costume, he had a heartbeat and was still breathing. His eyes were closed and he was still pale and sweating, but at least the latter symptom ruled out full-blown heatstroke—something I'd picked up from a long-ago first aid class. But it definitely looked like heat exhaustion, which wasn't anything to play around with.

"Mattie, fetch my phone!" I called over my shoulder.

The dog immediately trotted to the library, where I kept my cell plugged in during the day. Relieved I'd had the foresight to teach her that trick along with your basic *sit* and *stay*, I gave the unconscious man a small shake.

"Mr. Westcott! Harry!" I repeated. "Can you hear me? We need to get you out of that costume and into the air-conditioning. If you can't get up, I'm going to call 911."

I heard a whine behind me. Mattie, with my cell phone in her mouth, waiting patiently.

"Good girl," I told her as I reached around the screen door and retrieved it. Wiping a bit of dog drool off its case, I gave Westcott another shake.

"Last chance, Mr. Westcott. Open your eyes, or you're getting hauled out of here in an ambulance."

"No need," Westcott croaked, opening his baby blues just a crack. "I'm fine. But if you could spare a small glass of water…"

I snatched up my lemonade and, supporting his head, held it to his lips. He drained half the glass in a single long gulp and then handed it back to me.

"Much better," he muttered, eyes open all the way now and sounding somewhat restored. Then, glimpsing the phone in my hand, he flailed a bit until he had dragged himself into a sitting position.

"No ambulance. Just a little too much sun. Give me another minute."

I shook my head. Last thing I wanted was a crazy penguin guy in my house, but common decency wouldn't allow me to leave him out in the heat until I knew he was okay.

"Okay, we'll hold off on the ambulance," I told him as, setting aside the glass, I scrambled to my feet. "But I'm not about to let you wander off in your current condition. If I give you a hand, can you stand up long enough to get through the front door and into the parlor?"

He managed a nod. Since there was no way I could lift him on my own, I did the next best thing. Shoving my phone into my pocket, I grabbed the shoulder of his black fleece costume and tugged.

While he struggled to regain his footing, I dug in my heels and leaned backward as ballast. Once he was upright again, I slid my shoulder beneath one flipper and walked him past the screen door, then used my foot to slam the main door shut after us. Medical emergency or not, I wasn't about to pay to air-condition all of Cymbeline.

Cool air flowed over us as we stood in my main hallway that ran shotgun-style down the middle of the house. I had plans to eventually brighten up the narrow passage with a fresh coat of pale-coral paint. For now, however, I was living with decades-old dark paneling and remnants of the home's original portrait gallery: a couple of truly creepy oils featuring grim babies dressed like small adults, several hand-tinted photos of ethereal young women, and a battered daguerreotype of a teen-age Confederate soldier.

It occurred to me that, since the house had belonged to Westcott's great-aunt, presumably these were his long-dead relatives.

Mattie trailing after us, I steered him down the hall to the parlor. There I dumped him onto one of the two antique blue velvet sofas that were original to the place.

"Take that suit off. I'm getting some ice."

A confession: I'd never been much of a Suzy Home-maker, even when I was married. But despite lacking the foodie gene, I had fallen in love with my new kitchen. Heck, I'd even bought Julia Child's French cookbook. Not that I'd tried any of the recipes yet, but the classic volume sure looked good propped on a wooden book stand on the counter.

The kitchen itself was a brash combination of late-nineteenth-century architecture and early-twenty-first-century technology. The counter-to-ceiling, glass-front cabinets, painted a crisp white, were original to the home, as was the whitewashed floor with its scattering of rag rugs. And the farm-style stone sink that was big enough to bathe in had been plumbed in during the nineties—the 1890s—though I'd seen that same style featured in any number of recent decorating magazines.

Surprisingly, Westcott's great-aunt had also liked her modern bells and whistles. The stove was a ceramic-topped electric model, and the programmable electric oven and oversized microwave each came with an inch-thick manual. As for the refrigerator, it was a jumbo side-by-side with water and ice in the door.

I grabbed a vintage embroidered dish towel from a drawer and dispensed a double handful of ice cubes for a makeshift ice pack. Then, hoping I hadn't made a terrible mistake in letting the man inside, I headed back to check on my unwelcome guest.

TWO

I RETURNED TO the parlor to find that, per orders, West-cott had stripped off the penguin costume, leaving a puddle of black-and-white faux fur on my faded Persian rug. He lay equally puddled on the sofa where I'd originally left him. Mattie had parked herself on the floor, looking rather like a rug herself. Her wavy black, gray, and white–splotched coat and bobbed Aussie tail made her resemble a bear cub, though I'd never seen a bear with one blue eye and one brown like hers. Stoic as any bruin, her multihued gaze was fixed on our unwelcome visitor's unmoving form.

I stopped short and did a little staring, too.

Stripped of the yards of baggy faux fur that had previously enveloped him, Westcott had the long, lean look of a dancer. In deference to the heat, all he'd been wearing beneath that portable sauna was a pair of black bike shorts and a matching black tank top. The skimpy shorts emphasized tanned, muscled thighs, while the wife-beater shirt showed off a satisfactory amount of smooth chest and nicely rippled arms.

Then, reminding myself of my Florence Nightingale mission, I gave myself a stern mental shake and headed toward him again.

"You alive?"

I wasn't kidding with that question. Living in Texas

and Georgia all my life, I knew that heat really could kill. And even though he'd ditched his mascot costume and was lying in a nice, air-conditioned parlor now, he was still sweating.

I gave a quick prayer of thanks for the oversized doilies pinned to either arm of the antique couch. Antimacassars, I knew they were called—the nineteenth-century housewife's solution for protecting upholstered furniture from gentlemen's hair pomade. In his case, the fragile velvet was protected from an unseemly amount of sweat.

He opened his eyes and frowned, though whether it was at my questions or Mattie's penetrating gaze, I couldn't guess. Straightening into a more upright position, he answered in an ungracious tone, "Yeah, I'll survive."

"Well, don't overdo the thanks," was my own equally snide comeback.

I couldn't help it. Hunk or not, something about the man set my teeth on edge. Shooing Mattie to one side, I slapped the ice pack on the back of Westcott's neck, adding, "Here, hold this in place. It'll help get your core temperature down."

He winced as the cold bundle contacted skin, but he obediently raised a hand to support the ice-filled towel. While he huddled on the couch in sullen silence, I made a quick foray outside again for my forgotten lemonade.

What caught my eye first, however, was that ridiculous penguin head lying in the grass. If I'd left Mattie outside, no doubt she would have made a soccer ball of it already. Not far from the head was the lavender letter that had taken flight from the porch and now gently fluttered in a welcome bit of breeze. The matching purple envelope had landed nearby. I snatched up both and stashed envelope and letter in the rear waistband of my shorts. Then, grabbing the lemonade glass, I head back inside again.

"You might as well finish this off," I told Westcott as I thrust the half-full glass at him. "According to my grandmother, lemonade is an old folk cure for combating overheating."

Westcott obediently took the glass and began drinking again. Meanwhile, I retreated to the matching sofa across from him and debated my strategy.

Kick him out once the lemonade was gone and let him fend for himself? Or, let him stay a few minutes longer while I pumped him for more info so I could report back to my own lawyer on his wild accusation?

I opted for the latter.

"All right, first things first," I began. "Why in the heck are you running around town in ninety-degree weather in a penguin costume, of all things?"

"It's not a costume, it's a mascot outfit," he corrected in lofty tones. "I have a summer gig depicting Freezie the Penguin, mascot for the Taste-Tee-Freeze Creamery."

"Oh, yeah, that place on the town square with that big neon ice cream cone hanging in front."

He nodded. I'd stopped there the week before, mostly because of their great retro sign. But the decadent scoop of mocha I tried had been some of the best ice cream I'd ever tasted. Despite the soft serve imagery on the sign, this was the home-churned variety with the optional "slice and dice mixers" on a cold marble slab. And the rolled ice cream offerings in the freezer case looked like something out of a bakery. It didn't hurt that the husband and wife owners, Jack and Jill Hill—yes, really!—handed out plenty of samples.

Then I frowned, wondering how best to delicately put my next question. After all, a summer spent as a costumed character was a job more suitable for a high school kid than someone his age.

"So, uh, what led you to work as a mascot?"

"I'm not working. I'm acting. That's what I do…act."

The look he gave me was chilly as the scoop of mocha swirl ice cream had been. I gave a wary nod in return. When you no longer have to pull the old eight-to-fiver, it's easy to forget that not everyone else has that luxury. Not that I hadn't suffered through my share of grunt jobs back before the ex hit it big. But a grown man being paid to dress like a penguin was, well, kind of sad. As for the "acting" claim, I had to wonder a bit at that. Given his hunky good looks, Westcott probably could have landed a leading role on some cable TV show or another if he'd had even a smidgeon of talent.

"So, you're an actor," I went on with an encouraging smile. "Have you been in anything I might have seen?"

His expression went slightly more glacial, and I promptly realized my mistake. Kind of like asking a writer if I might have read any of her books, or asking a painter in what galleries his painting hung. The implication was that one should have been familiar enough with the artiste's oeuvre not to have had to ask.

"Probably not," he replied, "unless you go for survival horror flicks…you know, zombies and radioactive zoo animals and high school kids being stalked by something they dug up in the neighborhood cemetery.

That's pretty much my gig these days. Oh, I shot a pilot back before Christmas—an undercover cop series— that's supposed to be shopped around this summer."

"Great, I hope it sells," I replied, meaning it. If he did get a full-time gig, as he termed it, maybe he'd forget about me and the house. Speaking of which…

Reaching behind me, I pulled the letter and envelope from my waistband and, reflexively mimicking his previous actions, shook the former in his direction. "Now, it's time to talk about this."

"Hey!"

He set down the glass on the table—on a coaster, I was impressed to see—and flailed an arm in my direction. I noticed that his fingernails appeared neatly trimmed and recently buffed, unlike mine. He growled, "That's my property."

"Well, it was lying on my property," I reminded him, easily evading his attempt, "and you know what they say about possession being nine-tenths of the law. Don't worry, I'll give it back. I just want to see what's in it that makes you think you should have inherited this house."

I suspected from his outraged expression that, had he been feeling better, he'd have grabbed hold of my wrist and pried the letter from my hand. But he must have still been suffering the aftereffects of his faint, for he gave a grudging nod.

"Sure, read it. You'll have a chance to examine it when I take you to court, anyhow."

The return address was indeed mine: 1957 Pettistone Lane, Cymbeline, Georgia. As for the mailing address, it impressed me a little, since it was a PO box in Hollywood, California. Apparently, good old Harry—or,

rather, Mr. Harold A. Westcott III, as he was addressed
on the envelope—really was serious about an acting
career, though I suspected the PO box was for receiv-
ing mail only, and that he'd actually lived in one of
the seedier parts of Los Angeles county. The postmark
showed the letter had been sent the previous October,
which would have been a couple of weeks prior to old
Mrs. Lathrop's death.

I pulled the letter from the envelope, cleared my throat
(the perfumed paper was starting to get to me), and began
reading the elegant if slightly shaky cursive aloud.

My dearest Harold,
It was a pleasure seeing you last week. I do not
like to complain (though, as an old woman, some
would say I have earned that right!), but it does
seem that the rest of the family has forgotten me,
so I am doubly grateful for your attention. And
you do know that I have not been well these past
few months.

Fortunately, Hendricks checks in on me when
he comes out twice a week to do the landscap-
ing. Oh, and that lovely Gemma Tanaka from the
coffee shop—surely you remember her?—brings
me a nice meal every Monday. So whenever my
number is up, as they so crudely put it, there is a
good chance I will be found within a day or so.

But, enough of such morbid thoughts. In-
stead, let me get to the point of my letter. I will
be scheduling a visit with my attorney in the next
few weeks, as I feel it is time that I update my Last
Will and Testament a final time. As you obviously

are aware, your dearly departed great-uncles
both left substantial estates to their children—
your father, and your aunts and uncles. And that
meant, in turn, that you and your cousins would
be equally well provided for down the road.

Knowing that, my intention had always been
that my estate be liquidated and, save for a few
small bequests, have the proceeds given to certain
charities that I've supported over the years. But I
recently learned what your father did as far as his
own will, and I must say that I quite disapprove.

I paused and glanced over the letter at Westcott. I
had a feeling I knew what his dear old dad had done,
but I wasn't quite crass enough to ask. Fortunately for
my curiosity's sake, he confirmed my guess.

"It was the usual," he said with a careless shrug
that didn't mask a certain hardness in his expression.
"Wealthy, respectable real estate mogul father disap-
proves of his wastrel son's choice of an acting career.
Father threatens to cut off son without a penny unless
he gives up all that foolishness. Son refuses and tells
the father that he doesn't want the father's money. Father says fine, and cuts the son out of the will. The end."

"Tough break," I replied, feeling somewhat sympathetic as I resumed reading.

"As you know, I am a firm believer in real estate
as an investment," I recited; then, flipping the page, I
stopped short as I silently read the next line.

Westcott—or, rather, Harry, as I was beginning to
think of him, now that I knew his life story—gave me
a bland look. Of course, he had the letter memorized.

"Do continue," he urged. "We're just now getting to the good part."

You mean, the part you're going to hang your lawsuit on. But as I continued to hesitate, he leaned forward and in a swift move snatched the letter from me.

"Now, where were we?" he asked. "Ah, yes here we are." Ostentatiously clearing his throat, he took up where I'd left off.

As you know, I am a firm believer in real estate as an investment, and so I've changed my mind about letting my place be sold for cash when I'm gone. Instead, I have decided that I shall arrange for the house and its contents to go to you, my favorite young relative. I hope you'll be pleased with that bequest, and that you'll keep up the place for awhile before you sell it off. I know that you are the only one of the family besides me who truly loves this old house, so I am confident I will be leaving it in capable hands.

But, I must ask you to keep this information to yourself until all the documents are signed. I don't want anyone else—particularly your father—to find out about my plans and start badgering me to change my mind. Once all is settled, I'll send you a note to let you know that, no matter what else may happen in the future, you'll always have a roof over your head.

I shall sign off now and put in a call to the attorney's office. I hope you'll make it back here for Christmas, at least for a short visit. Until then, much love from your Great-Aunt Daisy Lathrop.

Finishing his reading, Harry refolded the lavender page and tucked it back into the envelope I'd set on the coffee table. He fixed me with a cool look.

"Unfortunately, Great-Aunt Lathrop died in her sleep a couple of nights before she was scheduled to meet with her lawyer, and so she never had the opportunity to change her will. But you can see from this letter that her intent was obvious."

I managed a casual shrug, trying to ignore a little frisson of panic welling in the pit of my stomach. Sure, he had a letter, but I had the executed deed along with the copy of the cashed check that had made this house owned by me outright.

Mine, mine, mine, I thought, and mentally stamped my feet for emphasis. But even though the place legally belonged to me, I had to admit that Harry Westcott had had good reason to believe he was supposed to inherit it.

Assuming, of course, that the letter wasn't some crazy forgery the man was trying to perpetrate. Or a clever con meant to scam me out of the house. He was an actor, after all. No way would I simply take him at his word.

Doing my best impression of Cousin Kit, Esq., I said, "I agree, Mr. Westcott, that your letter is compelling. But why did you wait until after the house was sold to me to bring it up? Why didn't you contest the will right away?"

"I was in Mexico shooting that pilot. I didn't even find out that Great-Aunt Lathrop had died until I got back to LA almost two months after the funeral. By then, the executor had already liquidated most of her assets and was putting the house up for sale."

He muttered a few expletives, and I ventured a quick assumption. "Let me guess, your father was the executor?"

"Give the lady a prize. You got it in one."

The barely contained outrage in his expression made him look like a brooding antihero from that cable TV series featuring lots of castles, dragons, and swords. Luckily, Westcott was unarmed at the moment; otherwise, I could see him whipping out an oversized dirk and slicing up my nice red velvet curtains as a substitute for disemboweling dear old Dad. No matter the legalities, the man truly believed he had a claim to this house. That, or he was a heck of an actor who deserved every award the Academy could hand out.

But, either way, I had a bad feeling that Harold A. Westcott III wasn't going to go gentle into that good night…not until he had his sneaky penguin flippers on my house.

Abruptly, I stood.

"This has all been most illuminating," I told him, "but if you're recovered enough, I think it's best you take your costume and leave. If you want to pursue this thing with your letter, you've got my attorney's contact information. Now, do you want me to call you an Uber, or can you walk?"

"I brought my own transportation, thank you very much."

With those lofty words, he rose from the sofa and scooped up the penguin suit. Then, Mattie doing her herding pup thing by literally dogging his steps, he headed for the door. "No need to show me out," he added over his shoulder. "I know this place like it was my own."

If I hadn't been suddenly terrified that my peaceful small-town life was about to go all to heck, I would have enjoyed the sight of those muscled glutes exiting stage right. As it was, I simply scampered after the pair, making sure Harry didn't filch a painting or side table on the way out.

Once he reached the porch, he turned and fixed me with a hard look. Then, quite to my surprise, he gave me a genuine smile—the kind of smile that belonged plastered on the cover of *People* magazine's latest "Sexiest Man Alive" issue.

"This whole your house/my house quandary aside," he said, "it was a pleasure meeting you. I'd heard the new owner was some big-city rich woman looking for a cheap investment. But I can tell you care about the place, too. And you didn't just roll me out to the curb when I was dying of heatstroke."

Then the 1,000-watt smile vanished. "See you in court, Nina Fleet."

So saying, he strode down the porch steps, scooped up the penguin head without breaking stride, and marched toward the front gate. The dramatic exit was marred somewhat when he paused there and pulled on the bulky penguin suit again. Only then did I notice the rusty red men's bicycle that had been leaning up against one gate pillar. He straddled said bike and balanced the penguin head in the wire basket attached to its handlebars.

Then, like Shane or Clint Eastwood's *Man With No Name*, he gave a push off and vanished from sight.

I glanced down at Mattie, who was sitting beside me, canine gaze fixed on the front gate. She hadn't gone off on the man like a hellhound, which I'd seen her do a time or two in Atlanta when we'd been approached by a sketchy sort. That meant Harry Westcott wasn't a physical danger to me. But if his case did make it to court, between the letter and his dramatic abilities, I could well find myself in an unpleasant standoff.

"I think I'd better get to know the enemy," I told Mattie, who gave a soft woof of agreement.

Forgetting about weeding, I hurried back inside and took a quick shower to remove the worst of the accumulated dirt and sweat. Then, leaving Mattie to lounge in the AC, I grabbed my keys, phone, and requisite sunglasses and walked the two blocks to Peaches and Java, the coffee shop on the town square, to check out the penguin's story.

THREE

SINCE CYMBELINERS TENDED TO rise bright and early, even on the weekend, plenty of my neighbors were out in the steaming Georgia morning. And so I did a lot of waving as I walked, even though I knew most of the folks only by sight at this point. I still found the ritual something of a novelty, given that I'd lived the past ten years in Atlanta. While the state's capital retained much of its original Southern charm, in a city of almost half a million people, no way were you going to greet every stranger you passed.

I reached the town square a few minutes later. As was typical in the South, it consisted of a small, park-like block with an old-style bandstand in its center. That white-painted wooden structure was large enough to hold the entire high school orchestra, and was still draped with red, white, and blue bunting left over from Memorial Day. Concrete walks stretched from the bandstand to each corner of the square, forming an X if you looked at it from a drone's point of view. A boiled-peanut cart parked on one corner of the square sold that popular regional treat. I gave the burly young man who owned the cart a smile as I walked past.

The remaining space was meticulously maintained grass, along with a few shrub arrangements and benches, plus a couple of mature live oak trees for additional shade. The streets surrounding the square were all one way, with angled-in parking along both the square itself and the four facing streets with their lines of shops. Here, amid a series of red-bricked, two-story buildings with neat white trim, the astute tourist found most of the town's Shakespeare-inspired business names... Sweets to the Sweet (a bakery), Perchance to Dream (a linens store), First Folio (a bookstore), and several more.

But most important to me, as a taxpayer, there wasn't an empty storefront to be seen in the Cymbeline town square.

As I'd hoped, morning rush was over at Peaches and Java. The lunch customers would not be out in full force for another half hour. That meant the owners, Gemma and Daniel Tanaka, would likely have a few minutes to chat while preparing for the noon shift. (As a side note, I'd previously asked Gemma, who was born and bred in Cymbeline, why their shop didn't have a Shakespearean-themed name. She'd pointed out that coffee wasn't common in England until after the playwright's death. Duh!)

On the walk over, I'd called Gemma to warn her that I needed to discuss my predecessor's family, so she was prepared. Barely had I taken a seat inside the coffee shop than she slid her slim, five-foot form into the chair across from me. I stared at her in mock dismay.

"How do you do it? If I were around this much good food every day, I'd be big as a house."

"Honey, I'd be that big, too, except that I run my butt off all morning long baking and setting up for two sittings."

Gemma wore her chin-length graying hair in twisted

locks, which she now gave a rueful shake. Then, with a glance at her husband, who was behind the counter mixing up a multihued pasta salad, she added, "You can see who doesn't do all the heavy lifting around here."

Daniel, who was perhaps two inches taller than me and close to two hundred pounds heavier, merely shot his wife a placid grin.

"Love you, too, honey." To me, he said, "There's some of my artisan peach cobbler left over from breakfast, Nina. You want a serving?"

My mouth began to water, picturing the dessert for which Daniel was famous…hence, the Peaches and Java name. Not only did he use locally grown fruit, but he piled the sliced peaches and spices into individual ramekins held down by a fancy lacework of buttery pastry that put the traditional lattice crust to shame. The sweet concoction was topped with a chilly dollop of amaretto-flavored whipped cream that beat the heck out of vanilla ice cream any day.

He didn't wait for my eager nod but strolled around the counter with a miniature porcelain baking dish overflowing with fruit and pastry and cream.

"On the house," he said. "It's the last one and won't keep until tomorrow."

I considered passing on the extra calories, but decided not to let it go to waste.

"So, what did you want to know about Mrs. Lathrop?" Gemma asked once Daniel had returned to his pasta and I was making swift work of the cobbler.

"It's not Mrs. Lathrop, it's some guy who claims to be her great-nephew and heir."

"You mean Harry Westcott? But how in the world

did you run into him? I thought he was living out on the West Coast."

I gave her a rundown of what had happened that morning with him and the penguin suit and the letter and his great-aunt's promises—and, of course, his threats to see me in court.

"I just wanted to be sure he is who he claims to be," I finished. "He didn't show me any ID or anything, and with that whole penguin routine…"

Gemma chuckled. "Don't worry, I've known Harry since he was a little boy. I used to babysit him while I was in nursing school. He spent most of his free time dressed up like it was Halloween, said he was going to be a movie star someday. With his looks, I can't believe he hasn't hit the big time yet."

Then her smile faded.

"Don't get me wrong, Nina. I'm on your side. You legitimately bought the house, and that's that. But I get where Harry is coming from, too. He was the only one of Mrs. Lathrop's family that kept in contact with her once the rest moved out of town. Even after he was all grown up, he still sent her letters and came by to visit a couple of times a year. I'm not surprised she planned to give him her house when she was gone."

Before I could digest that last unsettling bit of information, Daniel spoke up again.

"Harry's back in town? I haven't seen him around since last Thanksgiving. He landed a gig playing a zombie in that cable show they film up near Atlanta. He texted me a picture of him in makeup. Pretty cool!"

I nodded. Right now, however, my concern was

learning as much as I could about the guy in case the whole lawsuit thing did have legs.

"I guess if you text him, you must know him pretty well. What do *you* think of Harry?"

Daniel had finished with the pasta and was now working on an exotic version of tuna salad. He did some Food Channel–worthy flipping about of a pepper shaker before setting it down and shaking his head.

"Sorry, Nina, I don't know him that well. I mean, when he comes by the shop, we chat about the weather. You know, small talk. The picture was actually for Jasmine. He figured she'd get a kick out of it."

Jasmine being Daniel and Gemma's teenage daughter, whom I'd met a couple of times.

Daniel continued, "He's an okay guy for an actor. He knows his way around food and wine, not so much around sports. He won't drink coffee, though, only tea."

"That's it?" I asked, disappointed. I wasn't really looking for a rundown on his diet.

Daniel grinned. "Well, okay, since you ask. The ladies all seemed to like him…some of the guys, too," he added, his short black brows lifting meaningfully. "Come to think of it, I never did figure out which way he swings, not that it matt—"

He broke off midword to dodge the packet of raw sugar his wife had just lobbed at him.

"What? What did I say?" he cheerfully demanded, his round face a careful study in innocence as he met Gemma's disapproving gaze.

She snorted and pointedly turned her back on him. "You can ignore the politically incorrect barbarian behind the counter, Nina."

"Well, it doesn't matter to me, either way," I informed her. "With any luck, today was our first and last meeting."

Not that I truly believed that. Harry had been serious about his lawsuit. One way or another, I was going to hear from him again.

I was saved from further comment, however, when a jingle of small bells signaled that the restaurant door had popped opened. A trio of shopping-bag-laden women in their sixties dressed in the requisite jewel-toned tracksuits came bustling in.

Gemma jumped up from her chair, all business now.

"Sorry, Nina, gotta go. Looks like the lunch rush is starting."

I finished my cobbler; then, fortified for the walk back, I made my goodbyes and headed out again. Despite the glass of ice water I'd drunk to wash down the cobbler, sweat was pouring off me by the time I reached my house. To make things worse, a full-sized SUV with dark-tinted windows and a glossy gray paint job was parked at my gate, engine running. Since I'd already had one unwelcome visitor this morning, I approached it with more than usual caution.

The driver's side door opened, and a familiar if not exactly welcome figure climbed out.

"Well, hi there, Nee-nah," the middle-aged woman with frosted blonde hair cut in a severe pixie style exclaimed. Smoothing the skirt of her bright-yellow summer suit, she went on, "How *are* you this morning?"

"It's *Nine-ah*," I blandly corrected her. "I'm just fine, Melissa Jane. What can I do for you?"

Melissa Jane Green had been Cymbeline's mayor for

going on two decades now. She, along with the remainder of what I'd dubbed the town's Holy Trinity—Bob Short (banking) and Wally McFadden (insurance)—had joined forces and bought up the greater part of Cymbeline's historic town square a few years back. That speculative bit of real estate tucked beneath their collective belt, they had sat down with the other local business owners. When all was said and done, they'd created almost from scratch a booming arts and antiques district that had been attracting tourists to Cymbeline for the past dozen years. Thus, the lack of open retail space on the square.

I couldn't argue with the good they'd done for the town, reviving what had been a dying local economy. As a businesswoman, Melissa Jane impressed the heck out of me. But I'd already had an unfortunate run-in with Madame Mayor, and so I was predisposed not to trust her toothy smile.

She walked around to the passenger side of her behemoth of a vehicle and leaned a skinny hip against the fender.

"It's not what you can do for me, Nina," she replied, getting the name right this time, her accent dripping with thick Georgia honey. "It's what we can do for each other. Remember when you asked about that commercial zoning change so that you could operate a bed-and-breakfast, and I told you that wasn't possible? Well, I think I've found a way to make it happen, after all."

I shot her a slanted look. Soon after moving in, I'd checked into changing the zoning for my property from residential to commercial. Not that I was hurting for cash. It simply had occurred to me that, sometime down the road, I might get bored playing lady of the manor and want a job of sorts again. And turning the house into a B&B had seemed an ideal solution.

Unfortunately for my grand plan, Melissa Jane had informed me that the town had plenty of bed-and-breakfasts already, and my request was denied. But now she had changed her mind?

"What do you need from me to get that done?" I asked with an equally toothy smile. "Sell you my soul? Sign over my firstborn? Buy all the tickets to the upcoming Shakespeare festival?"

She gave a dismissive wave of scarlet-tipped fingers.

"Really, Nina, don't be silly. I have a true business proposition for you. I'll fast-track the zoning change and get you set up with the Chamber of Commerce. Wally McFadden will take care of the insurance details for you. The only catch is that we need you to open up your B&B first thing tomorrow."

"Tomorrow?"

I stared at her in disbelief. Harry wasn't the only person a few breads short of a loaf. Obviously, the summer heat was making the whole town go crazy.

"You're crazy," I told her. "Even if I could possibly open for business in one day—which I can't—it's not like I have any guests to stay here. What's the big rush?"

"Now, honey, would I make you this deal if I hadn't thought of all the details? Why, I have your first guests for you right here."

She waved the scarlet-manicured nails again, this time in the direction of her SUV. On cue, all three passenger doors opened.

I felt my mouth drop open, too. Crazy? This wasn't

crazy. This was downright lunacy. I blinked, and started counting. *One, two, three, four, five...no, six. Six!*

A moment later, they had all assembled in a neat line on the sidewalk in front of me. By design or happenstance, they were arranged in order of height—the tallest a good five inches taller than me, and the shortest somewhere in the four-foot-nothing range. Despite the heat, they were dressed identically in black, relieved only by a touch of white around their faces.

I clamped my jaws back together and turned to Melissa Jane.

"Nuns?" I squeaked in a voice high enough to make Mattie howl. "You want me to open a bed-and-breakfast for nuns?"

"These are not just any nuns. They are the Sisters of Perpetual Poverty. Reverend Mother, this is Ms. Nina Fleet. Nina, this is the order's Mother Superior, Mother Mary Francis."

She indicated the nun in the middle, who gave me a crisp nod. I guessed her to be in her seventies, with a ruddy complexion and a pair of oversized black-framed glasses straight out of the 1990s.

"Reverend Mother," I managed with a limp wave back, following Melissa Jane's lead in addressing the older woman.

"And the rest of the sisters. Sister Mary George... Sister Mary Julian... Sister Mary Thomas... Sister Mary Christopher... Sister Mary Paul," the mayor went on, starting with the tallest of the nuns and pointing down the line in turn. "Sisters, this is Nina Fleet, owner of this lovely home."

Then, while I still struggled for a reply, she went on,

"Their convent is right outside of town—that big Tudor Revival building in the middle of a field. You've probably seen their signs for artisan goat cheese."

I gave a faint nod, remember a cute billboard with a pair of gamboling white goats and the slogan THE HEAVENLIEST CHEESE IN GEORGIA. Not knowing that the *fromagerie*—the cheese-making business—in question was connected to a convent, I hadn't gotten the joke.

"I fear the good sisters have run into a small issue regarding their convent," Melissa Jane continued, assuming a somber expression. "You see, they don't actually own the buildings and surrounding land. It all belongs to a real estate developer—a Mr. Bainbridge—who has been leasing it to their order for the past twenty years. Unfortunately, their current lease is up, and he refuses to renew it. The property has increased significantly in value, and he wants to develop it instead."

"But couldn't the Church just buy the property from this Bainbridge guy?" I wanted to know. "Maybe they could sell off one of those undiscovered da Vinci portraits they've got hidden in the Vatican basement, or something."

Mother Superior gave me a look through those oversized glasses. But all she said was, "Let me explain, Ms. Fleet. While I'm not privy to all the details, my understanding is that negotiations between the developer and the archdiocese broke down before they even came close to talking real numbers. And so I fear there are no legal challenges we can bring to halt the eviction."

Melissa Jane nodded. "The convent's cheese operation has already been shut down, and the goats have been moved to a nearby farm. As for the good sisters, they're waiting for word from the archbishop as to re-location."

At that last, an audible sniff came from one of the nuns. Expression sympathetic, the mayor continued, "Obviously, the town council encourages residential development, but the optics on this one aren't pretty. We're attempting to convince Mr. Bainbridge to recon-sider his decision, but for now the nuns need a place to stay. And since all the other B&Bs in town are booked up, well, I thought of you and your lovely home."

She paused, and her grave expression promptly morphed into the familiar gleaming smile. "So, shall I bring the sisters back here with their luggage first thing tomorrow?"

She waited for my response, looking positively be-atific now. I glanced from her back to the lineup of nuns. Their expressions were placid, accepting of whatever might happen to them. *God's will*, and all that.

Except for the tallest nun—Sister Mary George, if I'd gotten the names right.

She appeared to be a good three decades younger than the rest of the sisters, putting her somewhere around my age. She was African American, tall and slender with caramel-colored skin and features that, even without makeup, seemed more at home on the cover of a fashion magazine than a convent. As I caught her wide brown gaze, she softly mouthed the word *please*. Not for herself, I knew, but for the row of el-derly women alongside her.

And how does a decent human being say no to that?

"No," I exclaimed, a bit more loudly than I intended. Then, when all seven women stared at me in shock,

I hurriedly clarified, "I mean, yes, I'll do it, but no, I need an extra day to get the house ready for guests. Can the sisters wait until Monday morning?"

Melissa Jane's smile returned. "I think we can persuade the sheriff to hold off one more day before starting the eviction process. See you on Monday."

Turning on her stiletto heel, she gestured the nuns back to the SUV. Last into the vehicle was Sister Mary George, who paused for a look back at me.

Thank you, she mouthed back.

I watched the SUV pull out from the curb, not quite believing what had just happened. First, I get accosted in my own home by a failing actor dressed like a sports team mascot. Then, I get blackmailed by the mayor into hosting six nuns. All I needed was to discover that the house was built on an ancient Native American burial ground for my day to be complete.

As I headed back inside, it occurred to me that Melissa Jane hadn't indicated who was going to be paying the B&B bill. That probably meant it was gratis, my hospitality in exchange for the zoning change. Which, if the hosting gig didn't drag on too long, was not all that bad of a deal. Maybe the sisters could teach me how to make cheese.

If nothing else, I'd enlist their prayers in making sure that the penguin who had started it all didn't prevail against me in court.

FOUR

SOMEWHAT TO MY SURPRISE, it actually did take the rest of the weekend to get the place ready for my B&B-ers. I'd yet to have any overnight guests since moving into the house, so I hadn't gotten around to changing the linens in all the bedrooms. That meant spending Saturday afternoon schlepping loads of sheets and towels and comforters downstairs to the laundry room and back up again. In between schleps, I signed for a courier package from Melissa Jane that contained my new business license issued by the Town of Cymbeline, along with miscellaneous other paperwork that included the promised rezoning notice.

After supper, Wally McFadden had shown up on my doorstep with a shiny new insurance policy in hand to match his shiny bald pate. To be sure, my first guests would be nuns who, I assumed, already came with some pretty big built-in coverage from The Guy Upstairs. But Wally had warned me that even divine intervention wouldn't provide sufficient protection for me should I find myself on the wrong side of a litigious guest.

Sunday proved just as busy. I'd already emailed Gemma with a heads-up about my new innkeeping venture and a plea for a bit of help on the cuisine end of things. After allowing myself to sleep in for what I suspected might be the last morning for some time to come, I fed Mattie and managed a quick shower. Then, after twisting my hair up into a messy bun, I threw on shorts and a Hawaiian-print linen top and hoofed it over to Peaches and Java. With the "bed" portion of my B&B pretty well handled, it was time to work on the "breakfast" end of things.

"We're down to a couple of homemade cinnamon buns left." Gemma greeted me with a harried smile while I squinted to read the whiteboard on the wall where the daily specials were posted. "If you want one, speak up now, or you're out of luck until next Sunday."

I knew the culinary bliss that was one of Daniel's oversized sticky rolls swimming in icing and topped with chopped pecans. I debated between that and another serving of his cobbler.

"Cinnamon bun and a cup of light roast," I hurriedly decided. "Oh, and a side of that maple-jalapeño bacon you have on the specials board."

"You got it." Then, with a glance around the packed room, she added, "Things should start clearing out in about twenty minutes. If you can wait a little while, I'll have time then to talk about your catering."

Given that it likely would take a good twenty minutes just to finish off the cinnamon bun portion of my breakfast, I nodded.

It was closer to half an hour later, however, when the crowd finally began to thin. Gemma dragged over a chair and sat with an exhausted but satisfied whoosh of breath.

"Here's our catering menu," she said, producing a brochure, which she set on the table between us. "We've got a special breakfast option that's probably what you're most interested in, and it includes Daniel's peach cobbler. But why didn't you say anything the other day about opening a B&B? I thought you told me a while back that the town council wasn't going to give you a zoning variance."

"Actually, this whole thing was the town council's—specifically Melissa Jane's—idea, not mine. If you want to know the truth, I got arm-twisted into it about five minutes after I left your place yesterday."

While Gemma stared in surprise, I gave her a quick rundown of my meeting with the Sisters of Perpetual Poverty and the devil's bargain I'd struck with Cymbeline's mayor. When I'd finished, the coffee shop owner was shaking her head.

"I'd say I'm surprised, but I'm not. I'd heard something was going on with the convent, but I didn't know Gregory was involved. Gregory, as in Gregory Bainbridge," she clarified for my benefit.

I nodded as I took a last bite of cinnamon roll, recalling Bainbridge as the name of the developer Melissa Jane had mentioned. But Gemma wasn't finished.

"That man is a real piece of work," she went on, tone growing heated. "He's the one responsible for that new development going up south of town...you know, Southbridge Acres. He claimed all the homes were going to be on minimum one-acre lots, and so the town council signed off on the deal that gave him approval to break ground. Then he found some loophole in the agreement and quadrupled on density. And that was after all the new streets were built, so traffic is a nightmare getting in and out of the development now."

"Yeah, it is pretty bad," I agreed, hoping I didn't

sound ironic. I'd been in that part of town a few times during what passed for rush hour in Cymbeline. Compared to Atlanta traffic, it was nothing. Still, folks living nearby who were accustomed to a couple of stop signs would see a hundred or so additional cars and two new traffic lights as major gridlock.

"Plus the town has to build a new elementary school now to handle all the families that moved in," Gemma continued to fume. "Which comes out of our tax dollars. Meantime, good old Gregory is rolling around in all that extra cash. I imagine he'll pull the same kind of stunt with the convent property."

She abruptly broke off as Daniel left his spot behind the counter, plate of pancakes in hand. He set the dish before an eager tween at one of the tourist tables and then sauntered over to where Gemma and I sat.

"Talking about the guy everyone loves to hate?" he asked with a snort. To me, he said, "Seriously, like she said, that guy is a piece of work. On top of everything else, he thinks he's some ladies' man. Do you know he actually tried hitting on Gemma right in front of me? Not that I blame him"—he paused and wiggled his eyebrows meaningfully at his wife—"but that's some kind of cojones to hit on a lady in front of her husband. Just let him try that again."

He drew his forefinger across his beefy throat in the cliché slicing gesture. I was trying to decide if he was serious or not when another, sour voice broke in.

"You're gonna have to stand in line, Danny boy."

The speaker sat at the table across from us, scowling over the top of his coffee mug. *Jack Hill, the ice cream shop owner.* Involved as I'd been in my conversation with Gemma, I hadn't noticed him come in. Tall, wiry, and in his midfifties, he had salt-and-pepper hair and lean features that verged on being handsome. He wore a black logo Taste-Tee-Freeze T-shirt that set off a pair of surprisingly big guns. Apparently, hand-churning ice cream and wielding a spatula and knife on a marble slab built up the old arm muscles.

"Yeah, that lowlife Bainbridge tried putting the moves on my wife, too," the man complained. "I told him I catch him doing that again, and it's lights out."

Daniel gave him a commiserating nod. "Don't worry, brah," he replied, the Hawaiian slang reminding me that, unlike his wife, Daniel wasn't a native Cymbeliner. "Not a jury in the world would convict you. Now how about I get you another cup?"

"Thanks," he said, putting his coffee down, "but I gotta get back to the store."

While Jasmine rang him up, I leaned a bit closer to Gemma. "Well, that was interesting. This Bainbridge definitely sounds like the kind of guy who wouldn't have any compunction about leaving a bunch of old nuns homeless."

"He's pretty darned lucky Laverna didn't catch him alone in a dark alley while the deal was going down. She would have changed his tune for him, right smart."

"Laverna?" I echoed, promptly picturing a very tall and very broad woman wearing a sneer and likely wielding a baseball bat. Obviously, Bainbridge had a target the size of Georgia on his back in this town. "What, is she Cymbeline's official enforcer?"

Gemma snorted at that. "Not exactly. If you met the

nuns, you met her…though you probably know her as Sister Mary George."

I'd been finishing the last piece of maple-jalapeño bacon. At her last words, I started choking and had to wash down the sweet and spicy scraps with a swig of coffee. When I could speak again, I demanded, "Wait, what? You're talking about the nun who could be on the cover of *Elle*?"

"Don't let that pretty face fool you. I've known her ever since she was in high school, and believe me, she sure wasn't holy back then. You see, Laverna is my brother's wife's younger sister. And Luther was already dating Simona—my sister-in-law—back when it all happened, which means I had a front-row seat to all the trouble Laverna was getting into."

I took another sip of coffee while I mentally unraveled Gemma's family tree. And while I didn't approve of gossip on principle—I'd been the subject of gossip myself while still married to the ex—I could see Gemma was dying to tell all.

Besides, how often did you get to hear dirt on a nun?

"So, what happened?" I asked her.

Gemma glanced about. Jack Hill was gone, and the remaining customers all appeared to be tourists who were yakking among themselves. Apparently satisfied that being overheard wasn't an issue, she turned back to me.

"Now, what happened went down about thirty years ago," she began in a low tone. "By now most people have forgotten the whole thing, which is how it should be. Laverna—Sister Mary George—is a true woman of God now. So you have to swear you won't talk about this with anyone."

"I swear," I swore, and pantomimed zipping my lips.

Gemma continued, "It started when we all were still in high school. Her and Simona's mother died in a car accident. That's a terrible blow for any child, but for girls that age…well, you know. Anyhow, Simona—she was a senior like me that year—coped by taking over her mom's role as best she could. But Laverna, well, she covered up her grief by acting out. And I'm not talking the drama club.

"She was only a freshman, but before long she was hanging with the wrong crowd. She started skipping class, drinking, smoking a little weed. Her dad tried to rein her in, but he didn't have much luck. I guess since he was the only parent she had left, he felt like he couldn't be too hard on her."

I gave a sympathetic nod. "I can understand that. But it still doesn't sound like Laverna did anything more awful than a lot of teenagers do."

"Believe me, it got worse."

The woman glanced over at Jasmine behind the coffee counter. Lattes and cold press appeared to be the last thing on the girl's mind, however. Instead, she was merrily laughing with a lanky, red-haired teenage boy sporting a Cymbeline High School Band T-shirt. Jasmine was just a couple of years older than Sister Mary George—Laverna—had been when her young life had been shattered. From the troubled expression that momentarily clouded Gemma's strong features, the woman had to be picturing her own daughter under such circumstances.

Shaking her head again, Gemma resumed her story.

"By her senior year, things had gone really bad for Laverna. She'd go out partying on a Friday night and not come home until Sunday. She was picked up for shoplifting a couple of times, though the stores never pressed charges. And she was pretty well on the road to not graduating because of all the skipping. But then, on one of the days she actually showed up to class, she accused some girl of stealing her boyfriend. She pulled a knife on her."

My mouth dropped open. *A knife-wielding nun?*

"Wow! So, what happened?" I managed after a few startled seconds. "Did anyone get hurt?"

"Thankfully, it was one of those little pen knives she was waving around, and Laverna swore she was only trying to scare the girl. But they scuffled, and the other girl got a cut on her hand, so they hauled Laverna off to juvie."

Juvenile hall, I mentally translated.

"Anyhow, Laverna was gone almost six months," Gemma remembered. "When she came home again, it was seriously like night and day. The first thing she did was announce to the family that she was converting to Catholicism and planned to join the Sisters of Perpetual Poverty as a novitiate."

"Well, it's not unheard of for people—even teenagers— to find God in jail."

"I guess not…though everyone thought it was a joke, at first. I mean, we're all good Baptists around here. We don't hold much with bells and smells."

I suppressed a grin, for I hadn't heard that particular down-home quip in years. Gemma referred to her church's aversion to the Catholic preference for incense and, well, bells during their services…basically, rejecting anything that smacked of ritual. For my part, I rather liked that sort of formality.

Gemma went on, "It turned out that one of the order's nuns came to the juvenile facility to counsel the girls on a regular basis, and whatever she said really resonated with Laverna. We figured she'd get over it, but she didn't. Just like she said, she became a novitiate, and after a couple of years she took her first vows. By then she had her new name, Mary George, and we all finally accepted that's who she was now. That brawling, backtalking Laverna was long gone, and this mild-mannered, soft-spoken nun lady had replaced her. Well, pretty much…"

She trailed off with a knowing look that I couldn't let pass. "What do you mean, pretty much?"

She grinned. "Well, there was this time about ten years back when some beer-swilling hunter wandered onto the convent property and started taking pot shots at the livestock. Luckily, he was so drunk he couldn't hit a barn, let alone a little goat. But that didn't stop Sister Mary George from going all Laverna on his sorry butt." Her grin broadened. "From what I heard, she grabbed his shotgun and chucked it into the stock tank, and then frog-marched the guy right off the property."

"Amen, Sister Mary George," I agreed with a matching grin. "I have a feeling the Lord probably let her slide on that one."

"Well, like I said, she's a woman of God now. And she watches over those old sisters like they're family…

which I guess they are. As long as they have her, they'll be okay, no matter where they end up after this."

Then, abruptly switching gears, she asked, "So, Nina, what do you want to do about the catering?"

We spent the next few minutes going over the list, settling on a basic menu of various quiches and a batch of Daniel's cobbler that Jasmine would bicycle over every morning around seven. I'd be in charge of coffee and hot tea, and I'd hit the grocery store for a selection of fruit and cereal (including prunes and bran, Gemma suggested, given the women's average age) and cheeses to supplement the baked goods. She also gave me a ten-minute crash course on food storage and presentation, since my last foray into restauranting had been as cashier at the Burger Castle when I was in high school.

"Normally, we'd do up a little contract," she said once we agreed on the details, "but since this is a fluid situation, let's play it by ear. Since the sisters are moving in tomorrow, I'll send Jasmine over starting on Tuesday. Just give me a heads-up the day before they leave, okay?"

"Perfect. You're the best."

With final goodbyes to Daniel and Jasmine—by now, the second seating was rolling in, so they were gearing up for that rush—I left Peaches and Java. The next item on my to-do list was a run to the nearby Piggly Wiggly to see about my portion of the food offerings. Though this grocery store had a smaller selection than the super-sized supermarket right outside town, it offered home delivery as one of its amenities. I made my selections, arranged a delivery time, and then headed back to the house to track down a coffee maker. The appliance in question unearthed from the back of the pantry, I carried my laptop into the kitchen and started inventorying.

That's the key to holding down costs, Gemma had assured me during my mini-course. *Set yourself up a spreadsheet of everything you're serving and update it every time you shop.*

Within a couple of hours, I'd put together a credible document that would hopefully also pass muster with my accountant. I was tweaking a final formula in the spreadsheet when Mattie woofed and scrambled to her fuzzy feet. A moment later, the doorbell sounded.

"Who the heck is it now?" I muttered in the Aussie's direction as I strode toward my front entry. The Piggly-Wiggly delivery kid had already stopped by earlier, and I wasn't expecting anyone else. With Mattie crowding at my heels, I peered out the sidelight window for a look.

Nobody I recognize.

This visitor was male, probably early sixties, maybe an inch taller than me. His regular features were, well, regular…though in his twenties and with a more youthful jawline and firmer cheeks, he had probably been considered a "catch." His catchability factor was diminished now by his wide fringe of gray hair that wrapped from ear to ear and verged on Bozo poufiness. But what caught my eye was the polo-style yellow shirt he sported, embroidered with one of those same tiny penguins that once waddled across the chest of almost every American male.

I frowned. He might be wearing a limited-edition reboot of that nineties fashion, which would mean he was rich and ironic…or he might simply have kept the pullover stashed in his closet all these years, which would mean he was cheap. All in all, however, he looked pretty harmless.

Tourist, I decided as I opened the front door and looked through the screen. "Yes, can I help you?"

"I do hope so," he replied, and sent a tight smile my way. "You are Ms. Fleet?"

"That's me. And you are…?"

"The name is Bainbridge. Gregory Bainbridge. I am—"

"I know who you are. You're the heartless SOB who kicked a whole bunch of old nuns to the curb." I cut him short and slammed the door in his face.

FIVE

NOT MUCH TO my surprise, the slamming-in-his-face thing didn't faze Bainbridge. He rang the bell again, followed by a genteel, "Ms. Fleet, I'd appreciate a moment of your time. It's important," called through the door.

I exchanged glances with Mattie, who didn't look impressed. For my part, I couldn't think of a single important thing the man could possibly have to discuss with me. Still, I couldn't help feeling a bit guilty at my rudeness, even though my reaction had been reflexive. Just because *he* was a Class A jerk didn't mean I should follow suit.

Grudgingly, I reopened the door. "All right, we'll try again. What do you need from me, Mr. Bainbridge?"

"Just a chance to tell my side of the story. I'm sure you've heard the worst, and, well…"

He paused and dabbed at his glowing expanse of forehead with a crisp white hankie he'd whipped from the back pocket of his khakis. "It *is* a bit warm out today. Perhaps we can do this inside where it's air-conditioned?"

"Fine, I'll give you five minutes," I agreed, and pushed open the screen. "But I'm pretty short on time, seeing how I'm getting the place ready for all those old nuns you dumped on the street."

"A rather harsh way to put things, don't you think?" he asked as he took a cautious step inside. "I prefer the phrase *facilitated their inevitable relocation*. Um, are you certain this dog won't bite?"

That last was asked with more than a bit of understandable trepidation, since the dog in question had her piercing blue-and-brown gaze fixed on the man's face. The fact that she'd begun a low growl deep in her throat probably wasn't helping matters.

"Back off, girl," I told her. "I'll let you know if I need you."

Mattie's ears drooped in disappointment, but she obediently shut off the rumbling and trotted to the corner of the foyer. She flopped onto the cool wood floor and kept both eyes fixed on Bainbridge while I closed the door behind him. Since this wasn't a social call, I didn't direct the man toward the parlor. Instead, hand on knob, I told him, "Like I said, I can give you five minutes. So what's this story you have to tell me?"

"Actually, it's more of a request for a sympathetic hearing. I'm hoping to reboot my image, so to speak, but it will take some outside help."

He tucked the handkerchief back in his pocket, expression bland now. "I'm certain that, as a newcomer to Cymbeline, you have a clear view of us. You come from a big city, so you're not shackled by a small-town mentality, unlike some of our fellow citizens who have lived here all their lives."

The obvious implication being that small town equaled not smart. But Bainbridge had read me wrong if he thought I'd be seduced by being told I was better than my new neighbors. Still, I said, "Go on."

"I would guess you have a fair idea of how small towns work. Everyone knows everyone else's business, and everyone has a long memory. Those people who opposed my beautiful Southbridge development are a prime example."

His voice rose, and he began wringing his hands in melodramatic fashion, so I was hard-pressed to keep a straight face.

"They failed in their efforts to stop me then, and their revenge now is that they find fault with everything I do. They're up in arms over the fact I intend to build a fabulous new golf community on property I've owned for years. The only thing they talk about is goats and nuns. What they forget is that I have every legal right to develop the land," he finished.

I considered this a moment. What he was saying about small-town memories didn't differ much from Gemma's discussion of Sister Mary George that morning. But what was legal and what was right weren't always the same thing. Unfortunately, guys like Bainbridge tended not to get that.

"So you're not Cymbeline's Man of the Year," I agreed. "But what does that have to do with me?"

"That's simple. You see, I have a lovely office on the main square over a charming antique shop. Once, it was a pleasure to do business in that location, but now, not so much. I can't even walk outside for lunch without feeling like I am traversing hostile territory."

He paused and gave an elaborate shudder.

"I've had to resort to wearing hats and overcoats to disguise myself just to walk from my office to the parking lot. That's why I wanted to give you my side of the story before the good sisters move in and turn you against me, too. Quite frankly, I'm in need of a friendly face in town, Ms. Fleet, and I have hopes that this face might be yours."

He sighed a little, expression pained, and despite the smarmy vibe the guy gave off, I couldn't help but feel a little sorry for him. It had to suck being everyone's favorite villain, even if you deserved the rep. I wasn't buying everything he was selling, but I'd give him a full hearing.

"You're not making it easy for yourself," I reminded him. "As far as most people are concerned, evicting a bunch of elderly ladies from a place they've lived for decades kind of puts you into the category of super-villain."

Bainbridge's pained expression hardened, contrasting sharply with his soft Georgia drawl.

"But that's the problem. I didn't capriciously evict them. I've been in negotiations with the archdiocese for years trying to avoid this very situation. The archbishop knew the lease was going to end, but his people refused to respond to my offers to buy me out. Heck, I even gave the sisters a six-month extension before I finally filed the papers for eviction. If you think about it, *I'm* the good guy here."

I suppressed a grimace. Much as I hated to admit it, if what he said was true, Bainbridge had a point...not that I'd go as far as calling him a good guy. But Melissa Jane had talked about optics. No matter how you spun it, the developer was going to come out of this situation looking bad. And while I might have been an open-minded outsider, I darned sure wasn't a stupid one. No way was I going to take Bainbridge's side, not if I wanted to be able to run over to Peaches and Java for coffee anytime I wanted to. But to be just as fair, I wasn't going to go around trash-talking the guy, either.

At least, not until I knew him better.

"Mr. Bainbridge—Gregory—I'm sorry you and the nuns both ended up in this situation, but I'm not going to take sides here. Consider me Switzerland. I'm going to let the sisters stay here as long as it takes to settle things, but I promise I won't yell nasty things at you if I see you in the town square."

"Well, that's something."

He gave me the first genuine smile I'd seen out of him. "Thank you for your time, Ms. Fleet... Nina. If you ever decide to unload this place and want a nice new modern home in a gated community, we're breaking ground on Westbridge this fall."

Then his smile turned sly. "And I work out special deals for, ahem, good friends."

And, there was the opening hit. If I'd had more time, Evil Me would have been tempted to lead him on a bit. But since I had my nuns to think about, I decided to take him literally.

"Well, if we ever become friends, I'll keep that in mind," I replied, and opened the door again to usher him out. "Now, you'd better get going before any of the neighbors see you talking to me."

Bainbridge drew himself up with a dignified smirk. "I assume you're having a little jest at my expense. But, yes, I'll be on my way."

I closed the door after him and heaved an exaggerated breath, earning a woof of agreement from Mattie.

"Well, that was special," I muttered as I peered

through the sidelight to make sure the man truly was leaving.

Fortunately, I could see him getting into a dark luxury sedan that had probably cost more than half the houses in Cymbeline. I could only hope that he'd keep his distance once the nuns arrived. Who knew, Sister Mary George might flash back to her youth and decide to go all Benihana on the man if he gave her any lip. And that was one fight I wanted to stay clear of.

Putting the developer firmly out of mind, I headed for the kitchen. More important things were at stake than Bainbridge's sneaky plans to win friends and influence people. Namely, I'd bought a tub of refrigerated cookie dough while I was at the store, and I had cookies to bake.

ON MONDAY MORNING, I'd barely finished dressing in a pink tailored shirt and cropped black jeans when the doorbell chimed.

"They're here," I told Mattie, who was lounging in the hall outside my open bedroom door. With the Aussie on my heels, I trotted to the front door and flung it open.

Gathered in a neat semicircle on the porch were my first guests, all wearing black calf-length habits with black stockings and brogues, their hair covered by white linen caps draped by matching elbow-length black veils. Gleaming against their chests were large gold crucifixes on chains.

Melissa Jane, wearing a sleeveless mint-green linen shift, stood behind them, beaming proudly. "We're here!" she said unnecessarily. "And I'm sure you're all ready for us. Right, Nina?"

"You bet. Welcome, Sisters. Please, come in," I said, and held open the screen.

They filed inside, each nun pulling a single wheeled black overnight bag behind her, so that they looked like funeral-bound flight attendants. Trying to be the helpful hostess, I asked, "Do you need me to grab the rest of your stuff out of the SUV?"

I heard a few stifled snickers as Mother Superior slanted me a look through those big glasses.

"My child," she intoned, "we're the Sisters of Perpetual Poverty. We don't have more 'stuff.'"

"Reverend Mother is right. That's kind of in our rule book." This from one of the younger nuns—meaning in her sixties—with cherubic cheeks and wide blue eyes. Sister Mary Christopher, if I remembered correctly.

"Everything else belongs to the archdiocese," added the freckle-faced Sister Mary Thomas with a smile as she let a curious Mattie snuffle her extended hand. "It's all packed up and going into storage until we figure out where we're headed."

"Oh, uh, sure," I agreed, giving myself a mental kick. This wasn't the Kardashian clan on vacay, after all.

But even though this was their chosen life, I couldn't help but feel a bit bad for them. All those years living at the convent, and their entire worldly goods fit into a suitcase that could be stowed beneath an airline seat. Heck, I needed more luggage than that for a three-day weekend.

On the other hand, I couldn't help feeling a bit jealous of them, too. It would be kind of nice to be able to pack all of one's worldly goods in a carry-on bag.

Melissa Jane, meanwhile, was saying, "I'm sure everyone will settle in just fine. Nina, can you take it from here? I have a meeting with one of our local contractors in about fifteen minutes, so I really must be off."

"Sure, I've got it. I'll call you if there are any problems."

"Problems?" The mayor gave a hearty chuckle. "What sort of problems could you have with guests like these?"

"I'm sure Ms. Fleet will be a credible hostess," Reverend Mother clipped out. "Thank you for all your efforts on our behalf, Madame Mayor. We appreciate your rushing through the permit."

"Not at all." Teeth bared in a campaign trail–worthy grin, Melissa Jane made her way out the door again.

I stretched my lips in an equally wide smile.

"I guess we're on our own now. Not that I expected the mayor to hang out with us. Though I'm sure she would have been glad to, if she'd had the time. Oh, and I had a couple of extra keys made. Maybe I should give them to you, Reverend Mother?"

I was perilously close to babbling. What was it about a roomful of nuns that made me nervous? Or was it simply first-time-innkeeper nerves?

"Nina," Sister Mary George spoke up as I helplessly trailed off, "perhaps you'd like to show us to our rooms?"

I shot her a grateful look. "Of course. Though I'm afraid some of you will have to share. Not you, Reverend Mother. But we'll have to do two to a room for some of the rest of you, if that's all right."

"The sisters don't mind doubling up," Mother Superior informed me with a cool nod. "And if necessary, I certainly can share my space with Sister Mary Paul."

The tiniest of the six nuns gave her veiled head a

vigorous nod. Her small face was wrinkled like the proverbial raisin, and her eyes gleamed like dark little currants. "Yes, yes," she croaked out in some vague Eastern European accent. "I am fine with roommate."

We made the short walk down the gallery of Ye Olde Ancestors to the main staircase. A second, more modest flight of stairs lay behind a discreet door near the kitchen. Back in the day, that stairway would have been used by the help. In these servantless times, it was handy for popping downstairs for a midnight refrigerator raid. But given that we were going for first impressions, I wanted the good sisters to see the real deal with its carved newel post and built-in under-stairs bench.

I couldn't help feeling a warm glow when they made all the appropriate noises of approval when they saw it and the parlor beyond. Not that I could take credit for the majority of the decor; still, I had added my own touches and made what I considered a few aesthetic improvements. The major change had come when I pulled up some unfortunate wall-to-wall carpeting that had been installed circa the 1960s, returning the wood floors beneath to their original polished bare state. On the other hand, I had kept most of the period wallpaper, which ran riot with flowers, curlicues, and stripes, often all in a single pattern. Overall, I'd pretty well kept the place as Harry Westcott's great-aunt had left it.

Harry Westcott.

With all the craziness of getting ready for my unplanned business opening, I'd pretty well forgotten the man in the penguin suit. I only hoped he hadn't gotten word about the B&B. Last thing I needed was another visit from his fleece-clad self riling up my guests.

"My apologies, Sisters," I said as the women hefted their bags and we started up the steps, Mattie following behind. "Unfortunately, all our bedrooms are on the second floor. Melissa Jane said that wouldn't be a problem?"

It had occurred to me two days before while I was hauling linen that upstairs bedrooms might not prove ideal for a bunch of elderly ladies. Heck, all that climbing had made *my* knees ache. And so I'd made a hasty call to our fair mayor expressing my concerns.

Melissa Jane had laughed.

Honey, those sisters are in better shape than you and me both. Remember, they spend hours each day herding up goats and milking them and carrying feed. And that cheese doesn't make itself, either. Don't worry, a little staircase won't stop any of them.

"Oh, don't worry about that, child," Sister Mary Thomas now echoed. "The convent building is three stories, not including the basement. We're up and down steps all the time. That's how we get our cardio in."

"Yes, and it's good for the glutes," Sister Mary Christopher agreed, with an approving glance over her shoulder at her own ample backside.

Since I'd seen a bit of improvement in my own admittedly neglected rear carriage after moving into the place, I had to third the observation.

A few more steps, and we had reached the second-floor landing. The paneled hallway that stretched to either side of the stairs was similar to the main hall downstairs. But here the dark raised paneling went from floor to ceiling, resembling a series of tall narrow picture frames set side to side. Depending on your mood, the effect was either cozy or claustrophobic.

"First things first," I told them. "We have a full bath here, and a half bath between two of the bedrooms. There's also a powder room downstairs near the kitchen. I'll let y'all work out the bathroom schedules among yourselves."

The nuns nodded in unison. With that established, I reached for the knob of the first guest bedroom. "Here we go. I call this one the Prince Chamber."

I'd given the room its sly moniker for a good reason. The walls were papered, floor to ceiling, with cascading images of purple flowers, from lilacs to tulips to orchids. Purple rain of the floral variety. Originally, the room's window had been hung with matching purple-print curtains, while the large rug covering most of the floor had been an unfortunate shade of plum. Those had been the first items to go. I'd tried to tone down the visual volume with crisp white curtains and white linen on the twin beds, but the place still looked like a shrine to the Artist Formerly Known As.

"Ooh, Prince... I get it!" Sister Mary Thomas cried with a clap of her hands, somewhat to my surprise. Though maybe she tuned in to the oldies rock station while doing farm chores and was familiar with the Purple One's oeuvre. "And I love it! This is my favorite color."

"Mine, too!" Mary Christopher gave an enthusiastic nod. "Mary Thomas and I call dibs on this room."

"Very well, it's yours," Mother Superior agreed, her lips twitching in what could have been a smile as the two nuns hurriedly dragged their rolling cases inside. "Now, why don't we see the next offering."

I walked down to the next door and opened it. "This room is a bit lower key," I said with a smile. "More of a country French feel to it, don't you think? Oh, and it has just the one bed."

Everyone merely peeked past the door frame, except Mother Superior. Leaving her bag beside the door, the nun walked all the way inside until she was standing a nose-length away from the toile wallpaper. Though I wasn't much of a toile enthusiast myself, I rather liked the faded robin's-egg-blue background with its brown pastoral scene.

"Very impressive. Hand blocked...original colors," Mother Superior murmured approvingly, pulling off her glasses to study the pattern on the wall. "You know, there's a lucrative market for original wallpaper of this era."

Since she was a nun, I assumed she wasn't planning to abscond with a couple of strips to sell on eBay once her stay with me was over. Smiling, I walked in to join her.

"I'll keep that in mind. I'm afraid the bedspread is a modern reproduction, though the colors and patterns match amazingly well. The furniture is fairly contemporary, too, probably midcentury."

"Quite homey," she decreed, putting on her glasses again and surveying the place.

I nodded. "Why don't you take this room for yourself?"

"But Sister Mary Paul—"

"Can stay with me," Sister Mary George declared

from the doorway, smiling as she put her arm around
the much smaller nun's shoulders. "This is so much fun.
I can't wait to see the next room, Nina."

"Then let's go."

Leaving Mother Superior to unpack, I led the remaining three nuns to the next room and threw open
the door. "I call this room Country Living."

Sister Mary George walked inside, eyes wide as she
looked about. The wallpaper in this room was a faded
cabbage rose pattern, almost more gray than pink. The
coverlets on the twin beds were a darker pink and edged
with white Battenburg lace that matched the white Battenburg lace curtains. The armoire, mirrored dresser,
and headboards on the twin beds were all plain pine. An
old-fashioned pitcher and basin set—antiques, as far as
I could tell—sat atop the dresser on a Battenburg lace
runner. Definitely a rural Georgia vibe.

Sister Mary George turned back to me with a broad
smile. "I love it. This reminds me of visiting my Nan
back when I was a little girl. Mary Paul, do you like?"

By way of reply, the little nun scurried into the room
with her bag. "Yes, I like," she declared in her thick accent, eyes gleaming.

Which left Sister Mary Julian. She was the only one
of the nuns thus far whom I'd not heard speak. Thin
with an olive complexion, she had the pale lips and
sunken cheeks of an ascetic. I suspected she might feel
right at home in the last bedroom.

The room had been empty when I'd moved in. A little
research into similar floor plans made me think it might
once have served as a lady's dressing room. Since the
current lady of the house was more than capable of get-

ting dressed in her own bedroom, I had decided to turn
it into a fourth upstairs bedroom. With that in mind,
I'd furnished it with a few of my own pieces: a simple
cherry four-poster and dresser. A teak lap desk sat atop
the tan counterpane and could serve as a breakfast table
or bedside stand.

The wallpaper here was in shades of sand and the
palest of pinks, with its design of tiny cranes amid bam-
boo evoking an Asian feel. Taking that as my theme,
I'd added a wall scroll I'd found at a garage sale, its red
kanji symbols representing love, wisdom, and health.
The window, I'd covered in a simple linen shade that resembled a miniature shoji screen. I'd told myself that, if
I ever decided to take up yoga or meditation, this would
be the room for it.

"Here you go, Sister. It's a bit small," I apologized as
I opened the door, "but you get it to yourself."

The nun rolled her bag inside and glanced about.
Then she smiled, the action transforming her expression from frighteningly grim to severely handsome.

"Lovely," she bellowed in a voice that made me jump.
I might have expected that volume to come from a Cymbeline High linebacker, but not from this sharp-edged
woman. In the same loud tones, she added, "I'll get un-
packed right now. Thank you."

Heaving a relieved sigh, I backed out into the hallway. So far, so good. My guests appeared to be happy
with their rooms. Mattie had her fuzzy head poked halfway into the Prince Chamber, where her new friend,
Sister Mary Thomas, had taken up residence. I'd been
a little concerned as to whether or not the Aussie would

be willing to share her digs with strangers, but apparently she was good with this particular group.

I whistled the dog away from the room and headed for the stairs. I'd give the sisters time to unpack—which should take about five minutes—and then I'd show them where the coffee and tea and my kind-of-homemade cookies were located. They'd also put in a request for a place to hold their daily prayers, so I'd rearranged the parlor to give them ample room. And maybe they'd want a look at the garden, or—

"Sisters," came Mother Superior's imperious nasal tones just as I'd started down the first step.

I turned to see her standing in the hallway. The other nuns promptly quit their rooms to gather before her. She glanced at the large, leather-strapped watch on her left wrist.

"It's nine forty," the nun confirmed. "Finish unpacking and attending to any personal needs, and then let's gather at ten am sharp in the downstairs hallway. We'll need time to pick up the signs, and then we'll want to be ready for the arriving tourists and the lunch crowd afterward. Oh, and you have permission to change into your outdoor habits. Any questions?"

The other sisters apparently did not. I, on the other hand, did. Signs and tourists and lunch crowds combined with nuns sounded a bit, well, strange. Plus, I felt somewhat responsible for the old women now that I was in charge of housing them. Reassuring myself I wasn't just being nosy, I raised my hand.

"Yes, Ms. Fleet?"

"Uh, where are you and the sisters going?" I ventured. "I mean, not that it's my business, but I need to know if I should put out the cookie platter and coffee after lunch, or if you'll be gone all day. Or if you want me to call you an Uber or something?"

Mother Superior gave me another of those looks through those oversized glasses, but her tone was mild as she replied, "We can walk, thank you. We're only going as far as the town square. You see, even though we've been evicted from our convent, we sisters haven't given up the fight. And so we requested a permit from the town. We're staging a protest outside of Mr. Bainbridge's office…and we shall show up there daily, rain and shine, until he reinstates our lease."

SIX

"Isn't this exciting?" Sister Mary Christopher warbled as the nuns walked, two by two, toward the town square. "I've never been in a protest before. Will it be dangerous?"

"This isn't the 1960s," Sister Mary George said with a smile. "The only danger is if you don't stay hydrated. Did everyone remember a water bottle?"

The "everyone" all nodded...me included. Still feeling like they were my responsibility, I'd managed to persuade Mother Superior to let me tag along with her and the other nuns. She hadn't seemed too keen on the idea until I bribed her with the cookie platter.

I felt a little conspicuous in my bright pink as I trotted down the sidewalk alongside them. They had changed into what apparently was the order's outdoor habit: medium gray instead of black, with short sleeves and a nape-length veil, and socks instead of stocking. And, of course, the usual gold crucifix. Doubtless this was a much more practical uniform than the 1940s-era long black habit for wrangling goats and making cheese.

"Do you think the townspeople will be on our side?" Sister Mary Thomas wanted to know. "What if they think it's better to replace the convent with the golf course?"

"The mayor has assured me that the majority of Cymbeline's citizens are on our side," Mother Superior replied. "What we hope to do by our presence is galvanize them to put pressure on Mr. Bainbridge to reverse his decision."

"You said you had signs for the protest?" I asked Mother Superior.

"Yes. Ms. Gleason, who owns the print shop on the square's west side, said she would print them up for us."

"Back in the old days," Sister Mary Julian loudly observed, "we used to make our own protest signs with paint and a cut-up cardboard box. We didn't buy them from the store."

"Yes, but Ms. Gleason kindly donated her services," Mother Superior countered. "It would have been rude to refuse."

We reached the town square a few minutes later. Given that it was a Monday, the place wasn't packed like it would have been on a weekend. But with classes out for the semester, plenty of schoolkids and college students on summer vacay mingled with the usual retirees and antique-hunting tourists.

Our first stop was Bard Printing. As with coffee, there apparently weren't any Shakespearean quotes about the printing press that could be twisted into a clever business name. Though at least the owner had made an effort. A string of tinkling bells announced our entry.

The inside of the neat red-bricked storefront was mostly a long white counter piled with books of forms and sample invitations. Half of the tan wall behind the counter was adorned with framed custom posters. The other half was decorated with framed, silkscreened

T-shirts in different colors. Each tee was printed with the business's logo: a stylized Shakespeare head with BARD PRINTING in Elizabethan-style block font.

"Good morning, Sisters... Reverend Mother," came a woman's cheery voice from the open doorway behind the counter. I'd met the owner, Becca Gleason, when I'd decided to send formal change-of-address cards to my relatives and friends and needed a printer. Childless, divorced, and currently not looking, Becca ran her shop single-handedly except for a couple of part-time college kids.

She walked to the counter while peeling off an ink-stained work apron. Beneath it she wore one of the logo T-shirts in an autumn orange hue that artfully set off her dark skin and the best afro since Pam Grier.

"We're here for the signs, Ms. Gleason," Mother Superior said. "As I told you on the telephone, it was very kind of you to donate them."

"Not at all." Her genial expression hardened. "Believe me, if there's any chance to put the screws to Greg Bainbridge, I'm glad to help."

Then, catching sight of me amid the bevy of nuns, she nodded. "Hi, Nina. Are you going to take part in the protest?"

"Just in charge of the refreshments," I answered with a smile, and raised the plastic bin of cookies. "I'm letting the good sisters do the heavy lifting."

"Well, *I'm* tempted to join them." Becca reached under the broad counter and pulled out half a dozen white corrugated plastic signs with wooden handles attached. "That sorry so-and-so Bainbridge conned my daddy into selling his property south of town for a third

of what it was worth. He did that with a lot of folks—
that's how he was able to build Southbridge."

As she spoke, she handed out the signs, one per nun.
"I did like you asked, Reverend Mother. The same slogan on one side for all of them, and then the different
slogans on the other sides."

"Very good," the old woman said with an approving
nod. "Let us pray they are effective. Come, Sisters. It's
time to march. We'll make our starting point the bench
on the square that faces Mr. Bainbridge's office."

We made our goodbyes and headed down the street,
where we turned at the corner. We passed a couple
of antique shops and the First Folio bookstore. Now a
small independent druggist and a real estate office lay
directly ahead of us. Beyond those businesses were the
Taste-Tee-Freeze Creamery and the antiques store above
which Bainbridge had his office.

It was warming up, and I was glad that Sister Mary
George had insisted on the bottles of water. The one
thing the town square lacked was a water fountain,
meaning you had to walk all the way to the public restroom one block over for water and other relief. Maybe
now that I was part of the Chamber of Commerce, I'd
suggest that we install a drinking fountain directly on
the square. Heck, if they'd put up a plaque with my name
on it, maybe I'd donate the fixture to the town myself.

I was so wrapped up in picturing my new commemo-
rative drinking fountain that, before I realized it, I was
lagging well behind the sisters. They'd already reached
the corner and were making their way across the painted
crosswalk to the designated protest bench on the square.

With a glance about to be certain the sheriff wasn't

lurking nearby, I decided to cross the one-way street midblock. I didn't hear the warning blat of a car horn until I'd already stepped off the curb and into the vehicle's path.

Barely had the first couple of years of my life flashed before my eyes when a strong hand clamped onto my shoulder. A heartbeat later, I found myself yanked back onto the sidewalk just as a land yacht of a sedan screeched to a halt right where I'd been standing seconds earlier.

As I struggled to regain the breath that had whooshed right out of me, the car's tinted front passenger window slid halfway down. A hunched-shoulder white guy somewhere past retirement age with an impossibly full head of equally white hair turned to look at me.

"Sorry, I wasn't paying attention," I gasped in his direction. "Don't worry, I'm fine… I, uh—"

The man didn't bother acknowledging my attempted apology. Instead, he lifted a pudgy wrinkled hand and silently extended a finger…and not the finger that would indicate I was Number One. Before I could react to that, the power window rolled up again, and the man drove off.

"Well, that was classy," came a male voice behind me—belonging, I assumed, to the Good Samaritan who'd pulled me from the car's path.

The man's words were muffled, but he sounded vaguely familiar. Trouble was, I was so shaken by the realization that I'd almost become a hood ornament that I couldn't focus enough to figure out who the speaker was.

"Don't let that middle-finger salute rattle you," he went on as he released his grip on me. "Mr. Tough Guy had a New York plate on his car. He's probably a snow-bird who forgot he's almost a thousand miles from home. It didn't mean anything."

The snowbird reference meant someone who spent their fall and winter down south and returned north for the spring and summer. While most of those part-time residents were lovely folks, some of them…well, weren't.

Nodding, I turned to agree with my rescuer.

"On the bright side," I began, "he probably—what the heck, *you*?"

SEVEN

"You!" MY RESCUER shot back at me through a layer of black-and-white fleece.

We stared at each other for a few seconds in mutual disbelief—or at least, I assumed he was as dismayed as me. It's hard to judge expression when the other person is wearing a giant bird head. For the person who'd yanked me from the jaws of death was none other than my old nemesis, Freezie the Penguin...aka Harry Westcott.

This time, the penguin head was in place—hence the muffled voice—but his right flipper was tucked to one side so that it bared his arm, which he'd used to pull me to safety. I shouldn't have been surprised to see him, since I'd just walked past the ice cream shop that was his home base. He must have exited the place for a round of mascotting on the square at the same time I'd done my death-defying move.

It looked like I owed Harry Westcott big-time. And that wasn't the sort of obligation I wanted hanging over me.

Sighing, I set down the cookie bin at my feet and stuck out my hand. "How about we call a truce, Mr. Westcott...at least, long enough for me to say thanks for saving my bacon."

For a few uncomfortable seconds, I was afraid he

wasn't going to reciprocate. Then the big penguin head nodded, and he shook.

"Fine, truce. But you're lucky I didn't recognize you from the back, or I might not have run so fast. You did something with your hair, or something."

"Yeah, I washed it and brushed it for a change," was my ironic reply, recalling that the first time he'd seen me had been while I'd been gardening, with my hair a sweaty, tied-back mess.

"Well, uh, it looks good."

Which half-hearted compliment probably burned his beak—er, lips—to say, but I'd take it.

"Yoo-hoo, Nina!" Sister Mary Julian bellowed from the corner of the square across from us. "Hurry up; we're about to start."

"On the way!" I called back, and smiled and waved in her direction. To Harry, I said, "Thanks again for the rescue, but I've got to go. I kind of talked my way into helping Mother Superior and the other sisters with their protest."

"You're with those nuns?" Harry asked, his penguin head tilting to one side in apparent confusion. The protest part of my explanation had seemingly blown right by him.

"Kind of. They're the first guests of my new bed-and-breakfast, so I'm giving them the full concierge experience. Homemade snacks delivered while they protest against their oppressor," I said, and raised the cookie bin so he could see its contents.

The penguin head snapped upright so quickly, I was sure he'd suffered whiplash. "Wait, what? You're saying you've turned my house into a B&B?"

"I've turned *my* house into a B&B," I corrected him. "Now, gotta go. Can't start the protest late!"

Not waiting for a reply, I glanced both ways this time before rushing across the street to the square. Once safely across, I passed the boiled-peanut cart and jogged toward the corner bench beneath a large shade tree where the sisters had gathered. The signs leaned at crazy angles against the bench arm in anticipation.

"Sorry, don't mind me," I panted as I reached the group. "I took a little detour to say hi to an old friend. Are we ready to start the march?"

"We are," Mother Superior said as the nuns gathered closer, "but first, we should ask for fortitude and guidance in our endeavor. Sisters—and Ms. Fleet—let us pray."

I listened politely as Mother Superior intoned the usual words of thanks and requests for protection. Following a chorus of amens, the nuns moved briskly back to the bench, where each old woman shouldered a protest sign. Mother Superior raised hers and swept a glance across their small group.

"When we passed the parking lot next to the square a few minutes ago, Mr. Bainbridge's automobile was parked there, meaning he is in his office."

She pointed in the direction of the Weary Bones Antique Shoppe. The second story above that business was unmarked, but a pair of open windows with fluttering lace curtains indicated it was occupied. I assumed the entry was a stairway to the rear in the alley, just as with many of the other second-floor businesses on the square.

The nun went on, "While it's not necessary for Mr.

Bainbridge to witness our efforts, it certainly does not hurt. Sister Mary George, you have the whistle?"

"Right here, Reverend Mother." The tall nun smiled, indicating a silver gym coach whistle that hung around her neck.

Mother Superior nodded. "Very well. Sisters, let us begin."

While I settled on the bench with my cookies and the water bottles to serve as cheerleader, the nuns fell into line and began their march around the square. I watched in interest, for their protest was unlike any I'd seen before.

No bullhorns, cat hats, or rocks here. Instead, the women trooped along the sidewalk in silence, spaced equidistant from each other and moving at a measured pace as they began to traverse the square. Tiny Sister Mary Paul led the procession, with the statuesque Sister Mary George bringing up the rear. The remaining nuns were arranged between them by size.

Interestingly, none of their signage seemed directed at Bainbridge personally. The fronts of all the signs read the same: God's Will Be Done. The backs varied: God is the Builder of Everything, Bless the House of Your Servant, and more. My favorite, however, was the one Sister Mary Thomas wielded—the one that read Goats, Not Golf!.

Each time the nuns reached the corner where Bainbridge's second-story office overlooked the square, they stopped and lined up, facing it. On some silent signal, they would flip their signs around so the "God's Will" slogans all pointed that way. If the developer was brave enough to glance out his window, no way could he miss seeing the sisters standing there in silent witness.

And the noiseless protest wasn't going unnoticed by the townspeople, either. As the sisters continued circling the square, passing drivers honked and gave them a thumbs-up, some even leaning out their windows to shout words of encouragement. The foot traffic on the square was equally enthusiastic, with passersby stepping out of the way to let the marchers go by.

But the nuns had a bit of competition. Out on the bandstand, Freezie the Penguin was bopping and moonwalking to faint music that I assumed must be coming from a boombox. *His* performance was attracting the kiddie tourist set. Over the next half hour, while the nuns marched, four or five grade school–aged boys and girls took turns dancing alongside the penguin while their parents presumably were hitting the nearby antique stores.

The occasional teen girls were focused on Freezie, too. More than once, I saw one or two of them rush up the bandstand steps to take a selfie with him before running off in a torrent of giggles. Those girls looked like locals, and I suspected they knew full well who was under the penguin costume. Hence the nervous giggling.

"Hello. May I join you?" came a man's raspy voice beside me as I kept watch on all the action.

Standing beside the bench was a gentleman in his seventies wearing putty-colored pants and a bright-blue pullover that set off his full shock of white hair. He had ruddy cheeks reminiscent of Ronald Reagan, but his otherwise pallid complexion seemed a reflection more of illness than of a basic lack of melanin-producing cells.

For a single surprised moment, I thought he was the New Yorker who'd earlier flipped me off. But a second look told me this was someone else. For one thing, he was smiling. And his soft drawl that I could hear despite his labored breathing did not originate from the Empire State.

"Sure, let me make room," I replied, and moved the water bottles and cookie bin to one side.

The man lowered himself onto the wooden slats, gripping the edges with large, gnarled hands. "Thanks. I've got a little lung issue, and I gotta set down every so often when I walk."

"How far are you going?" I asked in concern. Chances were the "little lung issue" was actually a big one, like emphysema or COPD. My ex-father-in-law had suffered from the disease, and I could recall the difficulty he'd had walking even a short distance unassisted.

"Don't worry yourself, ma'am," the newcomer replied, smile broadening. "I don't have much farther to go. I'm headed across the street to the printing shop to visit my little girl. She's the owner."

That last was said with a father's unmistakable pride, and I gave him a surprised look. "You're Becca Gleason's dad?"

"I sure am. And, yes, she gets her good looks from her momma."

He'd doubtless used that line numerous times over the years as a mild joke...or to stave off unthinking comments from people who were clueless regarding mixed marriages.

"Oh, I'm not surprised you're her father," I hurried to assure him. "It's just funny how I was talking to Becca less than a half hour ago, and she mentioned her dad. And now, here you are. I'm Nina Fleet, by the way," I introduced myself, sticking out my hand. "I moved to town a few weeks ago."

"Welcome to our little town. Travis M. Gleason, at your service. Just call me Travis." His handshake was brief but surprisingly firm for someone of his age and debility. "What's with the nuns and all those signs? They protesting the Pope or something?"

"Actually, they're protesting against the developer who took over their convent and left them homeless."

The man's genial expression abruptly hardened.

"You mean Greg Bainbridge? He's the same sorry SOB that screwed me and a bunch of other folks…pardon my French."

Which I already knew, thanks to Becca. I gave him a headshake to show I wasn't worried over his mild vulgarity. "That's okay. What happened, if you don't mind saying?"

"It's no secret," Travis replied with a shrug. "About five years back, he showed up in our neighborhood with some official-looking report that said all the ground-water there was contaminated with heavy metals. Said the scientists claimed we'd get cancer and all the new babies would be born with defects if we kept drinking it. Scared the holy hell outta us."

"I'll bet," I replied, pretty sure I knew where this story was going.

The man nodded. "Of course, no one wanted to give up their place, especially since most of the mortgages were already paid off. But folks had kids and grandkids, and we got worried. So Bainbridge bought us all out, paid us maybe a third of what the land was worth. He said he'd just sit on the property until someday someone figured out how to fix it so folks could live there again. And we was all real grateful to him."

Saint Gregory strikes again.

Travis continued, "Then, a few months after the closings, Bainbridge came back with a new report saying the first tests were wrong. Bad sampling, he said. The water was fine, he said. Next day, bulldozers were out clearing everything so he could build that new subdivision of his."

"That's terrible."

"Yeah. He gets his new subdivision. Meantime, I'm stuck in a trailer in a park with a bunch of other old geezers, instead of living in my nice, paid-off house where my late wife and I raised our baby girl. I retired ten years ago, but now I've gotta go back to doing handyman work again to pay my rent."

The bitterness in his tone was obvious. I could understand why Becca was ready to jump in on the protest. "I assume you talked to an attorney about the deal?"

"More than one. But all the lawyers who reviewed our case said they wouldn't be able to prove in a court of law that he'd done anything illegal." His gnarled hands tightened into blocky fists. "If I wasn't sick, I'd of taken him out somewhere and beat the crud out of him long ago. But my girl says not to worry. She says he'll get his comeuppance someday."

"Maybe the nuns will have better success than the

lawyers. Cookie?" I offered, hoping to lighten the mood a bit.

A flicker of a smile returned. "Thanks, young lady, but I'd better go. Becca said she'd treat me to lunch at Peaches and Java."

"Well, enjoy. And nice meeting you."

We made our goodbyes, and he ambled off in the direction of the printing shop. It was then that I heard the shrill bleat of Sister Mary George's whistle. At the signal, the nuns made a sharp turn and headed back to where I was waiting at the bench.

"We are taking a short break," Mother Superior explained once they'd returned and set down their signs again. "Perhaps you can distribute those cookies to the sisters now. We'll make a decision on lunch after that."

"Of course."

I opened the bin and began handing out napkins and snacks. Mother Superior, meanwhile, drew Sister Mary George to one side and asked, "How are all the sisters holding up?"

"I'm afraid Mary Paul is a bit overheated. She should rehydrate and rest for a while. And Mary Thomas appeared to be limping."

"Just a blister," that nun bravely confirmed as she bit into cookie. "Maybe we can find a bit of sticking plaster at the drugstore?"

"A good idea," Mother Superior agreed. "Mary George can handle that. Someone please make sure that Mary Paul sits down and finishes her water. Speaking of which, we should probably have someone go to one of the shops to refill our bottles. Sister Mary Christopher?"

"I'm on it, Reverend Mother," the nun replied, her

usual warble toned down a few notches in the heat. She
began gathering the reusable containers as swiftly as
the thirsty women drained them.

Mother Superior gave an approving nod. "As for the
rest of you, if you wish to visit the facilities across the
way, now is the time to do so. I plan to take advantage
of them myself."

"Anything I can do to help, Reverend Mother?" I
wanted to know.

"Yes. Please stay with Sister Mary Paul until I return, and make sure she drinks her water."

While the other nuns dispersed, I closed up the
cookie bin; then, spreading one of the extra napkins
atop it, I set the container in front of the bench where
the tiny nun was sitting. "Here, Sister, prop your feet
on top of the box so you're more comfortable."

"Thank you, child," she said with a smile, and complied as I sat beside her. "I just need rest for moment."

She leaned against the bench back and closed her
eyes. Once I was certain she was merely taking a snooze
and not sinking into some sort of heatstroke, I glanced
around the square.

It was lunchtime now, and the foot traffic was clearing out as people headed home or to one of the restaurants for a bite. Even the boiled-peanut guy was taking
a break. The gazebo was empty, too, except for a couple
of young boys chasing each other around it. My penguin
friend had apparently left for alternate climes, for I saw
neither hide nor beak of him. I pulled out my phone and
spent a few minutes checking my social media, reminding myself that I probably needed to set up a page for
my new B&B. Though, of course, I still needed to think

up a snazzy name for the place before I filed the official incorporation papers with the state. A few ideas flitted through my mind. Magnolia Manor… Peach Tree Inn…

By the time I looked up again, a quarter of an hour had passed, and Sister Mary Paul was the only nun in sight. I was mentally kicking myself for forgetting to pull a cookie for myself before turning the food bin into a footstool when I heard what sounded like a woman's scream.

The nun's eyes flew open. "What that?"

"I don't know."

I jumped from the bench and spun about, looking for the source of the cry, but saw no one. It had to be one of the teenage girls acting silly again, I told myself. *Ignore them, and when they don't get any reaction, they'll go away.*

But as I sat back down again, a plump middle-aged brunette came trotting around the corner from the Weary Bones Antique Shoppe. I noted in passing that she was wearing almost the exact same outfit as me. Her pink top was sleeveless and more blouselike, however, and she was wearing knee-length black shorts instead of cropped jeans.

She caught sight of me and halted. Then, to my surprise, she began jumping about and waving her arms.

"Help! Help!" she called. "You've got to call an ambulance!"

Tourist with heatstroke was my first guess. Maybe a heart attack. I glanced about the square again. Sister Mary Paul and I were the only ones in sight.

"Wait here, Sister; I'll find out what's wrong," I told Mary Paul, and rushed toward the jumping woman.

"What's wrong?" I demanded as I reached her. She merely shook her head.

Channeling Sister Mary Julian, I waved my phone and bellowed, "Look, lady, I know you're upset, but you need to get a grip. Tell me what's happened so I know what to tell the 911 operator!"

Eyes wide and brimming with tears, she glanced behind her, and then turned back to me. With a wail, she finally managed, "Someone's stabbed him. He's dead!"

My heart did the proverbial leap into my throat. *Stabbed? Dead?* Almost choking now myself, I demanded, "Who's stabbed? Who do you think is dead?"

"Him…that cute actor guy. You know, the one dressed up as Freezie the Penguin!"

EIGHT

I GRABBED THE woman by her thick, sunburned arm, fleetingly registering the bright-colored parade of tattooed cartoon bears wrapped around her beefy bicep. I'd seen that design before, but I didn't have time to recall what it meant.

"The penguin!" I demanded. "Tell me where he is!"

"He's lying in the alley behind the antique store. I—I was taking a short cut, and…no, no, I don't want to go back there again!"

But I was dragging her alongside the building toward the alley anyhow. I darned sure didn't want to see a dead guy, either—especially not one I knew. But if he really was dead, I needed to know where to direct the cops. Plus, I didn't trust the woman's diagnosis. Maybe Freezie—I didn't want to say Harry, because that made it way too real—wasn't dead yet. Heck, maybe he hadn't even been stabbed. Maybe he'd tripped on those big mascot feet and fallen on a ketchup bottle. Maybe…

"OhmygodHarry!" I choked out as we rounded the corner.

Sprawled ten feet away from us on the ground next to the dumpster was a motionless black-and-white figure. He lay on his back, one furry flipper reaching out in our direction. The other was flopped atop his belly beneath the upright blade of a very large kitchen knife that had been plunged into his chest. Just for emphasis, a bright red stain was beginning to seep through the oval of white faux fur that ran from chin to belly.

What could I say? He looked pretty damned dead to me, too.

Breathe, breathe, breathe, I told myself as the woman and I gripped each other for mutual support. Not that I liked the guy all that much, but he was young and vital and good-looking, and less than an hour earlier he'd saved *my* life. And who in the heck would want to kill an unemployed actor?

And then the flipper on his chest gave a barely noticeable quiver.

"He's still alive! We need the paramedics now! Wait," I shrieked as the woman pulled her arm free from my grasp. "Where are you going?"

"Away from here!" she shrieked right back.

She took off running in the same direction from which we'd come, leaving me alone with a guy with a knife in him. I took a swift breath and shut my eyes for an instant as adrenaline surged through me to dizzying effect. Or maybe it was simply the wafting odor of rotting garbage that was getting to me.

That first aid class I'd taken had helped when Harry had been on the verge of heatstroke, but this was a thousand times over my pay grade. One thing I did remember learning, however, was never to pull an impaled object from an injured person. Chances were said object was keeping the victim from bleeding out. So I used the best first aid tool I had at hand and started punching keys on my phone.

"Nine one one, what's your emergency?" the tinny voice in my ear asked.

The next few moments passed in the clichéd blur you always read about as I identified myself and relayed the information to the 911 dispatcher as best I could.

Having been assured that both an ambulance and the sheriff's department were on their way, I hung up, shoved the phone back into my pocket, and frantically wondered what in the heck to do next. But I already knew the answer. At this point there was nothing I could do for Harry except maybe pray.

Problem was, I was pretty rusty at that.

"There she is!" Sister Mary Julian bellowed from somewhere behind me.

Then, again, I could always find the right people to do that praying for me.

I whipped about to see Mary Julian and the other nuns clustered at the corner. Apparently, Sister Mary Paul had pointed them in my direction once they'd returned from their respective errands.

Mother Superior didn't wait for any explanation.

"Quickly, Nina, have you already called 911?" she demanded as she rushed past me and dropped to her knees beside the injured man. Sister Mary George was right behind her. The other nuns followed as well, lining up behind the pair and beginning a silent prayer.

I nodded. "The paramedics and sheriff are both on the way. Reverend Mother, I think he's still alive…but I didn't dare touch him."

Mother Superior nodded, glasses flashing in the sunlight.

"You did the right thing, my child. But we should remove that silly head so the poor man can breathe. And we should find out if there's someone on the square with medical knowledge—a doctor, or a nurse—who can help while we wait for the paramedics to arrive."

"My sister-in-law, Gemma Tanaka," Sister Mary George promptly exclaimed. "She used to be an emergency room nurse. Let me run to Peaches and Java and get her."

"No, let me," I broke in. "I can't just stand here and watch, and I'm not really good when it comes to praying. And I'm wearing running shoes."

Mother Superior gave me a curt nod, and I took off. I didn't bother trying to call Gemma on my cell first. It was lunchtime, and she probably wouldn't have her phone on her. And even if she did, she might not answer on the first try. By the time I could get hold of her and explain the situation, I'd already be on the shop's doorstep.

Actually, it was close to a minute later—hey, I said I was wearing running shoes, not that I was the Flash!—when I burst through the front door of Peaches and Java. Gemma was near the front taking an order from a table of four retiree tourists, and I all but fell into her arms.

"Nina, what in the heck?" she demanded, though her initial annoyance swiftly morphed into alarm as she saw the look on my face. "Girl, what's wrong?"

"We need a nurse. Sister Mary George said you could help. Grab some towels and a first aid kit if you have one, and let's go!"

To my relief, she didn't question me. Leaping into ER mode, she rushed behind the counter where Daniel was working. She bent and searched a moment, then straightened back up with a red plastic case in one hand and a stack of bar towels in the other.

"Emergency, gotta go," she told her husband, and gave him a quick peck on the cheek.

Daniel nodded, apparently flashing back to the old days when his wife was still an ER nurse and on call. "We got it, honey." Then, turning in his daughter's direction, he called, "Jazz, need you to fill in for your mom!"

"Where are we going?" Gemma snapped as the shop door slammed behind us.

I pointed. "The alley behind Weary Bones."

"Okay, let's move. Nine one one's already called?"

Still panting, I trudged after her. "They're on the way." To punctuate that, in the distance now I could hear sirens. "Mother Superior and the other nuns are with him."

"What happened? Someone pass out?"

"No, stabbed. It-It looks pretty bad. The sheriff's department is on their way, too."

I expected a shocked reaction, but apparently Gemma had seen it all in her hospital days. "You can't always tell with things like this. Any idea who the victim is?"

"It's Harry."

Gemma halted so abruptly I almost fell over her. "Harry? Our Harry? Harry Westcott?"

"Yeah, it's him. He was still wearing his penguin suit."

"Damn it, boy," she muttered, almost to herself. "I warned you. How in the—never mind." She broke off as she realized I was staring at her in confusion. "None of that's important right now. Let's go."

We reached the alley a few moments later. Not unexpectedly, other passersby had stumbled across the scene in my absence. Maybe half a dozen people were standing beside the nuns now, gaping at the fallen man… and, in the case of a few of the bystanders, recording the action with their smartphones.

Bunch of ghouls. Probably putting it up on YouTube, I thought in angry dismay. Suppressing my first impulse to grab every single phone and stomp them all into oblivion, I instead called, "Reverend Mother, Gemma's here to help."

"Please move aside, folks," Gemma commanded as she pushed her way past the knot of lookie-loos. "I'm a nurse."

I stayed back, ready to serve as bouncer if necessary. Besides, I didn't want a closer look. Though my view of the victim was fairly well blocked now by Gemma and the nuns, I could see the penguin head lying to one side.

Les Miserables redux, I told myself, fleetingly recalling the other time I'd seen that penguin head rolling around.

The sound of sirens was growing louder. Gemma was tugging on a pair of disposable latex gloves she'd pulled from her first aid kit. She glanced back at me from where she knelt beside the motionless man.

"Nina, run back to the square so you can direct the paramedics." To Mother Superior, she said, "Reverend Mother, can you and the other sisters make sure everyone stands at least ten feet back?

"And no photography," she added with a businesslike glare at the guilty parties. "There's a man clinging to life here."

While the nuns swiftly reassembled to form a gray

barricade, I rushed off to do as Gemma ordered. I'd barely reached the square again when I saw strobing red and blue lights.

I began waving my arms to catch the cop's attention, ignoring for the moment the shouted questions from some of the nearby business owners who'd heard the commotion and were peeking outside their shop doors.

The deputy squealed his cruiser to a stop a few feet from me, parking up on the curb. Thankfully, he'd turned off the siren, though he'd left the blue and red lights flashing. Bald, tall, and broad, and wearing a belt packed with pistol, handcuffs, and who knew what else over his tan-and-brown uniform, the African American cop radiated competency.

"You the one who called, ma'am?"

"Yes. The victim's back there in the alley," I explained and pointed. "A nurse is taking care of him while we're waiting on the EMS guys."

"Good. You a witness? I'll need to talk to you once I secure the situation."

He gave a brisk nod and immediately trotted off in that direction. Meanwhile, I could see down the main street two more sets of flashing lights headed toward the square.

Thank God, the paramedics.

I did a little jumping in addition to my arm-waving now. Between my gymnastics and the lights and sirens, it was pretty evident to everyone around the square that something big was going on. Fortunately, the EMS trucks reached me before any curiosity seekers did.

"This way!" I shouted, pointing as the lead vehicle slowed, and the female paramedic in the passenger's seat leaned out. "The victim's in the alley behind the antique store."

I followed on foot and watched as they swiftly parked and rolled out the big guns...meaning, of course, a gurney piled with bags of portable equipment. The deputy had already moved the growing crowd away from the mouth of the alley to the opposite street corner. Gemma still hovered over the motionless man, the nuns circling the pair.

He must still be alive, I thought in relief. Maybe he had a chance if they got him to Cymbeline General fast enough.

As I watched, two of the blue-uniformed paramedics promptly descended upon him with IVs and portable monitors. Gemma scrambled to her feet and huddled with the other two EMS officers. Apparently satisfied she was leaving Harry in good hands, she stripped off the latex gloves and gathered her gear.

"How's Harry doing? Will he make it?" I ventured as she reached me.

Gemma gave me an odd look. "I don't know. That's between him and God and the surgeons. But, Nina, that's not Harry lying there."

"Wait, what?"

Confused, I craned my neck, trying to see past her to the still form being worked on by the paramedics. I could hear clipped muttering from them... *BP*, *vitals*, *shock*, *internal bleeding*...none of which sounded very positive. Who they actually were working on, I couldn't tell from my vantage point. All I really could see was the costume. But why would someone besides Harry have been wearing the penguin getup?

And, more importantly, who was that someone?

"What are you saying?" I demanded in disbelief. "If it's not Harry, then who in the heck is lying there with a knife in his chest?"

"Yeah, who?" came a now-familiar voice behind me. I swung about and gave a startled little shriek.

"OhmygodHarry!" I cried for the second time in less than thirty minutes, feeling myself sway a little in shocked relief. Harry Westcott was standing before me, definitely *not* stabbed. "Thank God you're alive!"

And before I realized what I was doing, I leaped forward and gave him a big hug.

My first reflexive thought was that he might be on the lean side, but that was definitely muscle beneath the black T-shirt he wore over his black bike shorts. My second thought was that he was cold. Not in attitude, though I was aware he wasn't actually hugging me back. But his exposed skin and even his shirt felt way too chilled for someone standing outside in the Georgia noontime sun.

My third thought was that I was making a total idiot of myself.

"Sorry," I muttered, and quickly released him. "Nothing personal. I was just shocked to see you. I mean, I've been thinking that you were doing the old knocking-on-heaven's-door thing, and then I find out you're alive…"

I trailed off, feeling my face flush, but he didn't seem to notice. Instead, he was peering past me at the motionless man on the ground.

The paramedics had cut the penguin suit all the way off him and had stabilized the knife in place with what looked suspiciously like duct tape. On a count, the four paramedics lifted him high enough to slide him onto the gurney, leaving the faux-fur costume behind on the ground like a shed skin. Then, raising the wheeled stretcher to full height, they came rolling in our direction.

The three of us stepped back as they rushed past. Between the paramedics and all the equipment piled on the gurney, I couldn't get a good look at the patient's face. But once they'd gone by, I could see the back of the man's head—a head that looked surprisingly familiar.

"You're kidding!" I choked out. "*He* was the guy in the penguin suit?"

"He? He who?" Harry demanded.

Gemma nodded, her graying locks bouncing. "Shocked the heck out of me, too, when I expected to find Harry and saw *him* lying there instead." Then, with a glance at Harry, she asked, "Baby, are you okay? You look like you're shivering."

Indeed, he had his arms wrapped around himself as if trying to keep warm. The sight reminded me how his skin had felt unusually cold, as if he'd been standing under an air-conditioner running full blast.

"Yeah, well, you'd be shivering, too, if you'd spent the past half hour locked in a walk-in freezer."

"Wait, what?" I exclaimed.

I'd been saying that a lot recently, I realized. For her part, Gemma looked equally confused.

"What are you talking about, Harry?" she demanded, planting hands on hips. "What freezer…and who locked you inside it?"

"The walk-in at the Taste-Tee-Freeze. It was getting pretty hot out, so I took a break to get some cold packs to stuff inside the costume. I went into the freezer look-ing for them, and someone slammed the door shut be-hind me."

"On purpose?" I asked, frowning. "Are you sure? Maybe someone thought someone else had left the door open by accident, and they closed it."

Harry snorted. "Yeah, or maybe it was the wind."

He glowered at me and then turned back to Gemma. "We can talk about that later. What I need to know right now is, who was that guy wearing my penguin suit?"

"Oh, I thought I told you," Gemma replied. "Though I guess we shouldn't be surprised, since he's the guy in town everyone loves to hate."

Gemma and I looked at each other; then, in chorus, we answered, "Gregory Bainbridge."

NINE

BY THE TIME the paramedics rolled off in a blaze of emergency lights and a fury of sirens, the deputy who'd been first on the scene had dispersed everyone but us and the nuns. Now he was unrolling bright-yellow crime scene tape.

"I'll need you folks to move over here to the corner," he said, pointing. "As soon as I get a perimeter set up, I'll want to take your statements."

Then, when Harry started toward the abandoned penguin suit, he barked out, "Sir, do not touch the costume. We'll be bagging that as evidence. Now please join the others."

"Great, there goes the job," the actor muttered, but left what remained of the mascot outfit where it was. He let Gemma take him by the arm and lead him over to where the sisters huddled together.

"Don't worry, baby, you couldn't of worn it again, anyhow," I heard her tell him. "Not all cut up and bloody. I'm sure Jack will buy another one to replace it."

So where was Jack, anyhow? I wondered. Surely there was enough commotion going on that he and Jill would at least have stuck their heads out of their shop to see what was going on. And having done that, wouldn't they be concerned about Harry?

But Gemma was taking up the slack in the comforting department, though her manner was unmistakably maternal. As I watched, she gave Harry's bicep a comforting pat, and I recalled her saying how she'd been his babysitter when he was young. Despite the seriousness of the situation, I couldn't help but smile a little. It was obvious from Gemma's solicitous manner that she was stepping back into that mothering role. But as we joined up with the somber-faced nuns, she let go of Harry long enough to give her sister-in-law a hug.

"How you been, Laverna…er, Sister Mary George? I'm sorry it's been so long since I made it out to the convent for a visit."

"Now don't you fret, Gemma," the nun replied with a soft smile, returning the embrace. "I know how busy you are with the coffee shop and your family. And you can still call me Laverna…at least in private."

Then, smile slipping, she added, "Do you think Mr. Bainbridge is going to pull through?"

"The blade actually went in right below the rib cage. My guess is that it pierced his liver, probably nicked a lung, too. He was already in pretty bad shape by the time Nina brought me over. With the internal bleeding that's going on, I doubt he makes it to the ER."

"That's distressing news. Mr. Bainbridge is not a kind or honest man, but he *is* a child of God. We all will continue to pray for intercession on his behalf. And we'll pray just as hard that our sheriff finds the culprit who did this to him."

The deputy, meanwhile, finished marking off the crime scene site and taking pictures from various angles. Sticking the camera and remaining roll of tape in his belt, he marched over to us. "Folks, I need statements from you."

Since I was technically the first on-scene, I went first. While the deputy took notes, I gave him the best description I could of the screaming woman who'd gone AWOL on me—straight brunette hair, middle-aged, plump, pink sleeveless blouse and black walking shorts—and how she'd led me to Bainbridge.

The deputy shot me a skeptical look. "You know you're kinda describing yourself, don't you?"

I bristled a little at that. No way was I middle-aged, and while I might stand to lose a pound or five, I definitely wasn't plump.

Coolly, I replied, "It's strictly coincidental about the clothes. Oh, and she had a tattoo of cartoon bears around her right…no, left…upper arm. I don't have any tattoos."

"Doug," broke in a brusque voice, "why don't you hit the restaurants with that description, and I'll finish questioning your witnesses."

The newcomer was female, about my age and height, and wearing mirrored aviator sunglasses. She appeared to be a good fifty pounds heavier than me, though I suspected the extra weight was mostly muscle. Her brassy blonde hair was pulled back in a tight French braid that looked surprisingly girlish in contrast to her tan uniform shirt and brown tie and pants. And in case we didn't figure it out from her air of command, the big gold badge on her chest marked her as the local sheriff.

Deputy Jackson—I'd seen his name badge, which was engraved with the last name—meanwhile had snapped to attention. "You bet, Sheriff. On that right now."

The sheriff waited until he'd rounded the corner before addressing us.

"Good afternoon, folks. I'm Sheriff Connie Lamb. Sorry to keep you from your lunch, but as you know, we've got a situation here. I need to get statements from anyone who knows or who saw anything."

"Excuse me, Sheriff," Mother Superior broke in, dabbing at her forehead with a crisp white handkerchief, "but is it possible to move to a shaded spot? It's getting warm here in the alley, and several of the sisters are rather elderly."

I gave a commiserating nod. In addition to the growing heat, the noontime sun was beginning to do its job on the nearby dumpster, so that the faint whiff of rotting garbage I'd noticed earlier was rapidly becoming a tsunami of stench.

To our mutual relief, the sheriff nodded. "Certainly, Reverend Mother. Let me have a quick word with Deputy Mullins first."

She paused as a second deputy approached. This one was a young and wiry redhead wearing Horatio Caine/ *CSI: Miami*–style wire-rim shades with black lenses… which accessory, I suspected, he'd deliberately chosen to play up the resemblance. I'd also have wagered that he practiced whipping them on and off in front of a mirror, à la David Caruso's iconic character.

The two conferred a moment; then the sheriff said, "Deputy Mullins will assist Deputy Jackson with the crime scene. Why don't you folks walk back over to the gazebo with me so we can chat?"

The nuns made their statements first, taking their respective turns beneath the nearby shade tree where the sheriff was holding court. Gemma was next up but was back at the gazebo within minutes.

"Your turn, Nina," she told me.

Sheriff Lamb was talking on her shoulder mike as I approached. I heard her say "Roger that" before she clicked it off and turned her attention to me.

"Thanks for your patience, Ms. Fleet. I know you already gave Deputy Jackson a statement, so I appreciate your hanging around to answer my questions."

I nodded. We both knew this wasn't really a voluntary exercise, that she could make us all stay if it came to that, but I appreciated the polite fiction.

She flipped back a few pages in her notebook and then paused, fixing me with a look. She'd taken off the mirrored sunglasses—the better to seem less intimidating to us witnesses, I guessed—and I saw with interest that her eyes were the same ice blue as Mattie's one pale orb.

"You're Nina Fleet," she confirmed, though I winced as she pronounced in the old *Nee-nah* way.

"It's *Nine-ah*, actually," I corrected her, winning a nod and a scribble on her pad that I hoped was a pronunciation guide and not a note that said *troublemaker*.

She looked up again. "Any connection to Cameron Fleet, the professional golfer?"

"Unfortunately, yes. He's my ex-husband."

I'd considered going back to my maiden name after the divorce, but I had been a Fleet almost as long as I'd been a Chatham and had professional contacts under the former name. I had known that decision would leave me open to discovery, but I'd been lucky thus far. Besides my real estate agent, Debbie Jo, only a handful of people in town knew of my relationship to Cameron Fleet.

Those folks were golfers themselves or else fans who followed the tour on television. As such, they also had heard and read all the breathless tabloid accounts of Cam's philandering. The only upside of the whole situation—other than the generous divorce settlement, of course—was that, as the wronged wife, I usually got the sympathy vote.

Fortunately, Sheriff Lamb fell into the sympathetic category.

"Funny how it used to be just the football players and baseball players getting the bad press about their personal lives," she observed with a snort. "But now the pro golfers are giving those boys a run for the money. First Tiger, then Cameron, and I'm sure there's a few more the media hasn't figured out yet. Makes me glad I never let anyone put a ring on it," she finished, waggling her diamond-free left hand for emphasis.

Then, just as I was feeling a warm glow of sisterhood with her, the woman abruptly changed tactics. "Why was Mr. Bainbridge at your house yesterday?"

I stared back at her, momentarily speechless. I hadn't expected this question…mostly because I didn't recall mentioning my encounter with Bainbridge to anyone. Definitely not to Gemma or any of the sisters. But apparently someone had seen the real estate developer's car parked in front of my house the day before and made the sheriff aware of that fact.

I managed a shrug. "I didn't invite him over, if that's what you're asking. I never even met the man until he showed up on my doorstep yesterday looking for, how did he put it, a friendly face?"

"Uh-huh," she murmured, scribbling. "And what do you think he meant by that?"

"It was pretty self-explanatory. He knew I was new in town, and he was hoping I'd have an open mind about the whole 'evicting the nuns' thing. I guess he was tired of being the guy that everyone hates."

"And what did you tell him?"

"I told him to think of me as Switzerland."

"Uh-huh, neutral," she muttered, making more notes. "That'd make you about the only one. That's the problem with finding out who attacked him…pretty much everyone and his dog has a grudge against the man."

She wasn't kidding. Besides the Sisters of Perpetual Poverty, I knew of at least three more people—Becca, her father Travis, and Jack Hill—who all had serious axes to grind with Bainbridge. But since none of them had bothered to hide their enmity toward him, I wasn't going to name names.

The sheriff, meanwhile, flipped back a few pages in her notepad, and then looked up again. "I'd like to account for everyone's whereabouts around the time that Mr. Bainbridge was attacked. Your 911 call came at twelve twenty-two pm. Can you walk me through what you were doing for the thirty minutes before that time?"

I gave her the rundown—marching, breaking for cookies, everyone going off on errands while I hung with Sister Mary Paul—up until the time the brunette made her appearance.

She nodded in seeming satisfaction, and then asked, "So let me get this straight. Prior to the time you saw

Mr. Bainbridge in the alley, there's a period of about fifteen to twenty minutes where you can't corroborate the whereabouts of any of the nuns except Sister Mary Paul, correct?"

"I—I suppose so."

"What about Sister Mary George, specifically? Did you see in what direction she was headed during this time?"

"I think she was going to the drugstore to get some Band-Aids."

I frowned. Surely the sheriff wasn't implying that Sister Mary George had anything to do with the attack on Bainbridge! Still, who could deny that the Sisters of Perpetual Poverty seemingly had the strongest motive of anyone in town for wanting Bainbridge dead? And it didn't help that (a) Sister Mary George had experience with knives and (b) she had been in the general vicinity of the ice cream shop around the time Bainbridge had been stabbed.

Cue number four on my mental list of ax-grinders.

But Sheriff Lamb was already chasing another line of questioning. "Whose idea was it for the sisters to move into your bed-and-breakfast?"

"Mayor Green asked me to do it as a personal favor. She said all the other B&Bs in town were full."

The sheriff frowned. "Interesting. Just how long has your B&B been in business?"

"Officially? Since this morning."

If Sheriff Lamb had been the one sporting the *CSI: Miami* sunglasses instead of Deputy Mullins, now would have been the time she whipped them off, spouted a pithy one-liner, and put them back on again.

But all she said was, "You've been very helpful, Ms. Fleet. Do you mind if I ask a final question?"

"Be my guest."

"Do you have any idea why Mr. Bainbridge might have been wearing Mr. Westcott's penguin suit when he was stabbed?"

A very good question. But as I flashed back to the conversation I'd had with the man yesterday, I thought I had an answer.

"Actually, yes. Bainbridge told me that anytime he leaves his office, people yell insults while he crosses the square to the parking lot. So he started wearing disguises."

"Disguises?"

I nodded. "Overcoats and ball caps and such—anything that made it harder to recognize him. Since his office is right next to the Taste-Tee-Freeze, maybe he took a shortcut through their back door and saw Harry's costume hanging in the storeroom and decided it would make for better camouflage than a hat and coat."

Said aloud, my theory sounded fanciful, but the sheriff seemed satisfied. "That's very helpful, Ms. Fleet. I appreciate your cooperation. I don't believe I'll need anything more from you or Ms. Tanaka or the sisters, so all of you are free to go now."

While technically we'd all been free to leave at any time—back to that polite fiction thing—I smiled. "Glad to help."

The sheriff smiled back, momentarily looking far less intimidating than she had just thirty seconds earlier. "Oh, and there is one last witness I need a statement from. Could you let Mr. Westcott know I need to talk with him?"

I nodded again and hurried back toward the bandstand. I recalled Harry telling me he'd gone to high school with the sheriff. Would that give him a pass when it came to questioning, or would Sheriff Lamb be even tougher on him so as not to appear she was playing favorites?

I didn't have time to debate that question with myself, however. I saw as I climbed the bandstand's wooden steps that things had changed during the few minutes I'd been gone. The nuns now were standing in a circle, hands folded and eyes downcast while softly praying. Gemma was seated by Harry now, both of them looking even more somber, if that were possible.

Keeping my tone low, I said to Harry, "You're the last one up. Sheriff Lamb wants to ask you a few questions."

He nodded and silently rose, heading for the steps. I turned to Gemma.

"Good news for the rest of us. You and I and the sisters are all free to go. I know you need to get back to the coffee shop, but I'll stick around until the sisters are finished?"

"It might be a while. They've got some heavy-duty praying to do now."

I felt my stomach tighten into a fistlike knot.

"Why?" I asked, though I was pretty sure I knew the answer.

Gemma sighed. "While you were talking to the sheriff, I put in a call to a friend over at Cymbeline General. Greg Bainbridge died in surgery."

TEN

SAYING GOODBYE TO GEMMA, I left the sisters to their prayers and went back to the corner to gather up the signs we'd left at the bench. With the object of the nuns' protest confirmed as deceased, it went without saying that the march was now a moot point.

The three sheriff's department cruisers were still parked on the street alongside the antique shop. With the stabbing incident upgraded from attack to murder, doubtless the deputies would be redoubling their investigation of the crime scene and their questioning of witnesses.

"Nina! Yoo-hoo, over here!"

I spied the yoo-hooer immediately. Mostly because he was standing beneath the awning of the Weary Bones Antique Shoppe across the street from me. I left the signs propped next to the bench and crossed the street.

"Hi, Mason. Shocking, isn't it?" I somberly greeted the man.

Mason was Mason Denman, the sixty-something owner of Weary Bones. It was an eclectic place right out of a picker's dream, with goods ranging from gilded eighteenth-century French bed frames to nineteenth-century samplers to midcentury modern atomic wall clocks. Basically, it was *the* spot in town to find something you never knew you needed until you saw it artfully displayed there.

Mason was pretty eclectic himself. Trim and short, with a carefully coiffed black pompadour (the hair, probably real; the color, definitely not) and eyebrows like mutant black caterpillars, he was dressed in his usual uniform of dark dress pants and white long-sleeved shirt topped by a vest—today, blue-and-gray striped—and accented by a monochromatic gray tie. His one touch of color this day was a bright vintage handkerchief—turquoise polka dots on yellow—tucked in his vest pocket. It was always a different hankie every day, and I'd yet to see a repeat.

He gave his eyes a discreet swipe with the handkerchief before leaning in for his usual two-cheek kiss.

"Simply terrible," he said with a sigh, and shoved the bright cloth back into his coat. "That hunky Deputy Jackson just gave us the bad news. Greg didn't make it."

"I know. Gemma told me before she went back to the coffee shop. I know it sounds cliché, but you just don't expect something like this to happen in a nice little town like Cymbeline."

"Well, get used to it," a second male voice broke in. "And it's all Bainbridge's fault. He's the one building things up so more outsiders move in. Pretty ironic he's the first victim."

The speaker was Jack Hill, charter member of the "I Hate Greg Bainbridge Club." Today his logo T-shirt was bright yellow. But despite the cheery color, the creamery owner did not look happy. Maybe he was mad that the paramedics had sliced up the penguin mascot suit.

Hoping to defuse things a bit, I stuck out my hand.

"We saw each other at Peaches and Java yesterday," I reminded him, "but we haven't formally met. I'm Nina Fleet. I live a couple of blocks north of the square, and I really like your ice cream."

As I'd hoped, his lips flickered into a semblance of a smile at this praise of his product. "Thanks, glad to hear that. And please call me Jack."

"Nina bought Mrs. Lathrop's place," Mason informed the other man as we shook.

"So you're the one," Jack said, seemingly forgetting about the murder that had happened right behind his shop. "I've been to the house a few times back in the day."

"And that's how you knew Harry?" I guessed.

He shook his head. "No, he was living on the West Coast then. We never actually met before a few weeks ago."

"So you were a friend of Mrs. Lathrop's." I tried again, not sure exactly where his story was going.

"Actually, I did some work for her. This was back before Jill and I started the creamery, while I was still doing carpentry for a living. I'd been to her place enough times that I'd kinda taken a shine to it. When the house came up for sale, Jill and I kicked around the idea of buying it, but you beat us to it."

"It's a great house," I agreed. "I've decided to try running a B&B out of it and see how that goes."

"Yeah, that was Jill's thought. I told her we already have enough to do running the creamery. I just wanted to live there."

Then he switched subjects again. "I saw you talking to the sheriff a few minutes ago. Does she have any suspects? Are they about to make an arrest?"

"You know how it is. The police never tell anyone anything. I'm pretty sure at this point that everyone is a suspect."

Jack raised his palms in a gesture of protest. "You can take me off the list. Not that I wouldn't like to shake the hand of whoever did it, but I've got a dozen witnesses to say I was in the creamery when it happened."

Then, with a smirk in the direction of the antique store owner, he went on, "But Mason could've done it. We all know there's bad blood between him and Greg."

I shot Mason a surprised look. Could he be suspect number five?

"Not me," Mason protested, tearing up again. "I liked Greg. Well, mostly. We didn't get along so well that time I complained about the restroom plumbing and it took him three weeks to get it fixed."

"Gregory Bainbridge was your landlord?" I asked in surprise.

Mason nodded. "Bobby Short used to own our building, but he had some health problems a couple of years ago. Greg convinced Bobby to unload it so he'd have some ready cash in case things grew dire with his prognosis. He took Greg's advice and put it on the market, and then Greg turned around and bought the building himself."

"Yeah, he got it for a song, and then he practically doubled the rent once our leases were up," Jack added.

I looked at Mason for confirmation, and he shrugged.

"Well, there's that. On the bright side, we hadn't had an increase in almost eight years while Bobby owned the building. Greg said he was simply readjusting the rents based on the current market."

The ice cream shop owner gave a disbelieving snort. "Current market, my—"

"Jackie," a woman's voice interrupted. "You wanna give me a hand here?"

Jill Hill, Jack's wife and creamery co-owner, had stepped outside the ice cream shop door. She must have recognized me from my original visit, since she gave me a regal dip of her chin that I answered with a friendly nod. Mason got a long-distance air kiss, which he returned.

I'd previously pegged Jill to be a dozen or so years younger than Jack, making her in her late thirties. Like the previous time I'd seen her, she had the full "Real Housewives of Atlanta" makeup thing going, from the heavy drawn-on brows a couple of shades darker than her foundation to the full, bright-red lips. Her black hair lay in a sleek, jaw-length bob frozen into place with industrial-strength hair spray.

Even dressed in a yellow Taste-Tee-Freeze–logo T-shirt and jeans like her husband, she looked as if she'd just stepped out of a glossy magazine ad. The only exception to the perfection—what some might call a flaw, but I thought rather endearing—was the sprinkling of Meghan Markle–like freckles across her nose.

"I know we're upset about poor Greg," she went on, "but folks are still wanting ice cream. I think all the excitement heats them up even more than usual, so everyone's looking to cool down. I could use a hand."

"Sure thing, baby. I'll be right there," Jack promptly replied.

Once she'd ducked back inside again, however, he turned back to me.

"I still do a little carpentry on the side. A couple of weeks before she died, I did an estimate for Mrs. Lathrop. One of the stair hand rails was loose, and a couple of steps needed fixing. You know, stuff you don't want to neglect if you have guests staying there. I can stop by later this week to take a look, if you want. You can call me here at the store."

He paused and gave me that little half smile again. "And don't worry, I'll give you the neighbor rate. Just don't mention it to Jill."

I responded with a noncommittal nod, trying to reassure myself that my internal Creep-O-Meter wasn't going off. I waited until Jack had gone back inside before rounding on Mason.

"All right, tell me the truth about that *neighbor rate*," I demanded, putting finger quotes around those last two words. "Maybe I'm just reading the guy wrong. Is he on the level with that whole carpentry thing, or was that offer a code for something out of *Fifty Shades*?"

Mason gave a sputtering laugh and then gestured me to move farther down the sidewalk. "If you're asking if Jack plays around on the side, no way. He spends his spare time thanking the Lord Baby Jesus that he landed such a hot woman. But when it comes to Jill, we-e-e-e-e-ll…"

The black caterpillar eyebrows danced all over his forehead as he drew out the last word on a meaningful little tenor.

I gave him a look. "So you're saying that Jill is the one who—"

"Oops, got to go," he cut me short as he gestured toward a potential customer heading in his shop door.

"Don't worry, Jack's a pro when it comes to carpentry. He's built me a couple of cabinets way better than anything you could buy at Ikea. But if it's gossip you want, feel free to stop by anytime."

By the time I returned to the bandstand with the protest signs, the sisters were wrapping things up. With a final "Amen," Mother Superior opened her eyes and glanced my way.

"I assume Gemma told you the unfortunate news, Nina?" she asked, expression unreadable behind the oversized glasses as she moved toward me. At my nod, she went on, "We have prayed for the repose of Mr. Bainbridge's soul, and for justice to be served. And now we should return to your house. Sisters…"

They filed down the bandstand steps and headed back in the direction of my place. I shouldered the signs again and followed. I paused, however, for a look at the tree where Sheriff Lamb had been doing her questioning. She wasn't there any longer, and neither was Harry.

I frowned. I'd been wondering how his talk with the sheriff had gone. But it was strangely coincidental that Harry had been trapped inside the walk-in freezer at the same time Greg was murdered.

Unless Harry had faked that whole freezer thing as an alibi, and *he* was the one who had killed Gregory Bainbridge.

So shocking was that unexpected thought that I literally gasped aloud. Could Harry have been the one who murdered the real estate developer? Did he belong on my suspects list as number five…or was it six now?

The more I thought about it as I followed the nuns across the square, the more plausible it seemed. Harry was an actor. It would have been easy enough for him to feign friendly concern with Bainbridge over the fact that the real estate developer was persona non grata with the people of Cymbeline.

I warmed to my theory. Harry could have offered Bainbridge the penguin suit under the pretense of helping him make it to the parking lot unmolested. And once the man was in the costume, Harry could easily have stuck a knife into him. Afterward, he could appear alongside the rest of us telling the story of being conveniently stuck in the freezer as the murder happened.

The only thing unclear in this particular scenario was a motive on the actor's part.

I lagged even further behind the nuns as I felt my enthusiasm for this mental exercise seep out of me like air from an untied balloon. Possible? Yes. Likely? No. Quite frankly, Sister Mary George was a more viable candidate than he.

Still, I continued to play the hypothetical scene through my admittedly overheated brain (with no shade to block the sun, our walk from the square was turning pretty darned toasty). Deep as I was in thought, I didn't hear the fast-moving footsteps behind me until they were practically upon me.

And then a familiar voice directly behind me asked, "Uh, Nina, can I talk to you?"

ELEVEN

I GAVE A reflexive little shriek as I swung about and saw Harry Westcott literally on my heels. As I spun, the protest signs propped on my shoulder caught the opposite momentum. Totally unintentionally—at least, that's what I told myself—they went flying out of my hands, passing within inches of Harry's face.

He dodged and ducked and avoided the onslaught. We both stared a moment at the scattered signs; then, at the same time, we knelt to gather them up.

Had this been a "meet-cute," we would have clunked heads together and then realized as we clutched our bruised foreheads that we were meant for each other. Fortunately, we avoided that well-worn (and painful!) cliché, mostly because I was busy checking out his hands to make sure he didn't have a knife in one of them.

Once I had the signs back in my grasp again, I stood. "You were saying?"

"Right, yeah."

He glanced ahead in the direction the sisters were walking. "I'm going that way, too…to the parking lot," he said, gesturing me forward. "We can talk while we walk."

"Sure."

I waited an extra couple of seconds to see if he'd do the gentlemanly thing and carry the signs for me, at least until we got to his car. When he didn't make a move that way, I shouldered them again and resumed walking.

"What did you want to talk about, Mr. Westcott?"

"You can call me Harry. Remember I told you how someone locked me in the walk-in freezer right around the same time that Bainbridge was stabbed?"

I nodded.

He went on, "I mentioned that to Connie—Sheriff Lamb—while she was questioning me. She told me it was probably an accident. She seemed more interested in how Bainbridge got hold of the penguin costume. Bottom line, she's busy looking for someone who wanted Bainbridge dead, not for the person who tried to freeze me to death."

"She's the sheriff," I replied with as much of a shrug as I could manage with the burden of my signs. "I got the feeling she's pretty competent. Maybe she's right."

"She's not," he flatly declared. "It's a small enough freezer that you can't miss someone standing inside, especially with the light on. And even if you did, it's an old unit, so it's not exactly soundproof. It's a good thing Jill finally came back into the storeroom and heard me yelling and pounding on the door. She's the one who let me out. But I guarantee you, someone was after me. They trapped me in the freezer and figured I'd freeze or suffocate in there. But when they saw Bainbridge in the penguin suit, they probably thought I'd escaped, so they decided to finish the job with a knife."

I considered Harry's theory, not sure if it was just crazy enough to be possible...or just crazy. "Maybe," I finally conceded. "But does anyone have any reason to want you dead? Maybe someone you've threatened to sue recently…besides me, I mean?"

He had the good grace to look a little embarrassed at that, though I noticed he didn't answer the question. We'd reached the parking lot, and I saw with a surprising bit of sadness that Gregory Bainbridge's dark gray sedan was still parked there. Likely at some point the sheriff's department would tow it away.

"Guess I'll see you around," Harry said.

I nodded. "Sure."

As I caught up to the nuns, I spared another glance behind me at the parking lot, morbidly curious to see which car Harry would drive off in. Three-quarters of the parking spaces were empty now, when a couple of hours earlier the lot had been almost completely full. Doubtless the whole murder thing had sent the tourists scurrying. Heck, for the moment *I* didn't feel comfortable living so close to a crime scene.

Then a worse thought occurred to me. Chances were the Savannah and Atlanta news outlets—probably Huff-Post and Yahoo, too—would soon be splashing headlines about Bainbridge's murder all across their websites. Forget our neighboring state to the south. Once word got out about the penguin suit, Georgia would rival Florida for the nation's most offbeat crimes. For the town's sake, Sheriff Lamb and her deputies needed to solve this murder fast!

I tossed another look over my free shoulder. The actor was heading toward an older-model SUV with lots of rust. And then he sidestepped the SUV and made a beeline for the ancient yellow school bus parked in the furthermost spot.

I stopped outright this time and stared. Had I simply missed seeing some low-slung vehicle alongside it? Nope, he was headed to the bus, one of those short ones with only five windows on a side. The kind of bus non–politically correct people made jokes about. And, to confirm it was his, a familiar rusty red bicycle was lashed to the bus's backdoor rails. As I watched, he opened its bifold door and climbed inside.

I waited for him to start it up, but instead I could see him moving down the rows toward the back. When he didn't make any move to drive away, I threw up figurative hands and started after the nuns again.

Mattie woofed excitedly at our return, and I felt a little stab of amused jealously when she gave me a perfunctory lick on the hand only to yip and dance in excited circles for the benefit of Sister Mary Thomas. The freckled old woman appeared equally delighted at the attention, so I pretended not to notice when the Aussie followed her upstairs to her room.

I stowed away the signs in the laundry room and headed for the kitchen. I didn't know about the nuns, but cookies and water for lunch weren't enough to sustain me. I cut up some cheeses and sandwich meat, adding them to a tray along with crackers and fresh veggies. That, and a pitcher each of lemonade and iced tea, went on the sideboard. The remaining cookies from my plastic bin rounded out the repast.

"Mother Superior… Sisters," I called up the stairway. "I've got some munchies for you in the parlor if you're hungry."

Apparently, just like teenage boys, elderly nuns never turned down a snack, for a few minutes later they'd all trouped back downstairs again and were filling plates. Satisfied that I'd fulfilled my hostessing duties for the afternoon, I left them to it. Whistling Mattie away from the snack tray before she tried to join in, I headed with her out to the backyard.

With all the excitement of getting the place ready for my B&B guests, I'd not had much chance to relax in my gardens the past few days. That had been one of the draws of owning the place. In addition to the porch along the front and sides of the house, a vine-covered pavilion and a brick patio lay right off the back door. Every view was different, but all were equally pictur-esque.

Of course, when I said "my" gardens," that was re-ally not the case. The grounds pretty well belonged to Hendricks, and we both knew it.

The stooped, foul-mouthed old geezer had, by his account, been caring for the property's gardens for a good three decades. He had appeared on my doorstep within days of my moving in to inform me that he was willing to remain at his post, even with Mrs. Lathrop now gone. His one condition was that I wouldn't mess around with his plants.

I was allowed, however, to mow and edge and weed the lawn. And he'd graciously given me free rein to harvest all I wanted once the peach tree in the front yard bore fruit.

The result was that the rest of the property that wasn't grass was sculpted and pruned within an inch of its life. In addition to a parameter of showy hedges and specimen trees, the brick walkway leading from the patio and pavilion outside the back door ended in a fancy circular garden that was quartered into pie-shaped plots, with a three-tiered fountain in its center. That formal garden was one of my favorite spots to read or simply lounge with a glass of lemonade…or something stronger in the evenings.

There was, however, an exception to the "sculpted and pruned."

With the front door facing north, the east side of the property included the strip of lawn than ran the length of the house and that my bedroom overlooked. This would soon be Mattie's domain once I'd put in a little cross-fencing. The west side of the property had a narrow gated driveway instead of lawn. The drive led to the property's former carriage house turned detached garage. The area flanking the garage and a portion of the driveway had been left to its own devices…that is, as much as Hendricks would allow.

Instead of neat hedges or tidy raised flower beds, several immense rose bushes had been allowed to run amuck there. Almost as broad as they were tall, the ramblers covered one side of the detached garage like a thorny green blanket. Depending on the time of year, the sprawl of green might be overrun with red or pink or yellow blowsy blooms. A few smaller varieties clung to wooden trellises.

With Mattie literally dogging my steps, I entered the side door of the old carriage house. The section that once served as a stall area for horses had long since been walled off from the actual garage area where I parked my Mini and was set up as a workshop. Praying Hendricks wouldn't put in a surprise appearance and catch me borrowing his tools, I grabbed gloves, garden shears, and an old bucket.

I'd learned from Hendricks that my roses were not your garden variety. Rather, they were part of a class known as heirloom roses—hardy, nonhybrid types that had been brought over to this country by its early settlers and carried westward. Even when the cabins and shotgun shacks had long since vanished from the former homesteads, the rosebushes the pioneer women had so carefully planted to remind them of home continued to flourish. Rescued out of the wild many decades later and propagated by rose enthusiasts, they could stand up to the summer heat and drought.

I clipped a few blooms from the nearest bush and added the stems to my bucket. Hendricks had called this variety an Infant Something-or-Other. The ragged-edged blossom reminded me of a peony, with an ombré palette that started out dark pink in its center and faded to a pale blush at its edges.

"Oh, how lovely!"

I'd heard the back screen door slam shut a few moments earlier, so I wasn't surprised to find Sister Mary Thomas walking up to join me. She stared in admiration at the array of rosebushes, and then nodded at the bloom I held.

"*Enfant de France*?" she asked, giving the words what sound to my southern ears like a credible Gallic accent.

I did a quick mental translation and realized that had been the "infant" Hendricks had referred to when he'd told me the flower's name.

"Uh, yes, I believe so," I told her. "How did you know? Did you grow heirloom roses at the convent?"

"Hardly," she replied with a tinkling little laugh. "We had vegetable gardens, of course, but no flowers. I just happened to recognize that particular species because my mother had the same rosebush back when I was a little girl."

She held the bucket for me, and we spent a few minutes in companionable silence while I clipped a few more blossoms. Once that container was full, I returned clippers and gloves to their rightful spots. Then, Mattie trailing behind us, we headed for the patio.

"I'm so happy we're staying here," the nun blurted. "Not that the other bed-and-breakfast establishments in town we looked at weren't nice, but yours has such a charming, comfortable feeling about it. And the fact you have such lovely grounds to wander about makes me miss the convent a bit less."

"I know how painful it is to lose a place you've loved and lived in for many years," I confided as we took a seat on the patio benches. "That happened with me after my divorce. My ex-husband and I had a wonderful mid-century home where we lived for almost sixteen years. It was so hard to give it up."

I went on, "I spent the past year renting a soulless sterile condo near downtown Atlanta. It's only now that I've found this place here in Cymbeline that I've started to feel like I've got a true home again. But for you and the other sisters, it's not just your home; you've lost the routine of the cheese-making business, too. It's hard after working for a living all your life to feel at loose ends every single day."

"I knew you'd understand," the nun replied, nodding. "Melissa Jane is a lovely woman, but she thought we sisters would be glad to have an excuse to retire, as she put it. But I don't want to retire, and neither do the others," she ended on a defiant note.

Sensing the old woman's dismay, Mattie came up and laid her fuzzy chin on the nun's knee. Sister Mary Thomas smiled and gave the pup a soft scratch behind her ear.

Then her smile wavered.

"The hardest thing about leaving the convent was saying goodbye to our little goatherd. The other sisters took care of the cheese-making and the marketing, but Mary Christopher and I cared for the girls, as we called them. We'd feed them and brush them and clean their hooves. And milk them, of course. I know that we're not supposed to be attached to things...and that includes livestock. But I—I truly miss them."

She blinked rapidly, as if to hold back tears, and then leaned toward Mattie to give her another pat. Which gave me an idea.

"Oh, Mattie, you shouldn't be snuggling up to the sister like that," I mock-scolded the pup. "You're all smelly. Why don't you wait to bother Sister Mary Thomas until I've had a chance to shampoo you?"

To the nun, I said, "I'm so sorry. In all the excitement of getting the place ready for you sisters, I didn't give Matilda her usual Saturday bath. I promise I'll do that tomorrow so you don't have a stinky dog wandering after you."

The Aussie—who was not at all dirty or smelly—

shot me a canine side-eye. Apparently, she understood that she had been unfairly dissed.

Sorry, girl, it's for a good cause, I mentally apologized, sending lots of *who's the good puppy?* vibes her way.

Meanwhile, the old nun's expression brightened. "Why, Nina, I could bathe Matilda for you. That is, if you'd like. She's about the same size as one of my girls."

"Oh, but that would be too much bother for you."

"Not at all. I could make her nice and clean again in a jiffy," she declared, nuzzling against Mattie's fuzzy head while the Aussie wagged her bobbed tail in happiness.

And so, while Sister Mary Thomas made a dash inside for what she'd called her "goat apron," I went back to the carriage house. I retrieved the shallow tub, doggy shampoo, spare towels, and brush that were all part of Mattie's canine spa day ritual and set it all up in a sunny spot in the driveway. By the time the nun returned wearing a tan, pinafore-like garment over her gray habit, I'd used the hose to fill the tub and had plopped the long-suffering dog into the sudsy water.

Leaving the pair to it, I retrieved my bucket of cut roses and carried it inside to the kitchen. I found Sister Mary George at the sink drying the last of the plates she'd apparently just washed following the nuns' snack break.

"Sister, thank you, but that wasn't necessary," I told her as I opened up a lower cabinet and pulled out a mismatched trio of cut-glass vases. "You and the other nuns are my guests."

"Don't worry, Nina, we're happy to help out. You

know what they say about idle hands," she reminded me, drying hers on a second dish towel and hanging them both on the oven handle to dry. "Besides, you already put Mary Thomas to work.

"No, no, don't worry," she interrupted me as I opened my mouth to explain. "I'm sure you wanted to make her feel useful and take her mind off the goats. Believe me, the woman was happy as a clam when she came downstairs wearing that apron and telling me she was going to give that dog of yours a bath."

I smiled as I began arranging the roses in their vases. "Poor Sister Mary Thomas. She seemed so depressed about leaving her herd behind. I thought if she could shower a little attention on Mattie, it would cheer her up."

"I'm sure it has. Certainly, we can all use some cheering after what happened today."

The nun stacked the plates and placed them back on their shelf. She shut the cabinet door decisively and went on, "But I must say, now things are even more confusing with Mr. Bainbridge's passing. Will the development proceed as he planned? Or do we move back and try to restart the *fromagerie*?"

Mary George's French accent, unlike the other nun's, had more than a touch of Georgia drawl to it. She added, "Reverend Mother is on the phone right now to the archbishop's office letting them know about the situation."

"I have a feeling that's not going to be resolved with one phone call. But all of you are welcome to stay here as long as you need to."

By now I'd finished with my amateur attempt at flower arranging. Sister Mary George helped me carry the vases into the parlor. With my inner Martha Stewart satisfied, I left her browsing the bookcase filled with vintage novels that hadn't sold at the estate sale. I hadn't forgotten my conversation with Jack Hill and his claim that repairs were still needed around the place.

So I made a check of the main stairway as well as the back servants' stairs, giving the hand rails a thorough shaking. All those fixtures appeared sturdy enough to last another hundred or more years. I even checked the porch railing outside when I went to look at the steps. But they were secure, and no wooden steps were loose.

Maybe Jack had lied about the repairs, hoping to con a newcomer by doing work that wasn't needed. Of course, it was possible that old Mrs. Lathrop had hired someone else for the job, but I doubted it.

Or was this instead a ruse on Jack's part—an excuse to get back into the house for some reason?

I mulled over the question for a while but came up with nothing. I probably was seeing intrigue where none existed. And with a houseful of guests to worry about, I had more important things on my plate than creating drama. So why was I insisting upon assigning sinister motivations to every person in Cymbeline I encountered? Wasn't that Sheriff Lamb's job?

Except that I somehow had ended up the touchstone for everyone who'd had any unpleasant connection to Bainbridge. And chances were that one of those people was his killer. Which also meant that person likely was watching to see if he—or she—was under suspicion. And not just by the local constabulary.

But by me.

"Hold your horses, Nina," I sternly commanded myself, pretending that a shiver hadn't just made its way up my spine. "No more reruns of *Law & Order* for you. Just stick to innkeeping."

I spent the rest of the afternoon admonishing myself with similar platitudes. By supper time, I'd pretty well settled myself down. Except, with a murderer out there somewhere, I wasn't comfortable sending the nuns out to scrounge for their meal. Fortunately, Mother Superior apparently was on the same page. As it neared six pm, the nuns gathered in the parlor to mull over take-out food suggestions. Sister Mary Julian was the first to speak up.

"We could call for someone to deliver pizza pie!" she eagerly declared. "I've always wanted to try it."

Sister Mary Christopher clapped her hands. "I've never had pizza before, either. That's a wonderful idea!"

"I agree," said Sister Mary Paul. "I try the pepperoni one."

"Pizza it is," Mother Superior declared. "Nina, perhaps you can suggest a place that we might call."

"Romeo and Juliette's makes the best in town," I told her. (Juliette, by clever coincidence, was the pizzeria's owner's actual name.) Picking up my phone, I added, "But let this be my treat."

Of course, there were the expected protests from the nuns. In the end, I won them over by agreeing that Sister Mary Paul, who apparently had been a Cordon Bleu chef-in-training until she decided to join the order, could cook us all supper the next night. After a brief debate over toppings (we went with one veggie pizza and one pepperoni, sausage, and mushroom), I phoned in the order.

A half hour later, we were well into a game of charades when I heard Mattie's woof, followed by the door-bell ringing. I followed the now-incredibly-fluffy dog to the front door and opened it, only to find myself face-to-face with a Renaissance man.

I'm not speaking in a philosophical sense. The pizza delivery guy was dressed like a buff Henry VIII, with his courtier's short, red-and-black velvet doublet topped by a starched white ruff the approximate diameter of a turkey platter. A soft cloth cap with a curling feather hung low on his forehead, and his long legs were en-cased in a pair of matching black tights that showed to advantage muscled calves and thighs.

Definitely not how the Pizza Hut delivery guy dressed.

While I inwardly saluted Romeo and Juliette's for their cleverness in keeping with the theme, the courtier held out two flat cardboard pizza boxes.

"Your order," he said, addressing me in tones straight out of BBC America.

I reached for the pizza boxes with one hand and held out my tip with the other. And then I got a better look at the delivery guy's face.

With a resigned shake of my head, I said, "You."

TWELVE

HARRY WESTCOTT SHRUGGED. "Yes, 'tis I," he confirmed, still affecting the same British accent. "If you will, please take your repast. I have other pizzas to deliver."

I nodded and, holding said repast well out of Mattie's eager reach, handed over my tip. Harry eyed the five-dollar bill before pocketing it, if that's the correct expression for sticking cash into the slashed sleeve of his doublet. "Your gratuity is appreciated. And now, while parting is such sweet sorrow, I shall say good night."

And this time, Harry was the one who got my mental props for slipping in a *Romeo and Juliet* quote while delivering pizza from Romeo and Juliette's pizzeria while dressed in Elizabethan garb.

He turned smartly on his slippered heel and started down the steps into the early Georgia evening. His exit was marred only a little by the arrival of the usual mosquito onslaught that always hit at dusk. This resulted in some very non-courtier-like slapping at those biting insects as he made his way to the delivery car parked beyond the gate. Since I knew it would be a matter of seconds before I was next on the mosquito menu, I made a hasty retreat of my own back into the house.

As expected, the pizza was a huge hit with the nuns, though the whole eating-with-your-hands thing momentarily threw the Reverend Mother for a loop. But following my and Mary George's example, she soon was nibbling happily on a veggie slice.

There were no leftovers.

With dishes washed and pizza boxes disposed of, we resumed charades in the parlor. After the team consisting of me, Sister Mary George, and Sister Mary Christopher won, the nuns regrouped for their final evening prayers.

While the women sought divine intervention, Mattie and I did our nighttime lockup routine. Even in a town like Cymbeline, one didn't tempt Fate and the dishonest by going to bed with windows and doors unlocked. And given that one of our neighbors had just been murdered by person or persons unknown, leaving the house wide open to the night would be rash, at best.

The light at the top of the stairway was shining brightly for the nuns to make their way upstairs once prayers were over. I shut off all the downstairs lights except the pair of tulip-shaped glass wall sconces that flanked either side of the hall near the front door. Those I normally left burning overnight. They gave out just enough light that one could traverse the darkness from door to main stairway without bumping into walls or door frames. Lockdown duly accomplished, the Aussie and I retreated to our bedroom suite for the night.

The soft murmur of prayer from down the hallway was surprisingly comforting as I changed into a comfy oversized yellow nightshirt and settled onto my bed for some quality time with my laptop. I tried not to look at the news site that was my default opening page on the Internet. I already knew enough about the crime that I didn't need a recap. And I darned sure didn't want to read the snarky comments by the usual Internet trolls that were sure to accompany the story.

Unfortunately, I didn't click through fast enough to miss the headline at the top that read, Man Wearing Penguin Suit Fatally Stabbed in Georgia. Deciding that the obligatory run-through on Facebook and Twitter would probably yield similar drama, I opted instead for a game of Candy Crush. But after a few rounds of clearing rows of bright-colored sweets, I was still feeling antsy. And that is how I found myself on a well-known movie database plugging in Harry Westcott's name in the search box.

I wasn't sure what I'd expected to find, but it wasn't the respectably long list of television and movie credits that popped up. Not that he'd had starring roles in any of it. Still, he'd guested in several cable TV dramas over the past dozen years, a few of whose series names I actually recognized. He'd also had minor (okay, walk-on) roles—"Man in Bar," "Second Thug," "Party Guest #4"—in five or six relatively well-known films, too. The listing also confirmed that he actually *had* shot the undercover cop television pilot he'd mentioned, which was currently in postproduction.

Also, according to the database, he'd performed in various regional Shakespearean productions, which doubtless explained how he'd happened to have an Elizabethan courtier's costume handy.

My curiosity more than a little piqued now, I pulled up his bio. To my disappointment, it didn't contain much more info than he'd already told me. I did learn his actual height (six one), his date of birth (which made him two years younger than me), and the fact that he was a black belt in tae kwon do and could play the piano. There were a few pictures of him that I scrolled through, both professional headshots and on-set photos from a couple of roles he'd played.

A couple of the latter pictures showed him shirtless, and I paused over those probably a little longer than necessary. But beyond that, I was more impressed than I wanted to be by how he could go from looking like a matinee idol to a back-alley gangster with little more than a change of costuming and attitude.

Curiosity finally satisfied, I shut down the website and leaned back against my stack of pillows. Mattie, who was lounging on the foot of my bed, lifted her head and gave me a quizzical look.

"Yeah, that's what I say," I told her. "It's got to be tough for him, being this close"—I held forefinger and thumb an inch apart—"to fame, and ending up back in your hometown delivering pizzas and dressing up like a penguin."

Though it was a bit strange that someone who'd worked relatively regularly as an actor was hurting as much for cash as Harry obviously was. Otherwise, why else would he take jobs better suited for high school kids? Though maybe all his earnings had gone to student loans, or an ex-wife, or maybe his attorney, given his seeming penchant for lawsuits.

I couldn't help wonder again, too, about the bus I'd seen him climbing into that afternoon. Tiny houses were all the rage, especially ones that had begun life on wheels. Was it possible that's where he lived? Though that vehicle's exterior sure hadn't gone through the same transformation as the buses I'd seen posted on Pinterest.

No wonder the guy had been royally ticked to learn he had been screwed over when it came to inheriting his great-aunt's house.

"Not our circus, not our monkeys," I told the Aussie.

I was still silently repeating that mantra next morning when the doorbell rang at seven am. Fortunately, I'd dragged myself out of bed a half hour earlier, so I'd managed a quick shower and was already dressed in cropped denim capris and a crisp white man-tailored blouse tied at the waist. The sisters were already long out of bed, for I could hear the soft murmur of prayer coming from the parlor as I rushed to the front door.

Standing on the porch was Daniel's and Gemma's daughter, Jasmine, bearing white pastry boxes that held the expected breakfast. I opened the door and ushered her in.

"Here you go, Miz Nina," she said through a yawn.

Like me, Jasmine looked like she'd just gotten out of bed. Unlike me, she was wearing barely-there cutoff shorts and a sleeveless green T-shirt with the Peaches and Java logo on it. A matching Peaches and Java ball cap was crammed atop her riot of golden-brown ringlets. I smiled and took the topmost box from her.

"Late night with your friends?" I asked sympathetically as I led her toward the dining room.

She shook her head. "Not me. I was up late getting in some extra studying so I'll be ready for my junior year when school starts again."

Her expression as she set her box on the dining table was virtuous enough that she could have been a shoe-in for joining the Sisters of Perpetual Poverty. But when I slanted a disbelieving look her way, she dissolved into teenage giggles.

"Okay, so I was up late texting with my friends," she admitted. "Just don't tell my mom, okay?"

I grinned back. "My lips are sealed."

I helped her carry the boxes to the dining room, then grabbed up the ten-dollar bill I'd had ready on the sideboard. On the way out, I handed it to her. "Here you go. See you tomorrow morning."

She brightened perceptively at the sight of the cash, and I was glad to see that a Hamilton (if that was the current urban slang) was still real money to a sixteen-year-old. With a smile and a big "Thanks, Miz Nina," she rushed off.

Moving with slightly less energy, I returned to the dining room to set up the food on the marble-topped antique sideboard.

I had a three-tiered pastry stand I had impulsively bought years ago and never used. Somehow it had been among the kitchen items I'd brought with me to the new house. Pleased to finally have a use for the pretty vintage serving piece, I arranged the selection of mini cinnamon rolls and tarts on it. The presliced quiches went on paper doilies atop fancy china plates. I left Daniel's famous cobbler in its foil baking pan, though I scooped the container of amaretto whipped cream into a small vintage Pyrex bowl. Unfortunately, the peach tree in the front yard wouldn't bear fruit until the fall; otherwise, I'd have put a fresh peach at every place setting.

"This all looks wonderful, Nina," Mother Superior said with an approving nod as the nuns filed in a few minutes later. "I believe we need to give you five stars on TripAdvisor."

"Our *fromagerie* has a four-point-five-star rating," Sister Mary Thomas confided in a stage whisper as she sidled past me to join the lineup at the sideboard. "You can't please everyone."

Breakfast went off without a hitch. Afterward, I put up the leftovers and did the dishes before the sisters could take over those chores. Then, feeling virtuous, I paused to fill out my food spreadsheet so I could update Gemma later. Next stop on my innkeeping list was to make the guest beds and do a quick cleanup of the bathrooms.

But the beds were already done up with crisp hospital corners, and the bathrooms were cleaner than they'd been before. Obviously, nun DNA did not allow for an unkempt room. I imagined they'd have done the same had they been staying at the local Holiday Inn. Aware that future guests wouldn't be as neat to a fault, I used the allotted time to instead straighten up my own bedroom and bathroom to nun-approved standards.

By then it was a little past ten. Time for my next mission—one I hadn't realized was on my list until I was midway through my second slice of quiche. I wanted to track down Harry and get his take on Jack Hill, and also find out why he thought that he, Harry, might have been the actual target of the murderer. Something was rotten in the state of Cymbeline, and despite my lecture to myself the night before, I was in the mood to poke around.

Leaving Mattie in Sister Mary Thomas's care, I gathered sunglasses, phone, and purse and headed out. I'd barely passed through my gate, however, when I realized that something was different. The traffic, which normally on a weekday was almost nonexistent on my street, was heavier than usual. I saw an Atlanta television satellite truck rumble by, followed a moment later by a sister truck plastered with a Savannah network logo, and I realized what was happening. The little town of Cymbeline was officially on the national map in the wake of Bainbridge's murder.

I muttered a few bad words but kept on trudging. Then I heard my phone chime, signaling a breaking story on one of my news apps. I took a quick look at the headline:

CYMBELINE SHERIFF'S DEPARTMENT TO HOLD
10:30AM PRESS CONFERENCE ON GEORGIA
PENGUIN SUIT MURDER

Which, according to my phone clock, would be in about fifteen minutes.

My bad words got a bit louder. Still, I realized that the sheriff had to do this. Like it or not, the murder was newsworthy because of the blasted penguin suit. And on the bright side, maybe all the reporters would hang around to eat and shop afterward. Heck, if I'd had brochures already printed for my new B&B, I'd probably be on the square handing them out.

A couple of minutes later, I reached the parking lot where Harry's bus had been parked the day before. It was still there, but unlike yesterday afternoon the lot was now packed with cars, many with Florida plates, and several more with television or radio station logos emblazoned across their back windshields. No satellite trucks were in sight, however, which probably meant they were setting up shop along the square.

Harry, however, was still with his bus...though not exactly in the way I remembered. Sometime after I'd left him the day before, the parking spot alongside the battered vehicle had been transformed into tailgate city. A cooler, portable barbecue grill and a couple of folding lawn chairs with red webbing had been set up at one end of the space. The remaining open area was occupied by a full-length matching chaise. A camping table held a bottle of suntan lotion and a book, with brown leather huaraches tucked beneath it. Harry sprawled in the lounge chair, wearing wraparound sunglasses and red, white, and blue–spangled swim trunks, and nothing else.

I strode over to the foot of the chaise and stood there for a couple of moments waiting for him to acknowledge me. Then I heard a faint snore from his direction and realized that beneath the sunglasses, the man was fast asleep.

I smiled, debating whether I should let him sleep on while availing myself of some undeniably fine eye candy, or instead take a little revenge by startling him awake. Reminding myself that I could always go back to that movie database if I needed another beefcake fix, I opted for choice number two.

"Hey, Harry, wake up," I called, and gave the chaise a nudge with my foot. "I need to talk to you."

He leaped upright, sunglasses falling askew. "What in the—! I told you not to—! Oh, it's just you. What are you doing here?"

"Looking for you. You were snoozing."

"I—I was not," he sputtered, and adjusted his sunglasses. "I was resting my eyes and working on my tan."

"Well, it kind of looked like snoozing to me. I mean, you were snoring."

He shot me a look that probably would have knocked me dead had I been able to see his eyes. Meanwhile, he was shaking out the folded blue T-shirt that had served as his pillow. Tugging it on, he said, "You've found me. What do you want?"

"I want to talk to you about a few things having to do with Greg Bainbridge that aren't adding up. Do you have a minute?"

He pulled his phone from the waistband of his swim trunks and made a production of checking his calendar. Finally, he nodded and stood. "I think I can fit you in. Why don't you step into my office," he said, and gestured to the pair of folding chairs.

I sat in the farthest one while he slid his feet into the huaraches and went over to the cooler. Popping its lid, he said, "I can offer you bottled water, flavored water, orange juice, or special parking lot–brewed sun tea—unsweetened, of course."

"Bottled water is fine."

He pulled two bottles from the cooler and handed me one before taking the other chair. As we cracked open our ice-cold drinks, he asked, "So what doesn't add up…other than the obvious?"

Before I could answer, our phones simultaneously chimed. We both looked at the news banner that had popped up on our respective screens, and I saw him frown. "Connie's doing a press conference. What's up with that?"

"Bainbridge's murder is trending. Didn't you notice all the out-of-town cars?"

He glanced around. "I guess the lot is fuller than it was first thing this morning."

"Yeah, while you were doing your Sleeping Beauty routine, you missed all the satellite trucks rolling into town. Seriously, this is turning into a big deal. They're even calling it the Penguin Suit Murder."

"Catchy. If you don't mind, let's hurry and get this little talk over with. What do you want to know?"

"I'm curious about Jack Hill. I mean, is he a decent guy? Anything in his background that's cray-cray?"

Apparently this wasn't the subject he'd expected me to bring up, for he took a moment to answer. Finally he said, "I just met Jack a couple of weeks ago, when I took that mascot job. He's okay, as far as I can tell. The only thing cray-cray, like you call it, is that he's super jealous of his wife. He thinks every man in town is hitting on her."

"So why would Jack hire a superhot guy like you, then? I mean, that's kind of like putting the fox in the henhouse."

Most men would have blushed and hemmed and hawed over that overt compliment, but not Harry. Because he and I and everyone else in a hundred-mile radius knew that he actually was one…as in, a superhot guy. Instead, he gave me a considering look.

"Actually, Jill was the one who hired me. And that's how I found out that beneath the perfect hair and makeup she's a real party girl. She's the one who does all the hitting on. Day one, she made a pass at me. I couldn't afford to lose the job, so I told her I was gay."

I recalled Daniel's offhanded remark about both the ladies and the men admiring Harry. But no way was I going to fall into that politically incorrect trap by asking the man about his actual orientation. Instead, I asked, "Did it work?"

"She just laughed and said I wouldn't be the first gay man she'd turned straight. In fact, I think it made it more of a challenge for her. I couldn't turn my back on her without her grabbing my butt...or other things.

"And no, it's not a compliment," he added, apparently worried I was going to laugh. "That woman is a predator. I seriously considered quitting every single day, but like I said, I needed the cash."

"Hey, I feel your pain," I said with an ironic snort. "Not too many guys have the bad luck to experience firsthand the crap that women have been dealing with for years. But back to Jack. My cray-cray story is a whole lot different."

I told him what Jack had said about the needed repairs to his great-aunt's house, and the fact that nothing the carpenter turned ice cream mogul had mentioned as being a problem actually was. When I finished, Harry shrugged.

"Maybe the real estate agent had her own people fix it," he suggested. "Or maybe there wasn't anything wrong, and that was an excuse to see you alone."

He waggled his eyebrows suggestively, the gesture momentarily reminding me of Mason Denman. Except that Harry was taller and younger and more handsome. And probably not gay.

I shook my head. "I already asked Mason over at Weary Bones about that, and he said no way would Jack step out on his wife. No, I'm thinking maybe there's something that has to do with the house. He and Jill thought about buying it, you know. And Jack said a while back he did some repairs to some of the paneling."

"Hmmm…that sounds like a subplot of a movie I was in called *House of Death*. So you think maybe he saw something hidden in the wall while he was doing his fix, and now he wants to go back and get it?"

"Yes…maybe… I don't know."

Put that way, my theory sounded pretty idiotic. Unless it somehow tied into Bainbridge's death, and the possibility that Harry was actually the intended victim.

"Okay, this is even crazier than your movie," I warned him. "Is it possible that Jack thinks you know about whatever is in the house that he's trying to find a way to steal, and he wanted you out of the way so when he located it, no one would know it came from your great-aunt's place?"

"You're right," he replied in an admiring tone. Then, before I could bask in that unexpected praise, he slanted me a look and clarified, "That *is* crazier than my movie."

"No crazier than you claiming that you might have been the intended victim."

He didn't reply to that, his expression suddenly shuttered. Pleased I'd shut him down, at least temporarily, I took another swig of cold water. Why had I thought that Harry Westcott, of all people, could help me unravel my twisted thoughts? But even as I indulged my pique, something in his manner caught me short.

"Hold on. There really is a reason you think Bain-bridge's killer was targeting you, isn't there?"

He slowly nodded. "It's like this. I've got a stalker, and I can't get rid of her. She's been following me for almost two years now. At first, it was kind of amus-ing. I mean, I'm not Brad Pitt or George Clooney or Denzel Washington. I'm just your everyday C-list… okay, D-list…actor. Actually, I kind of felt like having someone obsessed with me put me in the big time."

"Big mistake, huh?" I said.

He sighed.

"After a few months, every role I landed, somehow she managed to get into a crowd scene, or she was serv-ing food at craft services or something. Most of the time she didn't even say anything, wasn't even close enough to touch. She was just always…there."

He hesitated, looking suddenly pale despite his tan.

"But about two months ago, things got pretty freak-ing scary," he continued. "It happened outside my motel in Austin. It was close to midnight after I'd left the set, and she was waiting in the parking lot for me. She opened this long raincoat she was wearing, and all she had on beneath it was her underwear. At first, I thought she was flashing me. Then I noticed this huge knife she had stuck in this fancy red garter she was wearing."

I reflexively caught my breath, picturing that scene in my head. But his next words were what sent a shiver through me despite the morning heat.

"She looked me right in the eye and told me that if she couldn't have me, then she'd make sure no one else could either."

THIRTEEN

"Wow," I SAID, a bit inadequately, given the situation.

He must have taken my muted response as disbelief, for he shot back, "So you think I'm imagining this wacko? You think I made up that whole knife thing?"

"Not at all," I hurried to reassure him. "Look, my ex-husband is a pro golfer. I know all about the gallery girls. And the ones the pros always joke about belonging to the PGA—the Party Groupie Association. And lots of names worse than that. Some of those ladies can turn pretty psycho. I remember one time back in Dallas when—"

"Hold on," he cut me short. "Your ex is Cameron Fleet? The golfer, Cameron Fleet?"

"I don't like to spread that around, but, yes. Why, do you know him?"

"I shot an allergy medication commercial with him last fall. You remember the one."

Of course I did. In fact, I'd given up network TV for a couple of months to avoid watching a high-def version of Cam pop up once every sixty minutes during prime time. But I didn't remember seeing Harry in it.

"I don't remember seeing you in it."

"Yeah, well, I was there."

Harry popped out of his chair and stood slightly bent, arms straight and hands clasped as if he were clutching an imaginary golf club. In a quite credible imitation of Cameron's good-old-boy drawl, he repeated the product's familiar phrase, "No sneezing…no wheezing. Life is pleasing."

He paused to sink the imaginary putt, and then looked up again, this time flashing an uncanny version of Cam's trademark shit-eating grin. "Do like I do," he continued in his Cameron voice. "Take an Allergone before you take on the outdoors."

He straightened again, abruptly coming out of character.

"I was hired to play his caddie," he explained, a hint of remembered outrage coloring his tone. "In the original version of the commercial, I had a line right after he made his shot. 'Great putt, Mr. Fleet,' was what I said, and then we were supposed to high-five."

Harry slumped back into his chair again. "Turns out your ex didn't like sharing the spotlight, so after the first take he had a little talk with the sponsor. Next thing I know, I'm hanging out over at craft services while the great Cameron Fleet does a solo performance. He cost me a decent chunk of change that day."

I felt Harry's pain. Good old Cam had cost me a decent chunk of change, too…and a pretty big helping of self-respect on top of that.

"Yeah, he's pretty much a jerk when the camera isn't on him," I commiserated. Then, recalling the true issue at hand, I went on, "So what about this stalker woman? Do you have a name, a description?"

"Her name's Lana… I think her last name's Harwood, but she might have been lying about that. Hell, she might have lied about the Lana part, too."

"And what does this maybe-her-name-is-Lana-and-maybe-it's-not look like?"

He shot me an annoyed look but answered, "Caucasian, probably in her fifties, about your height but heavier. Not fat or anything," he hurried to qualify, probably worried that I might go all militant female at the mention of a woman's weight. "Her hair is blonde... except sometimes it's brown. Oh, and once it was red. I don't know if she dyes it or if she wears wigs. She's pretty. Not so good-looking that you'd turn and look at her on the street or anything, but not bad."

I suppressed a snorting little laugh. "So, basically, she looks like almost every other middle-aged white stalker woman in the country."

"Except that she's got this cutesy tattoo on her left arm. It's a bunch of dancing gummy bears in different colors wrapped around her bicep."

I straightened in my chair like I'd been jabbed in the back.

"Not gummy bears," I slowly said as realization hit. "Grateful Dead bears...the marching cartoon bears like off that old rock album. My uncle had a tattoo like that. The fans who used to follow the band around to all their tour stops were called Deadheads, and those bears were this sort of this calling-card icon for them."

"So she likes musicians, too. What's that have to do with me?"

I swallowed hard. "Your friend Lana is right here in Cymbeline. And this time she's a brunette. I talked to her myself. She's the woman who flagged me down to tell me that you...well, Bainbridge...had been stabbed."

Harry was silent for a long moment. Finally, I asked,

"Did you mention anything to the sheriff about this Lana person?"

He shook his head.

"Well, what are you waiting for? We should let her know that we're pretty sure who murdered Gregory, and that up until yesterday she was still in town. Right?"

Instead of answering with a rousing *Right!* as I expected, he said, "I've got an idea. Give me fifteen minutes."

"I'll give you ten," I told him as he leaped to his feet and started for the bus. "If you're not back by then, I'm going to tell Sheriff Lamb about her myself."

While Harry was busy doing…well, whatever… I pulled out my phone and swiped on the news-feed headline that had announced the sheriff's press conference. Not that watching it was going to distract me from the realization that I might have been literally hands-on with a crazed murderer the day before.

As usual, start time for the live event was running behind. But the camera was panning the square, and I could see that the place was literally packed. Every parking spot except those blocked for official business— sheriff's department vehicles, the town council's cars— was taken. No fewer than four satellite trucks rounded out the media circus, with dishes raised high looming over everything.

As I squinted at the screen, Melissa Jane Green and the rest of the town council, followed by the sheriff, all made their way up the bandstand steps. Melissa Jane spoke first, bellying up to an elaborate, carved wood podium that I suspected had been borrowed from Mason's antique shop.

She introduced herself and talked about the virtues of the town and its people, saying how shocked we all were by this intrusion of big-city life. Finally, she wound down and introduced Sheriff Lamb, who took the podium radiating cool professionalism.

After a few words of thanks, the sheriff began reading what I assumed was the official statement. An instant of panic flashed through me as I wondered if she'd mention any witness names…most particularly, mine. The last thing I needed was a herd of reporters converging on the house trying to get first-person accounts out of me. And certainly I didn't want my nuns subjected to the same craziness, either.

And what if this Lana person put two and two together and figured out who I was? Harry might not be the only one who had to worry about knives in the night!

But to my relief, Sheriff Lamb mentioned only "witnesses" and "concerned citizens" when explaining how the crime scene had unfolded. Of course, I wasn't naive enough to think I wasn't going to see some blowback at some point. The *Cymbeline Sentinel* was bound to send a reporter my way sooner rather than later. But with luck, the sheriff would make an arrest before that happened.

I'd just listened to a brief description of the dead man's fatal injuries when a quavering voice beside me said, "Young lady, can you possibly help me out?"

I was on edge enough over the whole Lana situation that the unexpected question made me jump. However, the speaker wasn't a middle-aged female stalker. Instead, he was a grandfatherly type wearing baggy kha-

kis, a loud plaid dress shirt, clip-on sunglasses, and a
golf cap, and he was leaning over me.

More to the point, he was actually leering down the
neckline of my shirt, which, given the way I was slouched
in the lawn chair, gaped wide open.

I promptly sat up straight to block his view. Now
I understood why Mama had always admonished me
not to slump.

"What can I help you with?" I snapped.

He pointed an unsteady finger past the parking lot.
"I hear sumpthin's goin' on at the square this morning.
Do you know what?"

"The sheriff is holding a press conference about yesterday's murder. There's press here from all around the
state wanting to know—Harry?"

The man whipped off the glasses and gave me a
broad wink. Sure enough, Grandpa Lech was actually
Harry in disguise. I stared harder, realizing that the
transformation had been done with little more than a
wig and cap and old man's clothes. He wasn't wearing any makeup, but had I not been so close to him, I
wouldn't have noticed the lack of wrinkles and liver
spots. The attitude he projected was more than sufficient.

"All right, you got me. Pretty impressive," I told him.
"But what's the point?"

"The press conference is still going on, right? You
know how they say that arsonists have a habit of sticking around to watch the fires they set? Maybe Lana will
be on the square trying to find out if anyone suspects
her. And she'll probably be looking for me in the crowd

while she's at it. We should head over there and see if we can find her first."

Which kind of made sense. Except I had a feeling that Sheriff Lamb wasn't the sort to appreciate amateurs sticking their noses into official business. And what were we supposed to do if we spotted Lana? Pull a citizen's arrest or something?

Harry must have sensed my hesitation, for he pressed on.

"Look, Nina, you're not the one who's in danger. You think I want to spend the rest of my life looking over my shoulder and waiting for her to stick a knife into me for real? We can't count on Connie and her guys being able to find this woman, especially when I don't know her real name or what she really looks like. Heck, that ridiculous bear tattoo might be a sticker, for all we know. The best chance of her being found is for you and me to do the legwork."

Bad idea. Really bad idea, I told myself.

"Fine, I'll do it," I agreed, and stood.

Because, when it came down to it, this Lana person also knew that I could put her near the scene of Bainbridge's murder. If she had really done the deed, and she learned that Harry and I knew each other, I might be added to her list of not-so-favorite people. And knowing how the woman dealt with frustration, that was one list I didn't care to make.

"The sheriff still has the mike," I told him, taking another look at the live video. "If we get moving, we'll be there before the press conference is over."

But Harry apparently was working from a different playbook than me. "Speaking of moving," he interjected, "hang on a minute."

Sliding on the old-man sunglasses again, he trotted over to the back of the bus, opened the rear door, and pulled out what at first glance looked like a giant spoked wheel. As I watched, he fumbled with the contraption for a moment, unfolding it into what I realized was one of those lightweight wheelchairs. He relocked the bus door and then rolled the chair over to me.

"Voilà," he said with a wave of his hand as he sat down in it. "This is guaranteed to give us a free pass anywhere at the press conference. So how about a push?"

"Seriously?"

"Why not? It's been about five years since I've used this thing. I bought it at a thrift store to practice for the role of a paraplegic soldier. I got pretty good with it—heck, I could even pop a wheelie—but it's been a while. Besides, poor old Grampy Westcott isn't nearly strong enough to propel himself all the way from here to the square."

He sat back and gave me the satisfied look of a minor potentate waiting on his servants to carry him in his sedan chair.

I snorted. "You can tell Grampy Westcott that he's in charge of his own transportation. I'll help you look for Lana, but no way am I going to push you all over town. Besides, your little charade is kind of insulting to people who actually do have a legitimate disability," I said, and started walking.

He wheeled after me.

"It's too bad you feel that way," he observed as we weaved through the parked cars. "I thought we were pals now…which is why I'd decided not to let all those out-of-town reporters know that Cameron Fleet's ex-wife is involved in a murder. But with that attitude, I don't feel any obligation to keep my mouth shut."

I halted and swung about.

"Why, you—"

I bit off the first expletive that came to mind. This was just what I'd been worried about, although it hadn't occurred to me that Harry would play the role of leaker. Time to nip that plan in the bud.

"You sneaky snake," I finally compromised on. "Here I'm trying to help you avoid the pointy end of a knife, and you're threatening to stick one in my back."

"Hey, I'm just trying to help out our friends from the press with a human-interest angle. By tomorrow morning you'll have reporters camped all over your yard looking for dirt. But look at it this way. That should mean a lot of publicity for your new B&B."

Right. The kind of publicity I *didn't* want.

I gritted my teeth. "Fine, I'll push you to the square. But once the press conference is over and we've talked to Sheriff Lamb, you're on your own getting back here with that chair."

"Fair enough. Oh, and I'll have you know that several disabled-veterans groups compared my paraplegic soldier performance quite favorably to Gary Sinise's Lieutenant Dan from *Forrest Gump*."

Not bothering to reply to that, I grabbed the wheelchair handles and propelled him forward. Fortunately for him, all the street corners in the downtown area were ADA compliant, meaning I rolled him down ramps rather than bumped him off curbs. I noticed, though, that he was taking this role seriously. Somehow, he'd managed to contort and shrink his body deep into the chair so that he did look like a little old man being shuttled about.

Not that he had miraculously lost weight. By the time we reached the square, I was panting a little with the exertion of wheeling a six-foot-tall muscular man. On the bright side, I was getting a good glute workout. And the physical exertion had helped deplete a little of that extra adrenaline. But I forgot all of that in my reflexive gasp as we reached the square.

Seeing the crowd on my phone's small screen was nothing compared to seeing it in real time. The block looked like a festival, with the buzz of voices and energy high. And with that number of people, Lana could be anywhere.

"I can try to get you right up to the bandstand so you can scan the crowd from there," I told Harry. "But that might draw too much attention to us. It might be better to take the square one quarter at a time. Besides, if I were Lana, I'd be standing toward the back so I could see all the action."

I'd expected a bit of a debate. Instead, he gave a decisive nod.

"Good thinking," he said. "Let's try that."

While the reporters continued to throw questions at the sheriff, Grampy Westcott and I began our rounds. Unfortunately, my earlier flip description of Harry's stalker looking like every other middle-aged white woman in the country wasn't far off.

"Don't focus too hard on faces," Harry advised, sotto voce. "Lana's worked as an extra, so she knows how to blend in. Think nondescript clothes, nothing with a logo. And so you don't notice her face, she might be wearing a wig or a hat or big sunglasses. What you want to do is look at body shape, and look at behavior. If everyone is focused on something, except for one person, that's who you check out more closely. Oh, and keep an eye out for that tat."

But if Lana was somewhere in the crowd, she was doing a good job of maintaining a low profile. We'd barely scanned the first two quarters of the square with no luck when Melissa Jane took back the microphone.

"Thank you, Sheriff Lamb, and thank you, members of the press," came her magnified voice over the tinny PA system. "We'll have another update same time to-morrow."

"It's over," I said unnecessarily, watching as the town council and sheriff's department members began departing the bandstand. "We'd better grab the sheriff before she takes off."

"Right. Onward, James…er, Jane."

Ignoring Harry's feeble attempt at humor, I started in the general direction of the bandstand hoping to head off the sheriff before she reached her vehicle.

The reporters were dispersing, too, making beelines to their crews so they could file their individual reports. That left the tourists and the locals, who, curiosity temporarily satisfied, began spreading in all directions. But still no sign of Lana anywhere, though we kept looking as we headed toward where Sheriff Lamb had paused to speak with Melissa Jane.

And from their body language, it was a contentious conversation…at least, on Melissa Jane's part. She was doing a lot of head-shaking and arm-waving, her face far more flushed than the temperature warranted. Sheriff Lamb stood with arms crossed, letting the mayor do most of the talking.

By the time we got within earshot of the pair, the square was almost back to its usual mostly empty weekday self. And so, as we walked/wheeled closer, I caught the last part of what the sheriff was saying.

"—can't make an arrest just to make one."

Melissa Jane had opened her mouth to counter that when she abruptly caught sight of me and Harry. She promptly schooled her features into genial mayor mode.

"Well, thank you, Sheriff Lamb," she said, honey dripping from every syllable. "That's all very helpful information."

To me and Harry, she said, "Hello, Nina. And who's your gentleman friend?"

Not waiting for my reply, she rushed on, "I don't need to tell you what a terrible thing poor Mr. Bainbridge's murder was. But beyond that, all this notoriety…well, let's just say this isn't the type of publicity we want. People should feel safe here in Cymbeline. Right, Sheriff Lamb?"

"I totally agree, Madame Mayor. So if you'll excuse me, I need to interview more witnesses."

"Uh, Sheriff," I said as she turned to leave, "my, er, gentleman friend has some confidential information he'd like to share with you about this case. If we could speak in private…"

I trailed off with a meaningful look at Melissa Jane, who huffed a little.

"Oh, very well. But think about what we talked about, Sheriff."

The woman flounced off…well, as much as one could flounce in running shoes and a seersucker suit. And while it seemed she might have been tiptoeing across an ethical line with the sheriff in pushing for an arrest, I understood where she was coming from. She and her team had built up Cymbeline from a moribund small town into a thriving tourist haven. Seeing all that threatened by something out of their control had to be difficult.

Once the mayor was out of earshot, the sheriff pulled out her notebook and said, "All right, Ms. Fleet, why don't you introduce me to the gentleman?"

Before I could answer, Harry straightened in the chair and pulled off his sunglasses. "Hey, Connie, it's me."

"Harry? Harry Westcott?" At his nod, she gave him a sharp look. "Is this some sort of stunt, Harry? Why are you dressed like someone's granddad, and what's up with that chair?"

"I'm kind of in disguise," he replied. "That's what I needed to talk to you about. I've got someone after me, and I'm trying to keep a low profile."

"Right. Low profile." To me, she said, "And you're here, Ms. Fleet, because…"

"I'm here to corroborate Harry's story. We think we know who killed Gregory Bainbridge, and why."

I expected a bit more excitement out of her at this revelation, but apparently that wasn't how the cops— well, at least this particular cop—worked. Instead, she replied, "It's pretty hot out, so why don't we head over to my patrol car. I can turn up the AC and we can chat."

She indicated the coned-off VIP parking area, which happened to be a portion of the angled-in parking spots on the square right across from Peaches and Java. Three sheriff's department vehicles were still parked there.

While I pushed Harry in that direction, the sheriff fell back a little behind us. I overheard her talking into her shoulder mike again, catching a few words—*suspect... my squad... ETA under a minute*—but nothing that I could make any real sense of it. All I wanted now was to get this over with and head back home again, where, in the company of my trusty pup and my nuns, I could take a little break from the insanity.

I halted at the cop cars and waited for instructions. But when they came, they weren't for me.

"Mr. Westcott, I need you to stand up out of that chair now."

"Why so formal?" Harry asked, remaining seated. "I'd really rather not break character in case—"

"Mr. Westcott, I'm asking you one more time to stand. If you don't, I'll consider that resisting. Now please get out of that chair and step over here in front of this vehicle."

"Connie, what's wrong? What are you talking about?" he demanded, though he did as requested.

Sheriff Lamb looked in my direction. "Ms. Fleet, I need you to take that wheelchair and step back at least ten feet from us. Once you've done that, do not move from that position."

Equally mystified, I nodded and complied. As I did so, I saw Deputies Jackson and Mullins approaching from either side. Something was definitely going down, though I wasn't sure what.

But at the sheriff's next words, I figured it out.

"Mr. Westcott, turn around and place your hands on the hood of the vehicle. Now spread your legs. Wider... no, wider. I'm going to search you for weapons, so if you have any knives or guns on you, I suggest you let me know right now."

"Connie, this is crazy," Harry replied from his half-sprawled position as she pulled off his hat and wig and tossed them to Jackson. "I don't own a gun, and the only knife I have is one of those Swiss army ones."

Unsettling as this little drama was, it wasn't going unnoticed by the rest of Cymbeline. A few tourist types walking past stopped to stare, while a saggy pants–wearing teen recorded the action with his smartphone. Even worse, a twenty-something woman with a half-shaved head and wearing an Atlanta TV station–logo shirt had pulled out a camera and was snapping pictures.

Sheriff Lamb, meanwhile, had finished frisking Harry.

"He's clean," she told the deputies, and reached for the handcuffs on her belt. "All right, Mr. Westcott, I need your right hand behind you...now your left."

In a couple of quick moves, she'd slapped the handcuffs on both of his wrists. That accomplished, she nodded to Mullins, who reached for Harry's bound arms and pulled him upright again, then spun him around.

"Harry Westcott," the sheriff grimly said, "you're under arrest for the murder of Gregory Bainbridge."

FOURTEEN

WHILE THE DEPUTIES loaded an obviously stunned Harry into one of the vehicles, I abandoned the wheelchair and rushed over to the sheriff.

"Wait, Sheriff Lamb, you've got the wrong guy," I choked out, realizing as I said it that this was the cliché claim of every friend and relative when someone they knew was under arrest.

Still, I persisted, "Harry and I know who really did it. It's this woman who's been stalking and threatening to kill him. She obviously thought it was Harry in the penguin costume. Her name is Lana Harwood, and she—"

"Ms. Fleet, please don't interfere in sheriff's department business," she cut me short, sliding her sunglasses back into place. "If you'd like to make a statement to one of the deputies about the case, come by our facility later this afternoon, and we'll be happy to listen to you."

She handed me a business card with a big star stamped on it along with her name and the sheriff's department address.

The official sheriff's department blow-off move, I thought in outrage, watching as the car with Harry in it drove off. But before I could summon another argument, the sheriff's chill expression softened fractionally.

"Look, Ms. Fleet, I've known Harry since we were kids. He's a great guy, lots of charisma. But he'd been a little, well, *off* since that falling out with his family. And we do have an eyewitness who puts him with the victim at the estimated time of the murder."

She must have seen the shock on my face, for she added, "We're still investigating the incident, so if you think you know something that would point us in another direction, we want to hear it. But there's something you should remember. He might not be taking statuettes home on awards night, but Harry is one hell of an actor. I suggest you keep that in mind when he tells you about how innocent he is."

Leaving me with that unsettling thought, she climbed into her own vehicle and pulled out.

"Ma'am, ma'am!" I heard a voice behind me calling.

I turned to see a clean-cut blond kid in khakis and a pale-blue pullover halfway across the square waving a cordless microphone and running in my direction. He was trailed by a chunky, middle-aged black guy with a graying old-school Fu Manchu mustache lugging a camera on his shoulder. I was pretty sure I'd seen the blond kid on one of the Atlanta news channels back when I lived there. Just the person I did *not* want to talk to right now.

Telling myself I'd retrieve Harry's wheelchair later, I fled across the street and into Peaches and Java. In this prelunch gap of time, the coffee shop was sparsely occupied, and only by locals. I saw no sign of Gemma or Jasmine, but Daniel was busy cleaning one of the coffee stations.

"Quick, hide me," I told him as the man looked up in alarm at my hasty entry. "I've got reporters after me."

Like Gemma rushing to help the other day, he didn't

pause for questions but pointed me to the storeroom behind the main counter. I fled through that open doorway as the bells on the front door jangled. From my vantage point behind a mostly stocked open shelf, I could see both the reporter and his camera guy, but I was pretty certain they couldn't see me.

"Can I help you?" I heard Daniel say.

"Dave Bradshaw, *Live News Atlanta*," the reporter replied, panting a little from his run. "I'm looking for a woman who just came into your shop. Brown hair, white shirt, jeans. We'd like to interview her about what just happened across the street from you. Any idea where she went?"

"No one like that came in, brah. But if you want to sit down and order, maybe she'll show up later."

"Are you sure? I saw her run in your door maybe thirty seconds ago. Anyone else see her?"

All he got in return was a lot of head shaking from the locals who, thankfully, were banding together to protect a fellow Cymbeliner. I could see the reporter's frustrated expression, and I knew he knew everyone was lying. Not that he could do anything about that.

Then I heard the camera man speak up. "Hey, Dave. Maybe she went into the restroom."

I hastily slid over to the next row of shelves, changing my angle so I could see what happened next. Sure enough, good old Dave marched over to the store's single public restroom, the cartoon paintings of anthropomorphic male and female peaches on its door indicating it was a unisex facility. And then he began knocking.

"Hey, brah," Daniel called. "This isn't Starbucks. You wanna pee, buy yourself a coffee first."

"Just checking for that lady," Dave airily assured him, rattling the doorknob now.

The restroom door opened a moment later, and a tall black guy with glasses walked out, newspaper tucked under his arm. Giving the reporter a chilly "It's all yours," the man returned to his table and settled back in with his coffee.

Dave and his camera operator exchanged looks; then the former shrugged.

"Guess I was mistaken. We'll be back later for that coffee. In the meantime, y'all have a *Live* day," he finished with what I assumed was his station's tag line before gesturing the camera guy to follow him out.

I waited another minute in case Live Dave pulled a fast one and came back. Only when I was sure the pair was gone did I leave the storeroom again.

"Thanks, everyone," I said to the remaining customers. To Daniel, I said, "I appreciate your letting me hide. I seriously did not want to talk to that kid."

"Always glad to help," he said with a smile. Then he sobered. "This Dave guy said something just happened outside the store. What's he talking about?"

"I'll explain if you've got a few minutes."

After Daniel had poured us both a cup of fresh brew—iced for me, since I was still sweating—I gave him the rundown about Harry's arrest. While Daniel exclaimed over this, I went on to tell him about the mysterious stalker Harry claimed had threatened him, as well as Sheriff Lamb's warning that Harry might not be trusted. When I'd finished, the man was shaking his head.

"I'm not sure what to tell you, Nina. I know Sheriff

Lamb, and she wouldn't be arresting Harry if she didn't have some pretty strong evidence against him. You already told the deputy yesterday about the woman who was the first one to find Gregory in the alley, right?"

"Right. But at the time, I didn't know she was Harry's crazy stalker."

"And you still don't know that, do you?"

When I gave him a questioning look, he went on, "Harry was there in the alley with you and Gemma and the nuns. He could have overheard what you said and used your description to make up this whole stalker thing. That way, when the cops came back to you with more questions, you'd be corroborating his alibi. I mean, that's all pretty vague when you think about it—some middle-aged white gal who might have brown hair, or maybe it's blonde hair or red hair."

"But he described her tattoo to me," I weakly protested. Daniel had come up with a good counterargument. The problem was, I didn't want to believe I'd been taken in like that.

He shrugged. "You probably mentioned the tat when you made your statement. Remember, an actor and a con artist have a lot of the same skills. They know people, and they know how to put on a convincing performance."

The shop door jingled again, and he stood to greet the new customer. "You want my advice, Nina," he finished, "keep away from the guy, at least until the cops wrap this thing up. You've got enough on your plate right now trying to run a business and taking care of those nuns."

Which was what I'd already been telling myself. On

top of that, not only the sheriff but now Daniel was warning me that Harry might be using his acting chops against me. *Had* he been playing me the whole time? How had the situation gone from the man waving letters and threatening me with a lawsuit to the pair of us skulking about together in search of his supposed stalker, who conveniently might also be Bainbridge's killer?

I set down my cup with a clank. Time to kick Harry to the curb and let the professionals handle the situation. I'd already told the sheriff all I knew about Bainbridge's murder. It wasn't my job to play Harry's sidekick. He had a dialing finger and an attorney. He'd be okay.

Feeling something of the same sort of relief I'd had when I'd signed my divorce papers, I gave Daniel a wave and then headed for the door. I checked first, however, to make sure Reporter Dave wasn't lurking outside with his cameraman. Fortunately, the coast was clear, and Harry's wheelchair was still where I'd left it. I'd do him one last favor and roll the chair back to his bus, but from there the actor was on his own.

As on the day before, I was a bit surprised when I finally got back to the house to find it barely noon. But this time, the nuns had taken luncheon matters into their own hands. The leftover meat and veggies from yesterday's snack tray had been chopped along with a couple of hard-boiled eggs and a head of lettuce I'd had sitting around to make a hearty Cobb salad.

"I hope you don't mind," Sister Mary George said as she ushered me into the dining room. "You already had the ingredients, so Mary Paul whipped up some homemade dressing to go with the salad."

"Believe me, I never criticize a meal I don't have to make myself," I assured the nun with a smile.

But the salad with its homemade dressing, while tasty, couldn't hold my attention. I'd debated telling the sisters about Harry's supposed stalker, or the fact that he'd been arrested for Bainbridge's murder, but in the end I decided to wait. Why upset them until we knew for sure if Harry was actually going to be charged? Tonight at supper would be soon enough to break the news.

And so, to distract myself, I waited for a lull in their murmured conversation and then brightly spoke up. "Sisters, I need some advice."

The soft clank of forks against plates abruptly halted, and six expectant gazes fixed themselves on me… Mattie being content to remain under the table and not involve herself with human chitchat.

"Of course, my dear," Mother Superior replied. "If there's a problem—"

"Oh, no, nothing like that," I rushed to reassure her, my glance taking in them all. "I need your perspective as businesswomen. Your cheese-making venture was such a success, I'm hoping you can advise me on my bed-and-breakfast. I need some ideas on groups and events to target to bring in more guests."

"Weddings!" Sister Mary Christopher promptly replied, wide blue eyes growing even wider in excitement. Then, catching Mother Superior's slanted look through her oversized glasses, she amended, "I mean, of course, for those who aren't members of the Church. Your gardens are so lovely, they'd make an ideal spot to exchange vows. Except you'd need to build an arbor for the bride and groom to stand beneath."

"Right," Sister Mary Thomas agreed. "And if the day is nice, you could serve the champagne and wedding cake beneath the pavilion."

"Chickens!"

This from Sister Mary Paul in her thick accent. Then, as we all stared at her in confusion, Sister Mary Christopher tittered. "I think Mary Paul means hens, as in hen parties."

Then, when the older nun vigorously nodded, Sister Mary Christopher clarified for the others, "You know, bachelorette parties. You could serve cocktails and lady fingers and watercress sandwiches, and the girls could make wedding veils out of toilet paper."

Mother Superior said, "I think those are excellent ideas. And, Nina, you might consider advertising to literary groups and women's organizations. They often schedule destination events for their members and are always looking for interesting venues."

"What about targeting rosarians?" Sister Mary George wanted to know.

Before I could ask what rosaries had to do with anything, she continued, "I'm sure there are all sorts of gardening groups dedicated to cultivating heirloom roses who would love to meet somewhere new. And with such fine specimens as you have growing, all you need to do is take some professional photos of them and add an album of heirloom roses to your B&B website. You do have a website, don't you?"

"You must have a website!" Sister Mary Julian bellowed in agreement. "Can't do business these days without one."

"I don't have one yet, but that's next on my list," I assured her.

We spent the next several minutes bouncing ideas off one another. Finally, I shoved back my now-empty salad plate and said, "I should have thought to bring a pad and paper and take notes. You've all been most helpful."

And they had. Already I had a few new ideas percolating in my brain for targeting potential new customers. Beyond that, I had almost unlimited resources in the various local business owners who might be willing to partner with me on some advertising, or provide discounted food or services in return for a plug.

Standing, I added, "I'd better start cleaning up, and then I need to go write down some of what we talked about."

"Oh, Nina," Mother Superior spoke up as I reached for her plate. "I'm sorry, I almost forgot. You had a visitor while you were gone earlier."

I glanced up sharply.

"A visitor? What did she want?" I demanded, more brusquely than I'd intended.

Telling myself I was overreacting, I tried to tamp down a reflexive sense of panic as visions of a middle-aged tattooed woman with brown—or blonde, or red—hair brandishing a knife flashed through my mind.

"Actually, it was a gentleman. He didn't give his name, but he said you two had met the other day. He wanted to talk to you about doing some work here at the bed-and-breakfast."

I dialed back the panic reflex to good old everyday annoyance. Apparently, Jack Hill was stepping up his game and making the first move to search my house for hidden treasure.

Then I frowned, considering. Why not let him? Next time he came by, I'd have him give the place the once-over so he could quote on supposed needed repairs. But I'd channel my inner Mattie and dog his steps the whole time so I could figure out what about the house piqued his interest. And then, once I'd sent him on his way, I'd do a little treasure hunting of my own.

I managed a smile. "I think I know who that was," I reassured her. "If he drops by again, I'll deal with him."

We finished the meal and cleanup in companionable conversation. Then, leaving the sisters to their post-luncheon prayers in the parlor, I changed into grubbies and retreated to the carriage house. I needed something to distract me, and a bit of mindless sweat equity would do the trick.

Kicking on the carriage house's window unit—no way could a person manage inside in this heat without some sort of air-conditioning—I got to work.

One of the little side projects I'd been doing since purchasing the house had been furniture refurbishing. I'd already stripped and restained two battered side tables and been pleased with the results. My current project was a vintage vanity and bench seat that had been stored in the back of the garage. While it had good bones, it also had more damage than I had skills to fix. And so I'd decided to commit the cardinal sin of style purists everywhere and use a little chalk paint for the "love it or hate it" shabby look. Though it hurt my midcentury-modern self to admit it, even halfway through the process I was liking the look.

I'd been sanding drawer fronts and changing out hardware for almost an hour when a voice behind me said, "Nina, can we talk a minute?"

I yelped and jumped and swung about to find Sister Mary George standing in the carriage house doorway.

The nun gave me an apologetic smile. "I'm sorry I startled you like that. I knocked first, but I guess you couldn't hear me with the air-conditioner on," she said, indicating the window unit that was blasting equal parts noise and cold air.

I smiled back and set down my screwdriver. "No worries, Sister. Here, let me find you a seat."

Over her protests, I cleared a spot on a wooden bench for her and then took a seat on an overturned bucket. "Is there something else the sisters need?"

"Oh, no, everything is lovely. But I'm wondering why you didn't tell us that Mr. Westcott was arrested this morning for Mr. Bainbridge's murder."

Her tone wasn't the least bit accusatory, but I immediately felt guilty. I guess nuns have that superpower. And, given the fact that the sisters had been right there when we'd found Bainbridge in the alley and that they'd stood prayerful watch over him while we waited for the paramedics, they *did* have a vested interest in knowing all the details about the whole murder thing.

Sighing, I asked, "How did you find out?"

She reached into the pocket of her black habit and pulled out a late-model smartphone.

"Don't look so surprised," she replied when I, indeed, gave her a surprised look. "We may be nuns, but our order lives firmly in the twenty-first century. How do you think we handled all the goat cheese orders?

You can only sell so much fromage to folks who happen to stop by. Anyhow, I saw the story on my news feed. Someone posted a video of the arrest, and I saw you there while Harry was being handcuffed."

"I'm sorry, Sister Mary George. I was going to tell everyone tonight. I—I just didn't want to upset anyone. I'm still pretty upset myself."

"All the more reason you should have said something," was her firm reply. "I know we're nuns, and some of us are pretty old, but that doesn't mean we're fragile or frightened. We choose to live a life of prayer and labor, but we darned sure can handle the tough world out there, if need be."

I felt even more guilty, if that were possible. In an attempt to keep things "nice," I'd been both patronizing and ageist.

"Sorry," I repeated. "You're absolutely right. If you have a few minutes, I'll tell you everything that happened this morning."

I gave her the same rundown of events that I'd given Daniel earlier. But when I'd finished, unlike Daniel, she shook her veiled head and said, "We can't abandon Mr. Westcott in his time of need. I'm inclined to believe his account."

"I'd like to agree with you, Sister, but there's nothing to back up his story about the stalker. And then he's running around wearing disguises and claiming he's trying to smoke out Bainbridge's real killer. With all of that, what makes you believe him?"

"Faith." She gave me a serene smile. "Once, many years ago, someone believed me when no one else did… and that believing changed my life."

"All right, Sister. If you believe Harry, then I'll believe him, too."

Not that I'd trust him 100 percent yet, I silently amended. But if the sheriff cut him loose, then I'd give him a chance, while keeping a sharp eye on him. Because the whole murder thing notwithstanding, I was pretty sure he still had his beady penguin brain focused on trying to somehow steal my house out from under me.

Sister Mary George nodded. "I'm glad to hear that. Now, I'll let you get back to your project. Your vanity is going to look wonderful when it's finished."

Basking a bit in that compliment, I closed the carriage house door after her…and then gave way to guilt again. Despite what I'd told her, I wasn't as convinced as the nun was of Harry's innocence. Not that I'd come up with a motive for him to want the man dead. But apparently Harry's father was some sort of real estate mogul. Perhaps Bainbridge and the elder Westcott had been in some sort of deal together that, like seemingly every other Bainbridge project, had caused the other man financial ruin.

Or maybe Bainbridge had helped sell Mrs. Lathrop's house out from under Harry. Talk about motive!

"Not my circus," I reminded myself. For now, I'd let Sheriff Lamb handle all things Harry.

A short time later I'd finished the dressing table drawer fronts and started tackling the bench. The striped sateen fabric of the cushion was stained and ripped, but fortunately the seat portion was removable. I fought with the fabric for a while—just how many rusted old staples were necessary to hold the cloth in place?—

and finally called it a day once I was down to layers of dirty old batting.

Mattie came running out to greet me as I left the carriage house. I didn't need to glance at my phone to know it was 4 pm, otherwise known as doggy snack time.

"Let me wash the dirt off first," I told her as we went into the kitchen. There I found all the sisters except Mary George and Mother Superior gathered near the butler's pantry and making notes.

"Don't mind us," Sister Mary Christopher called in her cheery warble. "We're trying to decide what Mary Paul should cook for us tonight."

Leaving the menu to them, I went to my room and took a nice long shower, then threw on the same outfit from that morning. Mattie, meanwhile, was dancing impatiently about the room to communicate that she was at the point of total starvation.

"Right, girl, you're so undernourished I can see your ribs…not," I teased her. "Come on, let's get your snack."

We returned to the kitchen, where she peered nervously in the direction of the outside door, ears quirked as if checking out something. The rustle of the treat bag distracted her, however, and she did her required *sit, down, stay* in return for organic lamb treats stamped into the shape of little bones. She'd just finished the last one when I heard the doorbell ring.

Her ears went up in full alert mode. Mine did, too… at least figuratively.

"So that's why you were all antsy," I observed. "Probably our buddy Jack again. Come on. I'm going to want you along with me if I let him loose in the house.

Though maybe we can talk about the arbor idea that Sister Mary Christopher had."

The bell was ringing a second time as I reached the entry. I peered through the sidelight, then gasped and pulled open the front door.

"Harry, you're out of jail!" I exclaimed, stating the obvious. Then, frowning, I added, "Did Sheriff Lamb believe your story about your stalker?"

"Let's just say that, after a few hours of questioning, Connie apparently decided her eyewitness testimony wasn't quite as open-and-shut as she thought. For the moment, I'm free to go, though she gave me the old *don't leave town* speech."

"That's great," I cautiously replied. Frankly, it would have been easier on me if he'd spent a day or ten in the clink so I didn't have to keep tabs on him. Then, eyeing him more closely, I added, "What's wrong? You don't look very cheerful for an innocent man who was just set free."

Since his release, he'd apparently gone back to his bus, for he'd exchanged the old man khakis and checkered shirt for an outfit somewhere between hipster and nerd: tight black jeans and a short-sleeved blue chambray shirt. He'd rolled and looped a faded yellow bandana around his neck in a look that might have made sense if he actually worked outside. But it wasn't just the deliberately wrinkled shirt and late-afternoon stubble on his cheeks that gave him a world-weary look. If I'd had to interpret his expression, I'd have said he appeared uneasy.

"Can I come in?" he asked, furtively glancing over his shoulder. "I need to talk to you."

Which led to another question. Namely, why was his second stop after being sprung from jail my place?

Feeling a bit uneasy myself, I opened the screen door. Had I been alone, or had it been after dark, I'd probably have reacted differently, but for the moment my curiosity ruled. "The sisters are in the kitchen, so we can sit in the parlor. You know where it is."

Mattie followed us down the hall, ears back to their usual half-mast state, which I took as a good sign. In the parlor, Harry sat on the same blue velvet sofa where he'd lain a few days earlier. Once again, I took the threadbare sofa opposite him and waited for him to speak. When he remained silent, however, I prompted him.

"You said you needed to talk. So what's up?"

"Here's the thing. After Connie cut me free, I called an Uber for a ride back to the bus. I changed clothes, and then came back outside to collect my camping gear. Turns out a town ordinance forbids parking in public lots for more than a couple of nights running. I didn't want a ticket, so I figured I'd better pack up and find another spot."

I nodded and waited, not sure yet where he was going with this story. And then he hit me with the punch line.

"I went to fold up my lounge chair, and that's when I saw that someone had used a knife to slice up all the webbing."

FIFTEEN

SLICED THE LOUNGE chair webbing?

As a punchline, it was a letdown. My first impulse was to dismiss the action as petty vandalism. The culprit was probably someone who was ticked that Harry was hogging two primo parking spots. Except that I could see he believed otherwise.

"You think *she* did it."

It was a statement, not a question.

"Lana wanted me to know she knew where I was," he agreed, rubbing his temples as if he were in pain. "I mean, she obviously knew I was in town, but she wouldn't have any idea I was camping in the bus unless she followed me back from one of my gigs. I mean, it wasn't like I had a neon sign posted on it that said, 'Here Lives Harry.'"

"I'm sure that was pretty unnerving," I observed. "So what did you do next?"

"I tossed the chair in the dumpster, put everything else in the bus, and hightailed it out of there."

"What about making a report? I mean, if it really was Lana, you need to document what she did...you know, a paper trail. Did you call the sheriff?"

He looked up again and nodded. "I took a few pictures of the slashed chair before I trashed it and emailed them to Connie."

He pulled out his phone from his shirt pocket and poked at the screen a moment, then leaned forward to show me several photos of the vandalized lounge chair from multiple angles. Each section of once-taut webbing had been sliced in half, almost as if someone had run a circular saw's spinning blade down the chair, leaving only ribbons of webbing hanging from the aluminum frame.

Disconcerting, to say the least. Though the revived skeptic in me noted that Harry could just as easily have done the damage with the Swiss army knife he'd told the sheriff he had.

Harry, meanwhile, gave an exaggerated shudder and stuck the phone back in his pocket.

"Connie called me back and said some out-of-towner probably was mad that I'd take up two parking spots and did it out of spite. But she did say that she'd put the pictures in the file. And then she made sure I remembered about the ordinance having to do with staying overnight in public lots, which is why I drove off."

"So if you're not there by the square anymore, where's your bus parked now?"

"In your driveway."

And there it was, the actual punch line.

I felt my mouth literally drop open as I stared at the man. True, I should have heard the bus belch and clank and squeak its way up the drive, but I hadn't. All I could guess was that he'd made his move while I was in the shower. My fault for not keeping the driveway gate shut, though in my defense, regularly wrestling that iron barricade open and closed took a fair amount of strength.

When I finally could speak again, the sole question I could manage was, "How in the heck am I supposed to get my Mini out of the garage with that *thing* in the way?"

"Don't worry, I pulled it far enough over to the side so a car can get past. Which leads us to our next topic of discussion."

He leaned back against the sofa, assuming a confidential tone now. "You can see the problem. I can't sleep in the bus in this heat with all the doors and windows closed, because I'll cook alive. And I can't leave them open to catch a breeze, because that gives Lana the chance to sneak in while I'm sleeping and put a knife in my ribs. I checked, and every hotel and B&B in town is full because of all the press staying here. Bottom line, I need a place to stay…as in, I plan to stay here."

Here? This last was less another punch line than a figurative slap upside the head. Now I was the one massaging *my* temples. Things were going off the rails very quickly now. The only way I could see to cope would be to indulge in a moment of WWTND—What Would The Nuns Do?

They, of course, would smile and invite him to stay, which I really didn't want. On the other hand, if Lana truly was out there somewhere with another knife, I'd feel responsible if something bad happened to the guy.

On the third hand, since there wasn't a spare room to be had in the place with the sisters still in residence, I had a legitimate out.

"Look, Harry," I began, "I understand your dilemma, and I'd love to help you, but you're going to have to figure out something else. The sisters are staying here indefinitely until the whole situation with the convent is settled. There's literally no room at the inn."

At my words, a flash of that slightly frenzied anger I'd seen at our first meeting darkened his expression.

"You realize I don't really need to ask," was his taut response. "As far as my attorney and I are concerned, the house is mine. You're only here until we get all the legalities worked out. Technically, I could haul all my stuff inside and make myself comfortable, and there'd be nothing you could do about it."

And there he was, back again...the genuine version of Harry Westcott. The guy I knew and didn't love.

"Look, even if I believed your claim—and for the record, I do not—like I told you, I just don't have a place for you. The nuns are using every single room already."

"Not every room."

I shot him a confused look that slowly morphed into disbelief as it occurred to me what he must be meaning. Without a doubt, he was an attractive guy and, crazy stalker women aside, probably had his share of females lining up outside his door. But no way was I going to join that number and let him turn my bed into his own personal casting couch.

In glacial tones, I informed him, "Sorry, my bedroom is *not* up for grabs...with or without me."

Now it was his turn to look confused...and then, disbelieving. With a snort, he said, "I think you misunderstand. Not that I'm not, er, flattered, but what I actually had in mind was sleeping in the tower room."

"Oh," I managed, feeling my cheeks start to burn at the realization that I'd jumped to one heck of a wrong conclusion. But before I could wallow too deeply in my mortification, it occurred to me that I had no clue what he was talking about.

"Oh?" I repeated, this time in surprise. "Tower room?"

I pictured the cupola atop my house that was tucked between two eaves on the second-story roof, like a squat ice cream cone clutched in a child's hand. I'd been more than a little disappointed when I'd first walked through the place and found no staircase leading up to it. Later, Debbie Jo had told me that the cupola wasn't part of the square footage and instead was simply an architectural feature.

"Good try," I told him, "but there's no way to access it. That's what the real estate agent told me. She even had an old copy of the floor plan, and nothing on it showed anything about it being living space."

"Wrong."

Jekyll/Hyde-ing himself back into the charming version of Harry, the man shot me a grin. "I practically lived up there for three summers when I was a kid. Believe me, there's a way up to it."

Then he grew serious again. "Look, I'll cut you a deal. Like I told you, our friendly neighborhood sheriff has asked me to stick around, so I really need somewhere to stay. Let's call a temporary truce on who owns the place. Let me stay in the tower room until Connie gives me the green light to leave town, and I'll show you the secret stairway that leads to it."

I considered his offer. Could this secret staircase have been the mysterious whatever that Jack Hill had been looking for? If he was the experienced carpenter he claimed to be, he likely knew about old houses and their architectural mysteries. Maybe he'd been up there before and knew something of value lay within its circular walls...something that I, the clueless new owner, had no knowledge of.

Swiftly, I debated the benefits of having access to this hitherto unknown room—maybe filled with treasure!—against allowing a somewhat broken actor—and possibly his equally crazy stalker—having free access to my house.

On the "against" side, I had no guarantee that Harry would keep up his end of this so-called truce. And depending on local ordinances, nonpaying guests who stayed a certain length of time were automatically deemed tenants. Once that happened, the only way to roust them was through a formal eviction process that could take months. I could be risking that situation should I let Harry stay.

But on the "for" side, the possibility of accessing the tower made for an equally compelling argument. And maybe it was more prudent to have Harry where I could keep an eye on him rather than wondering what he was doing behind my back.

"Here's my counterproposal," I cautiously told him. "I'll agree to this truce, which does not mean that I think you have any sort of claim to the house, just that we're not going to argue about it. You'll show me the way up to the tower room, and if it's still habitable, you can stay there...but only for one week. And you're not my guest, you're a short-time renter. I'm going to write up a bill and charge you a token rate to stay there. Say, a hundred bucks—in advance—but that's only for the room. You're on your own for food. Oh, and you're not getting a key."

I had to give it to Harry; the man had one heck of a poker face when it suited him. I couldn't tell from his expression if I'd demanded too much or settled for too little. After a long moment, he nodded.

"I accept your counterproposal. Though it would have been kind of you to throw in breakfast. This is a B&B, after all."

"Hey, be glad I'm not charging you extra for parking that heap of a bus in my driveway. Now, show me the secret staircase."

A few moments later, we were upstairs in the hallway near the front of the house, not far from Sister Mary Julian's room. Fortunately, the sisters were all still in the kitchen or else in the parlor for another round of prayers. Even so, I made the effort to keep my voice low. I'd inform them about Harry's stay only after we determined that the tower room was fit for sleeping.

"Okay, the cupola should be just about on top of us. So where in the heck is your mysterious secret stairway?"

"Voilà!"

With a grin, Harry reached for the wall beside me and twisted a bit of trim on one of the raised panels, like he was turning a knob. That section of the paneling abruptly popped open, revealing a narrow doorway.

I stared in amazement. Because of the dim light and the raised-panel style of the wood, the door's outline was neatly camouflaged. I'd walked down this hall any number of times and never noticed the slightly wider spacing in the beveling surrounding that particular panel, or the gap in the trim that allowed the makeshift knob to turn.

Harry reached into the opening and tugged a length of string dangling there, lighting a bare bulb of minimal wattage mounted on the inner wall. Now I could see that the doorway gave way to a closet-sized room enclosing a wooden staircase.

I use the term *staircase* loosely. In reality, it was more like a heavy ladder which, though solidly mounted above and below, had a pitch far too narrow for it to be climbed without using both hands and feet. Peering up into the gloom, I could see what appeared to be a section of railed landing above.

I shot Harry a doubtful look. "Are you sure it's safe to climb up there?"

"Of course," he replied with only the faintest hint of boyish scorn in his tone. "I told you, I pretty much lived up there for a few summers when I was a kid. Come on, follow me."

Stepping inside, he nimbly mounted the first rung and confidently started upward. I proceeded a bit more slowly. Mattie, who had followed us upstairs, apparently realized that the stairs were beyond even her climbing abilities and retreated downstairs again to rejoin the sisters.

Heights and climbing never had been two of my favorite sports. Luckily, I was provided with sufficient distraction—the denim-clad butt above me, which, in all fairness, was about the only thing I could see as we made our climb.

Even in the meager twenty-five-watt glow, it was obvious that Harry had the glutes of a man who either (a) had been blessed by nature, or else (b) hit the gym on a regular basis. Since neither (a) nor (b) applied to me or my posterior, I made a mental note to (c) never climb ahead of him on these particular stairs and (d) seriously consider joining one of Cymbeline's two gyms.

Though, actually, navigating this stairway a few times a day would be a nice little workout, I told myself as we reached the landing above. Harry gave me a hand the last couple of steps, though I wasn't certain if he was simply being gentlemanly or if he was worried that I might not make the climb.

Once I was safely settled, he flipped a switch on the wall, which added sixty or so watts to the ambient lighting, and then gestured grandly. "This is it, the best view in all of Cymbeline."

Staring about the circular room that was perhaps twelve feet in diameter, I was inclined to disagree. Unless, of course, one's definition of the best view included sheet-draped furniture and a thick gray layer of dust on the wooden floor. As for the tower's half-dozen windows, they were shrouded in still more sheets, giving the place a faintly sinister air. And since the central air wasn't working up here, the room was almost oppressively hot.

Harry didn't notice my initial disappointment, however, for he was busy whipping sheets off the furniture and raising a cloud of dust in the process. The bed, side table, and chest of drawers he revealed were oak, just the sort of furnishings one might have found in a boy's bedroom back around World War II. Plain, but serviceable, and able to withstand roughhousing. There were also a couple of armless upholstered chairs of indeterminable vintage that, with their brown-and-yellow plaid upholstery, also fell into the plain-but-serviceable category.

While I sneezed, Harry tackled the windows, leaving a trail of sandaled footprints in the dust. Once the sheets were removed, I could see the delicate lace draperies that were visible from the outside. Close up, they were yellow with age and almost matched the faded striped wallpaper. Both definitely needed replacing.

Looking around, I saw a small porcelain sink standing on metal legs against the wall across the room from me, next to what appeared to be a closet door. A metal-frame shaving mirror, vintage World War I, hung over the tiny basin. Curious, I walked over and twisted the white china handle marked with a black cursive *C*, not expecting much. To my surprise, after a few gurgling seconds, a steady stream of somewhat rusty water poured from the vintage faucet.

Harry, meanwhile, was making a second round of the windows. This time, he opened all eight of them, letting in a warm breeze that didn't do much to lower the temperature but definitely dispelled the room's oppressive air. He paused after the last one and stuck his head out the screenless opening, then glanced back at me.

"C'mon, take a look," he urged, gesturing me to join him. "You can see the square and half the town from here."

I left my own set of footprints in the dust as I joined him to take the requisite look…and was instantly smitten.

"This is the best view in Cymbeline!" I exclaimed, echoing his earlier sentiment. "You're right, I can see most of the town square, and every backyard for blocks.

Look over there, where one of the news crews is getting ready for an evening broadcast."

Oddly fascinated, I continued to search the area for signs of life.

"Why, that's old Mr. Jamison walking his bull terrier," I said, glimpsing one of my neighbors.

"And not using poop bags," I added accusingly as I saw the pair scamper off from where the dog had just left a sizable deposit.

I went from window to window, taking in the changing view. "This is amazing. You can see what everyone's doing, and unless they're looking up, they'll never see you. Talk about an opportunity for blackmail. Was that what you did all summer when you were a kid, spy on people?"

"I prefer to call it studying human nature. Besides, it was great training for my career."

"Career as what, a Peeping Tom?"

"No, as an actor," he retorted, while I tried not to snicker. "People are more honest when they don't know they're being watched. They dawdle, they scratch, they sneeze without covering their mouths…"

"They leave dog poop behind instead of bagging it," I finished for him. "So what's that have to do with acting?"

He sighed, as if I'd just asked him to explain rocket science to a three-year-old.

"Think of how a chef keeps a well-stocked kitchen with all the basics: eggs, flour, milk, butter. Put those ingredients together one way, and you get a cake. Put them together another way, and you get a soufflé. But instead of food, an actor stockpiles physical expressions, gestures, accents."

I wondered if this was an explanation he'd made up long after the fact, or if he'd actually used this as an excuse back when he was a kid. Still, it explained how he was able to do his Grampy Westcott routine so well.

I turned from the window and said, "All right, the room looks like it's safe to sleep in. We'll give it a try for one week, like I said. I'll pull out some spare linen you can use, but you have to do the dusting and vacuuming yourself. And no talk about the house being yours. You break that rule and I can kick you out, no refunds. Do we have a deal?"

He hesitated for so long that I thought he'd changed his mind. Finally, he agreed, "Deal," and stuck out his hand. "I'll run out to the bus later and get you the cash."

We shook, and I pretended I didn't feel a little tingle at that brief contact. For his part, Harry seemed more interested in reclaiming his boyhood space, for he swiftly let go of my hand and hurried to grab the dusty broom propped near the closet.

While Harry did his thing, I went downstairs to round up cleaning supplies. By now, all the sisters were gathered downstairs. They'd seen the bus and were all atwitter to know what was going on. I gave them a rundown on Harry's current status, prompting a chorus of knowing *hmm*s and *ah*s. Then I told them about his stalker, in case the woman showed up at the house. This brought a refrain of stern *tsk*s and *oh*s. And when I explained that Harry would be staying at the house until he could make other arrangements, they all nodded and smiled.

Sister Mary Thomas clapped her hands.

"I can't believe we have a real live movie star staying with us," she gushed. "This is almost as exciting as the time Dolly Parton's tour bus stopped by the convent and her manager bought some cheeses for the stage crew."

Mother Superior shot the nun a stern look.

"Calm yourself, Mary Thomas. From what I understand, Mr. Westcott's acting roles are hardly suitable fare for God-fearing persons. We should give him his space, but also treat him as someone in need of our help and guidance, so that he may make better choices in both his personal and his professional lives."

Which sentiment drew a fervent "Amen" from all the nuns. I found myself rather agreeing with them.

While they plotted to save Harry from himself, I carried the cleaning supplies upstairs and left them at the foot of the ladder.

"Why don't I wait on the linens until everything is clean?" I called up to him through the drifting cloud of dust that was filtering down.

His reply was muffled; then he stuck his head over the railing, and I saw that he'd whipped off his bandana and tied it over his nose and mouth, bandit-style. Probably the first and only time the bandana would see practical use, I thought with an inner smirk.

He pulled the bandana down to his chin and said, "Hang on, I'm coming down."

Joining me, he swiped the sweat from his forehead, leaving a dusty stripe behind. Despite the grime, he looked far more cheerful than earlier. He grabbed the mop and bucket I'd filled with rags and spray cleaners.

"I found an old box fan in the little closet up there,"

he told me. "I'm going to put it in the window facing out to help clear some of the dust and heat. I'll close the door so you're not trying to cool the whole block."

"But what if the door sticks and you get trapped up there?"

"Don't worry, that can't happen. See, there's a matching twist knob on the inside of the door," he replied as he showed me where it was on the back of the door panel. "Once everything is clean, I can shut the windows and open up this door again so the cool air can start filtering in. Unless the landlady wants to spring for a window AC unit?" he finished with a hopeful look at me.

"Since this is a temporary arrangement, that would be a *no*," I told him in a pleasant tone.

He nodded, not discouraged. "There used to be screens on those windows. Someone must have taken them off last time they cleaned the outside panes, and they didn't bother putting them back on. We can check around tomorrow for them."

"Sure, *you* can. Oh, and when you take a shower after you're done, don't hog all the hot water. The sisters all like to take their showers in the evening."

On that note, I left Harry to his chores. Then, since supper was a couple of hours away, I decided to treat myself to one of the chocolate muffins left over from that morning. With the temperature outside bearable in the shade and breeze, I planned to settle on the front porch swing with the muffin and a tall glass of iced tea, along with the cat cozy mystery Gemma had loaned me the previous week.

First, however, I walked up to the front of my driveway and turned to check out Harry's parking job.

The drive was narrow enough and the garage set back far enough that his school bus wasn't noticeable from the street unless someone was really looking. I wasn't aware of any ordinances against parking a small behemoth on private property, but I darned sure didn't want the look of my home's charming exterior spoiled by his heap. I returned to the front porch. I had long since finished the muffin and was well into the third chapter of the story when I heard the slight squeal of the front gate and saw someone coming up my walk.

Brushing the last crumbs from my fingers, I set aside the book and waited until the man reached the porch. Then, as he mounted the steps, I stood and stuck out my hand in greeting.

"Why, hello," I said with a smile. "I have to say, I wasn't expecting to see you."

SIXTEEN

BECCA GLEASON'S FATHER, TRAVIS, smiled and nodded as he slowly managed the steps.

"Afternoon, Miz Fleet," he said with a wheeze as he took my hand. "Hope you don't mind me just showing up like this. Usually I'd have called first, but I don't have your number. I came by earlier too, but you weren't at home, so I thought I'd try again. I hope this isn't a bad time for you now."

"Ah, so that was you," I replied in surprise, sending a mental apology to Jack Hill for continuing to think he had designs on my house. "Mother Superior mentioned a gentleman had stopped by, but she didn't say who it was. And, actually, I was just taking a little break, so your timing is perfect. Please, sit down."

Curious as to what he could want, I gestured the old man to the white Adirondack-style rocker next to the swing. "Can I get you a glass of tea? Sweet or not sweet?"

"Sweet tea would be just fine, thank you, ma'am."

While he sat, I went inside. By the time I returned with the promised tea, a few minutes had passed. But Travis had managed to keep himself occupied in my absence. I saw in amusement that he had picked up my book and was studying the back cover, chuckling.

"Now, don't tell anyone," he said in a stage whisper

as he swapped book for glass, "but I like these books with talking cats in them. Gets your mind off of…well, things."

"I like them, too," I agreed, and resumed my seat on the swing while he took a long drink from his glass. "So, can I help you with something? Wait, there's nothing wrong with Becca—"

"Oh, no, no," he cut me short with a careless wave. "She's just fine. Actually, I'm here to conduct a little business."

At my encouraging nod, he went on, "See here, I won't beat around the bush. Since you've got this new bed-and-breakfast business going, it occurred to me that you might have some handyman work around here that you need done. I'm licensed electrical, but I can do any plumbing stuff that don't need permits, and I can do drywall and painting. Oh, and lookit here."

He reached into the pocket of his baggy pants and, somewhat to my surprise, pulled out a late-model smartphone. As Harry had done earlier, he brought up his photo app and started scrolling through pictures.

"With my arthritis and all, I can't do some of the big projects any more. I leave stuff like that to them young fellas like Jack Hill. But I started me a little sideline business that's doing good."

The pictures he showed me were of wooden fireplace surrounds, ceiling and baseboard trim pieces, and those intricate ceiling medallions. Seeing my confusion, he clarified, "You wouldn't believe how many folks buy these old houses just to rip out the original wood and make things all modern. Then, a few years down the road, they get tired of the place and sell to someone who wants to restore it back to its original state. Or maybe the house has all the original trim work, but some of it got damaged over time and needs replaced. That's where I come in."

"Got it," I said with an impressed nod. "You recreate vintage wood trim."

"Yep. I managed to buy some of the old-style machines, and I got a fellow who makes me the custom molding knives to match the trim profile."

Profile in this case meaning the decorative pattern of bevels and carvings and rounds specific to a particular style of trim. I'd learned something living in old homes over the years.

"The machines do the hard work, but some of the smaller pieces, I mostly do by hand with knives and chisels," he added in a proud tone. He indicated a final photo, which was a close-up of him using what looked suspiciously like a Bowie knife to make a delicate series of curlicues in a section of window cornice.

"Pretty impressive," I agreed, meaning it. "I'll keep that in mind if I ever need any of my wood trim repaired. Right now, I don't really have any projects—oh, wait," I stopped myself, recalling that I did. "Actually, Mr. Gleason—"

"Travis."

"Actually, Travis, I might have work for you. I'm looking at making the tower room livable again. I was thinking about adding a window air-conditioning unit, but I don't want to do that without someone to check out the wiring first. And there's a little sink up there that works, but it probably hasn't been used in twenty-five years, so I want to make sure there aren't any leaks."

"You've been up there?" he asked in surprise. "I did a little painting for Miz Lathrop once, and she told me the room wasn't fit for human habitation. You probably shouldn't be poking around there."

"Oh, the room itself is fine…it was just hot and covered in dust. I'm sure that's all she meant," I said with a laugh.

But the old man didn't look amused. He persisted, "Like I said, I wouldn't go poking around, not until I check it out for you and make sure it's safe. You wouldn't want to put a foot through the floor or something. Best case, it costs you good money to get it fixed. Worst case, someone gets hurt. Now promise me you'll take my advice."

"All right, I promise I'll keep your advice in mind," I told him. And I would… I just wouldn't follow it.

But my answer seemed to satisfy him, for he said, "Then it's settled. Just tell me when you want me to start."

"Let me find out how long my guests are staying so we don't have to disturb them with any contractor work. Do you have a card with your number, by chance?"

He reached into the pocket of the checkered shirt he was wearing—a shirt that resembled Harry's "Grampy Westcott" costume a little bit too closely—and pulled out a dog-eared business card. Black ink on white stock, it had his name and phone number, with clip art images of a hammer and plumber's wrench. The tagline LICENSED AND INSURED was printed across the bottom.

"Call me when you're ready. I can be here anytime. Well, except Sunday morning when I go to church."

He set the now-empty tea glass on the porch railing,

and I thought the gesture signaled that our little chat was at an end. But instead of getting up as I'd expected, he cleared his throat and shuffled his booted feet.

"Was there something else?" I prompted him.

He shrugged. "Just a little idle curiosity, I guess. Rumor has it you were right there on the square when Greg Bainbridge bit the big one. I heard that actor fellow—you know, Miz Lathrop's kin—got arrested for killing him. You know anything about that?"

I shrugged. "All I know is that the sheriff arrested him, but apparently whatever evidence she thought she had against him didn't pan out. So she let Harry—Mr. Westcott—go free, and the sheriff's department is still looking for Mr. Bainbridge's killer. And hopefully they'll find him—or her—pretty soon. I hear Sheriff Lamb is pretty good at what she does."

I wasn't going to mention anything about Lana, since it still was possible her role in Bainbridge's murder was all in Harry's head. But my noncommittal response apparently wasn't sufficient for his supposed idle curiosity,

"So, who do you think done it? I mean, you must have seen something that morning. Coulda been some crazy tourist, right? Or do you think maybe the killer is one of us...as in, someone we all know?"

A bit surprised at his persistence, I held up both palms in a "Hey, I'm innocent" gesture, just like Jack had done the other day.

"Sorry, Mr. Gleason... Travis. All I know is that it wasn't me, and the sheriff doesn't think it's Harry Westcott."

Travis's gaze sharpened.

He leaned closer, and I caught a whiff of Old Spice mixed with sweat. "Let me share a little something with you. This here is a fine town; lots of fine people. But we got ourselves some secrets. Some are kind of silly, but other ones not so much. Not too many folks around these parts are upset about what happened to Greg. And sometimes, it's best not to stick your nose into things you don't know nothing about."

Then, with a "Thank you kindly," he rose and made his halting way back down the walk again.

I stared after him. Why he thought I had a vested interest in the town's secrets, let alone Bainbridge's murderer, I couldn't guess.

Before I could puzzle over that, however, the front door opened and Sister Mary George stuck her veiled head around the screen door.

"I didn't want to bother you while you had company," she said. "May I join you now?"

"Of course."

She took the seat that Travis had just vacated and settled back, smiling a little. "I haven't sat in a rocking chair in years," she confided. "I forgot how comforting they are."

Then she stopped midrock, smile fading.

"I'm afraid we're going to need a lot of comfort in the next few days. I have some bad news, Nina."

"About the convent?"

She nodded. "Mother Superior spoke with the archdiocese again this afternoon. They have done additional due diligence, and Mr. Bainbridge's death won't have any impact on the convent lease. We probably could get an extension from the executor allowing us to stay until the estate is settled, but the goats are already gone and the equipment is all in storage. There's no point in trying to start up again, only to shut down for good in another year or two."

"So what does that mean?" I asked when she paused a moment.

"It means that once all the final arrangements are made on the diocese's end, His Excellency has directed them to send a van out to pick us up and take us all to Atlanta. From what Mother Superior told me, it likely will be the end of this week."

"That's too bad," I said with a sigh, though I wasn't much surprised. When you got down to it, the Church was basically a big corporation interested mostly in the bottom line. "I truly hate to see you sisters go, but I understand. So I assume your new convent is located in Atlanta, then?"

Mary George shook her head. "For the moment, they'll simply take us to the archdiocese's main campus there. As soon as they can, they'll split us up and reassign us to whatever convent can take us."

Her final words ended on a trembling note, and my surprise turned to shock. "Split you up?" I echoed. "You mean, send each of you somewhere different? But can't they find a place you can all go together?"

"There aren't that many places, Nina. So many convents have shut down because young women just aren't interested these days in a vocation. It's hard being a nun in the age of Snapchat and Instagram and Netflix. We're antiques…like rotary dial phones in a smartphone world."

She pursed her lips, and I could see she was on the verge of tears.

"It's not so much for myself that I'm worried," she went on, "it's for the other sisters. Nina, they've been together for almost fifty years. Fifty years! It's like splitting up a family. And even though they don't want to admit it, they're old women. Reverend Mother has terrible arthritis, and Mary Julian is diabetic. Mary Thomas and Mary Christopher both have thyroid and blood pressure problems, and Mary Paul has a bad heart. Of course, they never complain, and they never stop working. But I'm afraid this sort of change won't be good for any of them."

She reached into the sleeve of her habit and pulled out a snowy white handkerchief, which she used to dab at her eyes.

"I know this is God's will," she added, "and so we shouldn't question what He has determined. But the way this is all happening...well, Nina, it just tries your faith, you know what I mean?"

I nodded silently, hard-pressed not to shed a few tears myself. It had been difficult enough divorcing after twenty years, even though it had been by choice. But to be split apart from the people who had been your family for decades without any say in the matter... I couldn't even imagine how that would affect the sisters.

"I really am sorry," I told her. "I wonder if Bainbridge had any idea what his decision would do to all of you. Maybe if he'd known, he would have thought twice about not extending your lease."

Sister Mary George gave a very un-nun-like snort.

Tone verging on anger, she replied, "Oh, he knew. And he didn't care."

With that cryptic response, Sister Mary George tucked away the hankie and put out a restraining hand.

"Now, Nina, please promise me you won't say anything to the other sisters about this," she said with a guilty look back toward the door. "Only Reverend Mother and I know that we won't be all together once we leave here. She wants to wait until we know the Atlanta plans are finalized to tell them."

"I promise I won't say a word," I solemnly agreed, earning a grateful smile from the nun as she rose and went back inside.

I gathered my things and followed more slowly, leaving the empty plate and glassware in the kitchen before heading to my room. Given the current situation, I was afraid that even reading about clever crime-solving cats wouldn't be enough to take my thoughts off "things," as Travis had put it.

What I needed was action.

Because Travis's comments had started me thinking that maybe I *should* stick my nose into this particular bit of town business. I'd been right there on the scene after the stabbing happened, and I'd likely been one of the last people Bainbridge had talked to before he died. While I agreed that Gregory Bainbridge was a Class A jerk, it wasn't right that pretty much nobody cared about the fact that he'd been murdered.

But if I were to be truly honest, I also had a personal interest in seeing this whole murder thing resolved. Now that I was officially in business, my primary concern was making my bed-and-breakfast venture a success.

My advantageous location a mere two blocks from the town square wouldn't be a selling point if people were put off by the idea of sleeping the same short distance from the scene of an unsolved grisly murder.

While I had every confidence in Sheriff Lamb, Travis was right on one point. From what I'd seen, not too many people in Cymbeline were concerned about who had actually killed him. If they knew—or at least, suspected—who that person was, more than likely they wouldn't be sharing their suspicions with the authorities.

But maybe they would talk to a fellow business owner like me.

I sat at my desk and, sliding my laptop to one side, pulled out a pen and small notebook. I was becoming more doubtful about the whole Lana situation. Had she actually stabbed Bainbridge, thinking it was Harry in the suit, she'd have long since hightailed it out of town. Even if she was still fixated on Harry, I suspected she wasn't so cray-cray that she would deliberately stick around and risk arrest.

On the other hand, I knew of several Cymbeline natives who each had a strong motive to murder the developer.

Swiftly, I drew a line down the center of the blank page and started writing names. When I was finished, I had two lists: one of possible suspects, and one of people I doubted could have done the deed but might have valuable information. At the top of the latter list was my antique shop buddy, Mason, who'd had an in with Bainbridge.

Besides, I had the perfect excuse to see him. The other week I'd found an old oil painting wrapped in a dusty pillowcase and stashed in the linen closet. The partial painted signature I'd spied had sent dollar signs flashing before my eyes. Common sense told me that what I had was likely a knockoff, but a little voice kept asking, *What if it's for real?* Bringing the painting for an appraisal gave me a plausible reason to drop in and casually question Mason about the murder.

Finding out I had a heretofore unknown Picasso on my hands would simply be a bonus.

But it was well after 5 pm, and Mason would be preparing to close his shop for the day. Though I was sure he'd stick around a little longer for me, it would be hard to remain casual if we both had one eye on the clock. Better to plan to be there in the morning soon after he opened.

That decided, I closed the notebook and slipped it into one of my desk drawers for safekeeping. Then, curiosity getting the better of me, I decided to see what sort of progress Harry had made in the tower room.

SEVENTEEN

PUTTING A SET of linens and towels in an extra laundry basket, I carried them to the closed tower room door and knocked. Hearing a muffled "Come in," I did.

By the time I'd made my awkward climb with the laundry basket, I was slightly out of breath. Still, I managed a sincere "Wow!" as I took in what Harry had accomplished.

In little more than an hour, he'd mopped and dusted the room into submission. Even the window panes behind the yellowed curtains were gleaming. All the cover sheets were neatly bundled by the ladder, ready to be hauled off to the laundry room to be washed.

Now *that's* the way to impress the ladies, I thought with a reflexive grin.

"Not finished yet, but not bad," Harry said with pardonable pride. "I scraped up probably ten pounds of dust. Next up is moving the furniture around a little."

"Here, let me help you."

I lifted and carried one end of every piece of furniture—some of them, more than once—about the room until he was satisfied with the results. By the time he called it quits, I had to agree that the place looked pretty livable.

With the space divided into roughly thirds, there was a sleeping area, a sitting area, and near the sink, a dressing area: a neat little studio apartment minus the full bath. He'd found somewhere a couple of small lamps and a few tchotchkes—a red glass vase, a bright-yellow candy dish, a chalkware horse statue—which we arranged atop the dresser. The box fan was propped in one of the windows and doing a tolerable job of pulling out the remaining dust and hot air. Once the sun set, it would cool off enough to close the windows and pop open the door so he could get some actual air-conditioning.

"I'll bring up some of my clothes and things now," Harry told me. "And then I'll grab a shower and go get food for tonight. There should be someplace on the square open past six."

There was a questioning note in his tone, and I rolled my eyes. I knew what he was hinting. Unfortunately for me, I was getting soft in my old age.

Before I could think the better of it, I said in a rush, "I know I told you that you were responsible for your own meals, but why don't you join me and the sisters for supper tonight? Sister Mary Paul is a Cordon Bleu chef, and she's whipping up a feast for us."

His eyes widened in appreciation before narrowing as he shot me a suspicious look. "What's the catch?"

"No catch. It's just that you worked hard to clean the place up, and nothing's worse than being exhausted and having to cook for yourself. Why don't you get your clothes and such arranged, and then we'll see you downstairs around six thirty?"

At precisely six twenty-nine, Harry appeared in the dining room wearing fashionably distressed jeans that clung to him almost as closely as the black ones had. Over the pants, he wore a dark-brown, nubby-textured shirt that I determined was made of some outrageously expensive—but doubtless 100% organic!—natural fabric.

Since he looked in need of a task, I sent him off to find my wine opener and stemmed glasses in the butler's pantry. The mini wine refrigerator already had bottles of white and rosé chilling, and so I told him to pick one of each.

The sisters, meanwhile, were finishing setting the table with what I recognized was my wedding china. After the first couple of years of marriage, the expensive set had stayed in the cabinet except on major holidays. And after a few more years, it never came out at all.

Sister Mary Christopher caught my look of surprise.

"Oh, dear, I hope it's all right that we used the pretty china," she warbled in concern as the other sisters bustled about bringing in side dishes. "It's just that it seems a shame to save it for special occasions. Why not enjoy the nice dishes all the time?"

"You're right. I'm going to start using them more often from here on out. Besides, this is the first time we've all sat down together for a big meal. And, technically, that makes it special."

Harry, meanwhile, was busy opening and pouring wine with an efficiency that made me guess bartending had been one of his side jobs while he looked for acting work. A few minutes later, everything was on the table and we'd all taken our seats: me at the head of the table, Mother Superior at the foot. Somehow, Harry had ended up to my right. Quite the dinner party, I decided in approval.

With everyone settled, Mother Superior addressed me.

"Nina, I trust you do not mind if we say grace first?"

"Not at all," I told her, quickly putting down my wine glass, from which I'd been preparing to take a well-deserved gulp. "I think we'd be pretty remiss if we didn't give thanks for this fabulous feast Sister Mary Paul whipped up."

And feast was not an exaggeration. The nun had done the culinary equivalent of fishes and loaves. She'd transformed a tray of chicken thighs I'd had in the freezer and some staples from my refrigerator and pantry into a magnificent herbed entree served atop a creamy pasta base and accompanied by a side of steamed veggies. A small salad and the wine finished off the menu. Should I ever decide to add a supper option to my B&B menu, I'd definitely give this dish a try.

With a nod, the nun launched into a prayer that, while, relatively brief, still managed to cover all the bases of food and friendship and hope for the future. I was a bit surprised when she ended to hear a fervent "Amen" from Harry beside me. Apparently, all that time spent among the Hollywood crowd hadn't completely knocked his childhood religion out of him.

Once the food had been passed around family-style, Harry raised his wine glass. "I'd like to propose a toast. To our gracious innkeeper, Nina Fleet, who kindly opened her home to us all when we were in desperate need of lodging and has made us all feel welcome."

I shot him a disbelieving side-eye. Our earlier negotiation process could hardly be termed "gracious," and I suspected he knew I'd caved only because it was the easier choice. The nuns, however, took him at his word.

"To Nina!" they chorused with smiles as they raised

their own glasses and took a drink in my honor. Plastering a gracious smile on my face, I waited until the official toasting was done to pick up my own glass.

"Thank you," I told them, feeling an unexpected hint of melancholy sweep me. "I've been on my own for a while now, and I didn't realize how much I missed having friends and family around. And so, I've made my decision. I'm going to stay in the bed-and-breakfast business, at least for the foreseeable future."

"Hear, hear!" Sister Mary Julian bellowed, taking another gulp of wine while her sentiments were echoed by the rest.

Once that final bit of hoopla died down, Mother Superior raised her fork. "What are we waiting for? Let us, as they say, dig in."

The meal lasted a pleasantly long time, fueled by anecdotes about goats and cheese on the sisters' part, and movie star gossip on Harry's. For a group of elderly nuns living in the country, they were surprisingly up-to-date on the latest television and movie and reality stars.

"Of course, we don't watch all these shows," Sister Mary George, to my left, quietly confided as Harry recounted an amusing incident he'd witnessed involving Dwayne "The Rock" Johnson and a macaw on a movie set. "Very few of them are morally uplifting. But we hear all sorts of chatter from our customers, particularly when a tour bus stops by. That's how we keep current. It's important to know about these things, even if we don't approve of them."

All too soon, we'd all pretty well licked our plates clean. But barely had the compliments to the chef recommenced when Sister Mary Paul decreed, "We not finished. Dessert!"

She trotted off to the kitchen, returning with a glass bowl filled with layers of cubed cake, pudding, and whipped cream and topped with sliced strawberries left over from breakfast. She began spooning up the confection in small bowls, while Sister Mary Thomas brought in a pot of coffee that had just finished brewing.

"Mary Paul made the trifle out of leftover muffins," Sister Mary Julian bellowed as the dessert was passed around. "It was a good thing you had a package of pudding in your cupboard, Nina."

By unspoken consensus, we remained at the table until we'd finished our coffee and Harry had polished off a second serving of trifle. But when I finally rose to start clearing the table, Sister Mary George put out a restraining hand.

"Don't you trouble yourself, Nina. Me and the other sisters—and you, too, Harry—will take care of the cleanup. Why don't you have a little chat with Reverend Mother in the meantime."

Knowing that, as with the Borg, resistance was futile when it came to opposing a group of nuns, I graciously acquiesced. While Harry and the other nuns began gathering dishes, Mother Superior and I made our way to the parlor, where the former closed the pocket doors behind us.

"Sister Mary George told you about our situation... most particularly, about the fact all the sisters will be split up after we reach Atlanta."

She said all this without preamble once we were seated opposite each other on the two blue velvet love seats. When I gave a sober nod, she went on, "Perhaps Mary George didn't share the fact that she and I both knew about this eventuality long before we moved out of the convent. It has been a sad and frustrating few weeks, especially since we decided to spare the other sisters the bad news until we knew when the move to Atlanta would be."

She sighed, and then summoned a smile to continue. "We have so enjoyed your hospitality, Nina, despite the terrible events concerning Mr. Bainbridge. In a way, it's been like a vacation for us, but we should be leaving in a few days. When His Excellency calls, we must answer."

"I understand. And I am so sorry that things are ending this way for you and the other sisters." Then, as another thought occurred to me, I asked, "Are you allowed to go... I mean, because of the murder investigation?"

"I've talked to Sheriff Lamb, and the answer is yes. If she has further questions, the archdiocese will know where to find us."

She paused, and her smile took on a wry little twist.

"But you're not getting rid of us immediately. It turns out that Mr. Bainbridge was raised Catholic. His family contacted the diocese and asked if we sisters might conduct a Rosary service for him at the convent chapel on Friday night, since his funeral is on Saturday. So we shall be staying here at least until then."

"Wait, you said yes, after what Bainbridge did to you?" I blurted before I had time to think.

Mother Superior's gaze through her oversized glasses sharpened, but her scolding was of the mild variety. "Of course we did. Mr. Bainbridge may not have lived an exemplary life, but that is not for us to judge. If we can be of service and comfort to his family, we shall."

Knowing there wasn't much more that I could say after that, I rose. "I'd better see how things are going in the kitchen. Harry's pretty good when it comes to sweeping and dusting, but I'm not sure I trust him yet with the good china."

It turned out that I needn't have worried. The dining room was my first stop, and I saw that the table was cleared and the leftovers put away. In the kitchen, the nuns were halfway through the dishes already. Being far taller than any of the women other than Mary George, Harry had been designated the official putter-upper, replacing the dishes in the cabinets as they were washed and dried. Despite my sorrow over the nuns' situation, I couldn't help but smile a little as I peered around the kitchen door frame and watched them work with the handsome actor.

A sleek brown heron among the penguins, I thought with a regrettable snicker.

The rest of the evening was spent in the parlor, with the nuns softly chatting or reading. I'd reclaimed my cat mystery and was doing my best to enjoy the felines' fictional antics. Harry had already retired to his tower room, claiming he intended to finish unpacking his duffle bag full of clothes. Sister Mary Julian and Sister Mary Paul were busy knitting what appeared to be tiny caps using soft pale yarn.

"For early babies," the former explained when I paused after a couple of chapters and admired her skillful work. I realized after a moment that she meant the preemies who needed the caps for additional warmth in the NICU. "We make many and send to hospital."

By nine pm the nuns had called it a night and rose to go upstairs. I turned out the parlor lights and followed them down the half-lit foyer toward the main stairway. Mattie had slipped behind Sister Mary Thomas and was keeping her head low so that I, the unobservant human, wouldn't notice what she was doing.

Knowing that the nun would have but a few more chances to snuggle with the pup, I didn't bother whistling the Aussie back. Instead, I smiled and said, "Sleep tight, everyone. Don't forget, I'll have breakfast ready again at seven."

They made their individual good-nights, with Mother Superior the last one to mount the steps.

"Thank you again, Nina," she told me, pausing to grasp my larger hand in her two wrinkled ones. "We will remember this lovely evening for a long time."

"No, thank you," I told her. "I'll remember it, too."

EIGHTEEN

DESPITE THE UNSETTLING day before, I slept quite soundly that night, waking to my alarm clock at six am so I could get a shower and feed Mattie before Jasmine arrived. I felt mentally recharged and, to quote Travis Gleason once again, ready to stick my nose into things. Which meant as soon as breakfast was over, I'd follow my plan from the day before and start with a visit to my friend Mason. Depending on what I learned from him, I might chat with a few other folks on my list, too.

I gave my head a rueful shake. Maybe it was the nuns' influence rubbing off on me, but I was beginning to feel that I owed Bainbridge something. Not because he was a great person, but because I was…or rather, I strived to be. And if the nuns could put bygones behind them after how he'd upended their collective lives, the least I could do was ask a few questions about who wanted him dead.

Plus, if I could figure out who was responsible for the developer's murder, I'd be that much closer to bidding Harry Westcott goodbye.

The Aussie had slipped out of Mary Thomas's room sometime in the night and come back into the billiards suite to snooze with me, so she was waiting patiently at the porch door for me to let her out for potty. She and I both performed our morning ablutions before I pulled

on a pair of white denim jeans with rolled cuffs and a
short-sleeved linen blouse in a summery pink, white,
and gray print. I'd prepared Mattie's food and had the
coffee, juice, and cereal already staged when Jasmine
rang the doorbell promptly at seven.

Once again, she looked like something the cat had
dragged in...well, as much as a naturally beautiful teenager could look bedraggled.

"Hi, Miz Nina," she said with a yawn as she let me
take the top box again and then followed me to the dining room. "Ugh, these early mornings are killing me.

"Uh, not that I mind or anything," she hastily back-
tracked when I glanced her way. "I mean, I like delivering to people and all. It's just it's so early, and—"

"Don't worry," I cut her short with a smile. "I hate
getting up early, too. But when you've got a job to do,
well, that's life."

"I guess," she replied, not sounding much convinced
as she set the box down on the table.

But, like the last time, her expression brightened significantly when I gave her the usual tip. "Thanks, Miz
Nina. See you tomorrow."

I smiled and walked her to the door. She was almost
skipping as she rushed off the porch and down the front
walk. I figured out why when I glimpsed a tall figure
with red hair on a bicycle waiting just beyond the gate.
My smile broadened. Apparently, she'd convinced the
boy she'd been talking with the other day to haul his
butt out of bed at the crack of dawn, too, and keep her
company on her ride.

I closed the door and headed for the kitchen. Light
seeped from beneath the closed pocket doors in the par-

lor, and I heard the faint murmur of morning prayers that would continue for another thirty minutes before I headed into the kitchen to get the coffee started—and almost bumped into Harry standing at the kitchen island.

He was wearing the same distressed jeans and nubby brown shirt as he'd worn the night before. Like Jasmine, he looked like the cat had given him a good dragging... and, similar to Jasmine, he appeared as disheveled as a guy with movie-star good looks could.

"What are you doing up this early?" Then, noticing he clutched my favorite I ♥ Aussies mug in one hand, I added, "And what are you doing drinking out of my personal coffee cup?"

"Roy boss," he croaked in a sleepy voice, and toasted me with the mug.

I blinked. "Roy who?"

"Rooibos," he repeated, this time carefully making the two syllables into a single word. "It's a kind of tea, filled with antioxidants. I drink it every morning. Would you like me to make you some?"

"No thanks, my oxidants are just fine. And I expect you to wash my mug when you're finished."

Doing my best to ignore his presence, I fired up the coffee maker and started pulling down plates. But it got increasingly difficult to pretend he wasn't there while I sliced up fruit and arranged the quiches and pastries. Not that he said anything, but I could feel his gaze following me...or, rather, following the food.

Almost as bad as Mattie, I thought as I started moving everything into the dining room. Though at least he refrained from drooling all over the floor. That is, until I whipped the foil off Daniel's latest freshly baked cobbler. As the sweet peachy aroma wafted through the kitchen, I could have sworn I heard a small whimper from his direction.

It was just half past seven when I heard the pocket doors slide open again, and the nuns came filing into the dining room.

"Oh, Nina, this looks even better than yesterday's breakfast," Sister Mary Christopher warbled—though in fact it was the identical spread, other than blueberry muffins instead of strawberry. But I told myself it was the presentation, since I'd double-plated and done a little fancy folding with the napkins.

Harry had come into the dining room, too, and was watching as the nuns filled their plates at the buffet station. I saw his eyes grow large as he took in the bounty, but he limited himself to a longing sigh as he pulled a granola bar from his shirt pocket and made a production of reading its label.

I shook my head. In another minute, he'd have the bar unwrapped on a plate and be cutting it with a knife and fork into miniscule squares. Next would be savoring each bite like a grateful Tiny Tim nibbling a bread crust. And, of course, all the nuns would then insist that he join in their breakfast.

Might as well bow to the inevitable and ring down the curtain on that dramatic performance before it started.

Besides which, when I'd gone back into the kitchen a few minutes earlier, I'd found my I ♥ Aussies mug already washed and neatly replaced in the cabinet. He got points for that.

"Harry, why don't you save the granola bar for later and join us all for breakfast?" I suggested with a sweet-as-peaches smile.

I didn't need to make the offer twice. Harry promptly tucked the granola bar back into his shirt pocket and took his place at the end of the line. And somehow when we all were seated, he managed to grab the chair next to mine.

A few minutes later, we were all making swift progress through Daniel's tasty cooking. Even Mattie got a little sliver of quiche from Sister Mary Thomas, though only after she'd asked for my blessing.

As with supper the previous night, adding Harry to the mix perked up the conversation level. This time, however, he was the one asking questions, drawing amusing stories about cheese-making and tourists from the nuns. Even Mother Superior deigned to share an anecdote—hers about the time when the sisters went head-to-head with a group of brash young priests from a New York seminary in a cheese competition.

"You should have seen their faces when the old women brought home the blue ribbon," she said in re-membered triumph. "And the prize money came in handy for upgrading our kitchen."

Her grin at the memory made her look a decade younger and brought answering laughter from Harry and the other sisters. Except for one. As I glanced to-ward the end of the table, I noticed that Sister Mary George wasn't smiling.

In fact, she appeared downright perturbed as she stabbed at her quiche with her fork. Apparently not sat-isfied with mistreating the egg dish, she picked up an apple from the fruit basket along with a paring knife and began slicing the former with the latter. So vigorously did she wield the small knife that the sight set a frisson of alarm vibrating through me.

I recalled our conversation the day before, and the way the nun had gone from the verge of tears to suppressed anger as we talked about what Bainbridge had done.

Oh, he knew. And he didn't care.

From what Reverend Mother had said, Sister Mary George had known well before the nuns left the convent that their little religious family was going to be broken up as a result of Bainbridge's foreclosure action. Her outrage at that had been genuine. Was it possible she could have run into Bainbridge at the ice cream parlor the day of the protest and impulsively decided to exact a little back-alley revenge?

I shook my head, trying to settle my thoughts. When I'd made my statement to Sheriff Lamb, I had been disbelieving when she had implied Sister Mary George might be a suspect. But much as I hated the thought, I'd watched enough cop shows on television to know that a nice circumstantial case could be built against her.

Motive, opportunity. And, most importantly, the fact that she'd been convicted of doing bad things with a knife once before.

But even as I tried to counter the thought, the clanking of silverware against crystal glassware refocused my attention. Mother Superior set down her butter knife and waited for the chatter to quiet. Then, gaze stern, she said, "Sisters, I've received important news from the archdiocese."

I stared back in surprise. Surely she wasn't going to announce the dissolution now!

But to my relief, she instead said, "We have been asked by the late Mr. Bainbridge's family to conduct a Rosary service for him at the convent chapel on Friday evening. I have told them we will be happy to do so. But this also means we'll need to make a trip back to the convent tomorrow after breakfast to ready the chapel and public rooms. Mayor Green has the keys and will drive us there."

"Back to the convent, Reverend Mother?" Sister Mary Thomas echoed with a wide smile, while the other nuns murmured excitedly among themselves. "Why, that would be wonderful. Oh, not that we're not enjoying our stay here, Nina," she assured me, "but it would be lovely to see our old home once again. We left in such a hurry..."

She trailed off, smile abruptly fading as her lips began to tremble. Sister Mary Julian gave her a comforting pat on the hand, while Mother Superior mildly said, "Enough of that, Mary Thomas. We won't have time for moping while we're there. We'll have a lot of work to do. Apparently, a large crowd is expected."

"Probably wanting to make sure Bainbridge is really dead," Harry muttered, presumably for my ears only.

But when it was apparent from the disapproving gazes suddenly sent his way that he'd spoken loudly enough for the whole table to hear, he added, "What? All I said was, I think that's a really fine way to pay respect to the dead."

"Then we'll expect you to join us for the service, Mr. Westcott."

The nun's declaration drew a faintly alarmed look from Harry, who obviously had had no intention of going and likely realized he couldn't say no now.

Mother Superior, meanwhile, was continuing, "Apparently, Mr. Bainbridge had a large extended family and a good number of business acquaintances, many of whom have said they will attend. Oh, and there is a catered wine-and-cheese reception planned in the convent dining hall immediately following the service."

Which explained the expected turnout, I thought, learning from Harry's mistake and saying that silently to myself.

Breakfast ended shortly afterward. With help from the sisters, the dishes and leftovers were cleared away. I saw Sister Mary Paul sneak a large square of cobbler onto a plate and hand it off to Harry, and I pretended not to notice as he beat a hasty retreat with his prize.

It was closing in on nine am by the time everything was back in place. The nuns, meanwhile, had moved to the back gardens for what Sister Mary George had told me was a meditative walk along the brick paths.

"Rather like a labyrinth walk," she'd explained with a smile. "That nice circular walkway around your lovely fountain will serve a similar purpose."

I had nodded in interest, trying not to remember that half an hour earlier I was thinking of her as a possible murder suspect.

"I've got a couple of errands to run on the square," I'd told her instead, "so please spend as much time out there as you like. And, remember, there is lemonade and iced tea in the refrigerator."

I'd considered taking Mattie with me—Mason didn't

mind well-behaved dogs in the store—but a glance now out the back window showed her placidly watching from the pavilion as the nuns walked in a measured gait around the fountain. Leaving the pup in charge of the guests, I went back to my room to grab my keys and purse.

I slung the latter over my shoulder; then, after a moment's hesitation, I went to my desk and retrieved the little spiral journal where yesterday I'd jotted the names of my suspects. Feeling somewhat foolish, I stuffed the notebook inside the handbag.

Just in case I need to scribble a few names or numbers after talking with Mason, I assured myself. Then, going to the linen closet to grab the painting that was my excuse for this little excursion, I headed out the door.

As I reached the square a short while later, I saw that the nearby parking lot and spaces around the shops weren't nearly as full as they had been in the past few days. No network satellite trucks were in evidence, either, though I spied a logo van from Reporter Dave's news station parked at the corner where the boiled-peanut guy had his cart. The square activity was almost back to its usual weekday summer self—a few locals, and about twice that many obvious tourists.

Apparently, with no new leads or suspects in the offing, the media had begun to lose interest in the Penguin Suit Murder.

"Whew," a woman's voice behind me spoke up. "I think we're getting back to normal again here."

I glanced behind me and jumped a little when I saw that the speaker was Becca Gleason. Hers happened to be one of the names on my list…in the first, longer column. I'd put her there because I recalled her reaction the day of the protest while the nuns and I were picking up the protest signs. It had been a few years since her father and his neighbors had been cheated out of their property by Bainbridge, but she was still furious on Travis's behalf. Definitely a motive…and with her printing shop nearby, she'd certainly had the opportunity to do it.

Possibly more damning was Travis's reaction yesterday. Maybe he had his own suspicions. Maybe he feared his daughter could be considered a suspect, and he'd been trying to protect Becca by warning me away.

But right now, the woman was looking at me expectantly. Realizing I had dropped the conversational ball, I pulled myself back to the present.

"Yeah, normal," I agreed with the best smile I could muster. "I was just thinking to myself that all the media folks seem to have left town. I guess since the sheriff doesn't have a firm suspect in the stabbing that they're getting bored and moving on to something more juicy somewhere else."

"Well, I hope so. I know it's only been a couple of days, but it feels like this has been hanging over us forever."

She paused and gave me—or rather, the bundle I was carrying—a curious look. "It's probably none of my business, but what are you hauling around in a pillowcase this early in the morning? It's the wrong shape for laundry."

I chuckled and rolled down the cloth to reveal a bit of the painting.

"Check it out. I found this masterpiece in a closet…

something left over from when Mrs. Lathrop owned the place. I wanted to have Mason Denman take a look in case it's actually worth something."

"Seriously?" Becca wrinkled her nose and echoed my laugh. "You're an optimist, Nina. I'll admit I'm not much on abstract art, but that's pretty awful. And I think I see three hands on that woman."

"No, it's only two. The third one belongs to an unseen person standing behind her," I cheerily assured her, and wrapped the painting back up again.

Then, deciding I might as well take advantage of having one of my "listees" standing in front of me, I added in a casual tone, "So, uh, is there any gossip going around town about who might have stabbed Greg Bainbridge? I mean, I keep hearing that lots of people held a grudge against him, but is there anyone who'd actually stoop to murder? You know, since the sheriff already released her only suspect so far."

Becca's smile vanished, her manner turning suddenly frosty. "Why do you ask? I don't know anything about any gossip. Why should I? Because I don't."

I took a reflexive step back. Her tone had been low but oddly vehement for someone who claimed not to be in the gossip loop. Or maybe she simply was inordinately sensitive about being thought to be a busybody. Either way, my questioning technique obviously left something to be desired, since she'd shut down after only a single casual query.

I gave myself a mental kick in the pants. *Good going, Nina.* If Becca knew something, chances were she wasn't going to share with me now.

"Oh, I'm sorry," I hurried to assure her. "I wasn't

implying you were a gossip. I just thought...you know, as fellow business owners...that we should know what people are saying. Because something like this murder can hurt our bottom line. I'm not just talking the tourists, but the locals. Folks can get pretty testy with all the hoopla, and everybody being suspicious of everyone else. And like they say, forewarned is forearmed."

I was afraid for a moment that I'd overdone the apology. To my relief, however, her expression thawed slightly.

"Yeah, I see what you're saying. Between the press hanging around and those news conferences on the square, my regulars have been keeping their distance. And I'm guessing no one wants to book a B&B in a town where there's an unsolved murder, either." She paused and gave a thoughtful nod. "You're right, it probably wouldn't hurt to head off any rumors at the pass."

"Agreed. So I guess let's both keep our ears open."

I hefted my pillowcase and added, "I'd best go see if Mason is going to tell me that I'm sitting on a cool couple of million here."

Becca's smile returned. "Good luck. If you win the oil painting lottery, don't forget your friends here in Cymbeline."

We parted on that friendly note, and I took the catty-corner route across the square toward Weary Bones. Since my first attempt at cross-examination hadn't gone so well, I'd need to up my game when I talked with Mason. As in, ease into mentioning subjects like *stabbing* and *murder* rather than rushing right in.

Fortunately for my cover story, I was the only customer in the shop when I walked in, an electronic bell discreetly announcing my arrival. I made my way down the main aisle, waiting for his pompadoured self to pop out from behind the register. When he didn't, I called out, "Mason, it's Nina Fleet. Are you here?"

Just as I'd begun to worry, picturing the antique shop owner sprawled in the alley like Bainbridge, I heard some shuffling from the back of the store. A moment later, Mason came walking up.

"Sorry, Nina. I was inventorying some ephemera and I didn't want to lose count."

He wore navy dress slacks and a white dress shirt topped by the usual vest, this time made of pale-blue summer wool, which held his signature hankie. He halted before me and plucked out that cloth square, patting his forehead with it while I observed him in concern.

The man's dyed-black pompadour had lost much of its usual pouf, and the dark circles under his eyes were even more noticeable because of the pallor of his face. As for his signature handkerchief, rather than the usual vintage square, this day's example was run-of-the-mill white cotton without even a monogram to distinguish it.

"Mason, are you all right? Are you coming down with something?"

He tucked away the hankie again and waved me off with a faint smile. "I'm fine, Nina, just not sleeping well. This whole situation with Greg—well, you know."

His voice broke a little on those last words before he rallied and went on in a stronger tone, "So, what brings you by this morning? Should I deduce there's some-thing interesting in that pillowcase you're clutching?"

In my concern for him, I'd almost forgotten the painting. Now, with a surprised little laugh, I admitted, "Interesting is probably putting a good face on it. I found this painting stuck in a closet and hoped you might take a look. It probably should go in a garage sale, but I thought just in case I should show it to you first."

More carefully than I probably needed to, I pulled the painting from its makeshift wrapping and handed it to him.

Including the carved wooden frame, the oil was about ten by twelve inches. Even my untrained eyes identified the style as cubism, given that the painted figure's head, limbs, and torso were broken into distinct blocks of line and color and then rearranged out of order. The color palette was mostly shades of browns mixed with black, with a bit of dark rusty red and a few splotches of white to relieve the gloom.

Ugly as sin had been my first thought when I'd found it. And then I had glimpsed a bit of painted signature at the bottom of the small canvas that the frame hadn't quite covered.

The letters *PIC*.

Mason, meanwhile, was *hmm*ing and *ah*ing as he studied the painting from various angles. Then he asked, "Do you mind if I remove the painting from the frame?"

"Be my guest."

He gestured me to follow him, and we walked over to the counter where the cash register was situated. Mason set the painting facedown on a section of countertop that had been padded for such purposes and pulled on the pair of white cotton gloves lying there. While I watched in anticipation, he used a small screwdriver and pliers to remove the various screws and staples that held canvas to frame. That accomplished, he turned the painting upright again.

Flipping on the extendable lighted magnifying lamp clamped to the counter's edge, he began his examination. Just as I'd started mentally composing the Sotheby's auction catalog listing, Mason smiled and looked back up at me, shaking his pompadoured head.

"I'm afraid what we have here is a nice effort by a hobbyist painter attempting to emulate the cubist style."

"What about the signature?" I asked, holding on to one last bit of hope.

His smile broadened—obviously, he knew what I'd been thinking—and he pointed to the fully revealed signature. "Sorry, Nina. It's Picardie, not Picasso,"

I leaned in and confirmed his assertion, my sigh one of equal parts amusement and disappointment. But Mason offered a consolation prize.

"It's not a total loss," he replied. "The painting might be crap, but you've got yourself a lovely nineteenth-century Italian frame wrapped around it. The wood carving is exquisite, and the gilding is real. I'd give you a hundred dollars right now, just for the frame, but you could put it up on eBay and probably get two or three times that, if you're lucky."

"Oh, I think I'll hang onto it. The painting's kind of growing on me," I told him, smothering a grin. I would do a little checking at Cymbeline's historical society. If this Picardie turned out to be a long-lost relative of Mrs. Lathrop, I'd give the painting to Harry as a good-bye present when his weeklong stay ended.

Mason, meanwhile, nodded and stripped off the gloves. "Hey, whatever floats your boat. If you like it, it's good art. Let me run to the storeroom for some new fasteners, and I'll put that back together for you in a jiffy."

Leaving me at the counter, he headed toward the rear of the shop. I was studying a small glass case filled with mourning jewelry on the other side of the register when I heard a muffled exclamation.

I straightened. "Mason, what's wrong?"

Then, when he didn't immediately reply, I hurried in the same direction he'd gone. I spied him bent over a heavy wooden box sitting on a display shelf. "Is everything all right?"

He straightened, his expression one of distress. The box in question was a vintage flatware box, stained a deep brown with a strip of lighter inlaid wood along its edges. It was open, and I could see its purple velvet interior. The box held a set of antique silver serving utensils: oversized forks, various spoons, and a couple of knives. Nice, but hardly unique.

I was still puzzled by why he was making a big deal over it when Mason pointed to the one slot in the velvet that was empty.

"I don't believe it. Look. Some miscreant stole my carving knife right out from under my nose!"

NINETEEN

A STOLEN KNIFE? My thoughts instinctively flashed to the memory of an oversized carving knife sticking out of Gregory Bainbridge's chest. Could that murder weapon have come from the shelves of Weary Bones?

I tore my gaze from the empty slot to stare back at Mason. The same possibility obviously occurred to him, because his eyes widened and the black caterpillar brows shot skyward.

"I'd better call the sheriff."

"You'd better call the sheriff," I echoed almost simultaneously. Then, getting a grip, I added, "Wait, before we go off half-cocked, let's talk this through. The murder happened Monday, and you're just now noticing the knife is missing?"

"Well, I've been distracted," he shot back, tone defensive. "It could have been gone as early as Monday. With all the hoopla, I've not been keeping up with things in the shop like I should have been."

I gave him a sympathetic nod. "I can certainly understand that, especially since the murder happened in the alley behind you. But are you sure someone actually took the knife? Maybe they picked it up for a closer look and walked around a minute, then set it down somewhere else. People do that at the grocery store all the time."

Mason took a steadying breath and nodded back. "You're right, Nina. It's probably on a shelf somewhere."

We spent a few minutes searching up and down the aisles. For a combination antiques-and-collectibles shop, Mason's place was surprisingly well organized and un-cluttered, unlike the standard frumpy chaos of a thrift store. Anything out of place, particularly a knife, would be obvious.

But our scouring of the shelfs produced no AWOL knife. Either it was well hidden…or it had been taken. The question was, when? And the next question was, why?

"This isn't good, Nina," the man said, wringing his handkerchief between his hands. "If nothing else, it's a liability. But if it's been gone since before noon on Monday…well, that could be really bad. I mean, what if it turned out to be *the* knife?"

He trailed off, while I pictured some as-yet-unknown person slipping into the store and absconding with a vintage but quite serviceable blade. If it was *the* knife, as Mason had put it, how better to make sure the murder weapon couldn't be traced back to the killer? Something stolen out of here wouldn't have any handy purchase history from Amazon or a big-box store attached to it.

I took a steadying breath of my own.

"I think we were on the right track a minute ago," I told him. "You should notify the sheriff's department. It would take probably two seconds for them to deter-mine if this set matches the knife the killer used. And then you'd know for sure whether the person with sticky fingers is a premeditated killer or just a run-of-the-mill shoplifter."

Mason's brows danced about in an even more alarming manner. "Premeditated?" he repeated, voice squeaking on that word. "I'm calling right now."

He rushed past me back in the direction of the counter. By the time I rejoined him, he was already speaking to the sheriff's office dispatch.

"Yes, I just discovered it was missing. Right, it was part of a set. Yes, we already looked, and it's not anywhere else. Yes, I'll be waiting right here."

He hung up and shot me a nervous look. "They're sending a deputy over. The dispatcher agreed it was a long shot but said they'd want to follow up anyhow."

He paused, head drooping. "If it really was my knife that killed Greg, I—I don't think I could forgive myself."

I frowned a little at this last. Was this just Mason being his usual overly dramatic self, or was he deliberately laying it on thick? Even though his name was on the shorter column of my list, I hadn't totally eliminated him as a suspect. Assuming the murder weapon did turn out to be his, how better to deflect suspicion than to have a witness present when he presumably discovered the missing knife?

Aloud, I merely said, "Mason, no one would blame you. Now, do you want me to stay with you until the deputy shows up?"

Not that I had any intention of leaving until I knew whether or not the murder weapon had come from the flatware set. I just didn't want to be obvious about it. To my relief, he nodded.

"I'd be most grateful. Now, let's put that horrible

painting of yours back into its lovely frame while we wait."

Barely had he completed the minor restoration when the electronic door buzzer sounded. Deputy Mullins, aka Horatio Caine's younger brother, stepped in.

He whipped off his omnipresent *CSI: Miami*–style sunglasses and hung them off his shirt pocket while we went through the formalities. At the dispatcher's earlier direction, Mason had left the box untouched on its shelf. The intros made, the shop owner walked the deputy to the back aisle and showed him the flatware box.

I, of course, trailed after them.

While Mason explained why he'd just noticed the loss, Mullins took photos of the box in situ, and then several close-ups of the various utensils. Finishing a final shot, the deputy stuck the camera back into his pocket and returned his attention to us.

"I think you're in the clear here, sir. The murder weapon is a standard kitchen-style instrument. I'm assuming your missing knife matches the rest of these utensils, which are lots more ornate. So I'd say unofficially that your stolen property wasn't involved in Mr. Bainbridge's murder."

"That's good news," Mason replied, dabbing his forehead with the hankie again. "Do you want to take the box with you anyhow?"

"Not necessary, sir…although I would ask that you remove it from the shelf and hold it somewhere safe for a couple of days, just in case. But I'm sure Sheriff Lamb will agree with my conclusion once she reviews these pictures and compares them with the actual knife."

With those words, Mullins put back on his shades.

We headed back to the counter, where I waited while Mason escorted him the rest of the way. Only when the door had closed after the deputy did I allow myself a small sigh.

I could likely take Mason off my list now. His distressed reaction to the whole knife thing had seemed legitimate. And if he ever did murder someone, I suspected his next act would be to confess to the first person he saw.

I was putting my restored painting back into the pillowcase when a subdued Mason rejoined me.

"I may have to go home and lie down a while after this," he said with a groan, still dabbing with the hankie. "Though I guess I should move that box back into the storeroom first. Darn it all, I'll have to piece out the utensils to sell them, since I don't have a full set anymore."

"What about video?" I suggested, and glanced toward the ceiling. "With all this expensive merchandise, don't you have cameras all around the shop? Maybe you could review the tapes and see if you caught the shoplifter."

He gave the handkerchief a careless wave.

"I used to have a system set up through my computer, but something got messed up with the software and it was too hard to fix. Besides, I don't want my customers thinking I'm spying on them."

"Well, you don't want your customers pilfering antiques from your shelves, either," I pointed out, though I understood where he was coming from. Small-town shopping equaled small-town friendliness, and security cameras kind of spoiled the effect.

Tempering that last small criticism with a smile, I

said, "Thanks again for taking a look at my painting. Do I owe you anything for the appraisal?"

"Always on the house," he replied, sounding more positive as he returned his hankie to his pocket with a flourish. "You find anything else you think qualifies for the *Antiques Roadshow*, bring it on by."

A few moments later I was back outside. Painting tucked under my arm, I surveyed the square before me, squinting against the sun. At a little past ten thirty am, the temperature was well on its way toward the usual summer highs; still, activity had picked up while I was in Mason's shop. At least half of the angle-in parking spaces were full now, while a few tourists were making their rounds. The boiled-peanut guy was on his usual corner, getting his cart set up for the day.

A logoed television station truck that I didn't recognize was slowly making its way down the street. *So maybe the Penguin Suit Murder is still news, after all.* I could see that someone in the passenger seat had stuck a handheld video camera out the open window and was panning the square. The vehicle slowed a little as it drew closer to me…looking for possible interview subjects?

Just in case that was their plan, I made a strategic retreat into the next door over, which of course happened to be the Taste-Tee-Freeze. Which happened to belong to another of the people on my list, namely, Jack Hill.

I'd added Jack's name partly because of his outright enmity toward Bainbridge and partly because of the handyman thing. If I was going to hire him to build an arbor or do any other improvements, I needed to know he didn't have some hidden agenda. Earlier, I hadn't been quite sure how to go about that. But now it occurred to me that I had the ideal opportunity to put him to the test, courtesy of the nuns. I just needed to bait the trap.

Inside the Taste-Tee-Freeze it was darker and much cooler than the square. I waited for my eyes to adjust, and then saw Jack behind the counter. Best I could tell, it was just the two of us. No other customers yet, though given the relatively early hour, that was hardly surprising. Where Jill was, I wasn't certain. Maybe in the storeroom?

No matter. If I was going to do this, I needed to do it while she wasn't around.

Jack, meanwhile, had looked up from whatever he was doing. "Hi there, Nina. Out shopping?"

Smiling, I walked up to the counter. "I had to stop by and visit with Mason for a few minutes so he could appraise something for me. Then one of those TV news trucks came by, and I kind of ducked in here to hide."

Which probably wasn't the best opening line. But Jack didn't seem to take offense. Instead, he shook his head. "Yeah, it's like a plague. I hope the sheriff makes an arrest pretty quick. This whole murder thing hanging over the square isn't doing much for business."

It hadn't done much for Greg, either, I was tempted to point out. Instead, curious to get Jack's reaction, I replied, "That was pretty unexpected, the sheriff arresting Harry Westcott and then cutting him loose. I wonder why she decided he was a suspect."

He gave me a sharp look. "I'm sure she had her reasons. He's an actor, and they're all a bit off, know what I mean? Jill wanted me to fire the guy the day he started, but he worked cheap and brought in the customers, so I kept him on."

I frowned. This wasn't quite the story Harry had told me. In his version, Jack was the one who'd wanted him gone.

Striving for a casual tone, I shrugged and replied, "Well, there were enough people around when it happened, so there's a good chance someone saw something. The sheriff's office probably has all sorts of tips being called in that we don't know anything about."

"Maybe. So, can I get you anything while you're hiding out?"

"Sure."

I could take a hint—besides which, he'd be more likely to agree to my request if I were a paying customer. And while I didn't usually have ice cream for my midmorning snack, I was willing to make the sacrifice. I did, however, try for something somewhat healthy.

"A scoop of French vanilla with chopped pecans and cherries topped with praline sauce in a waffle bowl, please."

Okay, maybe not *that* healthy.

"You got it."

I watched with awe as he scooped out the vanilla, added my toppings, and then wielded knife and spatula like a Japanese steakhouse chef to fulfill my order in under thirty seconds. My ice cream customized, he scraped the chilly confection into its edible container, drizzled the praline syrup, and stuck in one of those flat wooden spoons.

Plopping everything onto a layer of napkins, he slid

my order across the glass countertop toward me and asked, "Anything else, Nina?"

"Actually, yes."

Feeling a bit nervous now, I glanced over to see if Jill had slipped into the shop during all the rolling and chopping. Even though she hadn't, I leaned in a bit closer.

"You mentioned the other day about quoting me on some repairs," I reminded him. "I'd really like to get that done, and I've got a perfect window of time when there won't be any guests. The nuns who are staying with me have to go back to their old convent for a few hours tomorrow, so I was hoping you'd drop by in between your busy times. Maybe around two?"

Jack glanced around, as if also looking for Jill. Then he nodded. "Yeah, I think I can break free around then. It shouldn't take too long to check out things, especially since I already know what to look for. And then I can email you a quote."

"That would be great."

I hesitated, like a thought had just occurred to me... which it had, since I'd forgotten I needed an excuse not to be there. I added, "I almost forgot; I have to take my Australian shepherd to the groomer tomorrow. How about I leave a spare key behind the front-door screen? That way, if I'm not back by the time you get there, you can go on in without me."

He nodded again. "Sure. I know the place, so I don't need you to show me around. And, no offense, but I can get things done a lot faster without anyone looking over my shoulder."

Which was exactly what I had in mind.

"Perfect," I told him. "Here's my number"—I paused and scribbled my cell number on a napkin—"in case there's any change of plan. Just lock up when you leave and put the key back in the same spot. And then you can let me know what you think needs fixing."

I handed him my money and took my change; then, juggling both the painting and my bowl of ice cream, I headed out as a cluster of noisy preteens were making their way in.

It wasn't easy to eat while simultaneously hauling a bad Picasso knockoff, but I managed to do it. By the time I reached the house, I was down to the final bite of waffle bowl and definitely feeling the calorie rush. I put the painting back in the closet and then found the sisters in the parlor, knitting and reading.

"I'm back," I announced unnecessarily, bending to give Mattie a pat when she trotted over to greet me. She accepted the tribute, but a scratch behind the ears wasn't what she was looking for. Instead, blue and brown gaze fixed expectantly on me, she sat and raised a paw.

I smiled. "And here I thought my pupper loved me for me."

I unwrapped the bite of waffle bowl I'd been saving and tossed it her direction. She caught it in midair with a neat snap of her jaws and swallowed the piece whole.

Sister Mary Christopher had been reading when I walked in. Now she dropped the slim volume into her lap and gave Mattie an enthusiastic little clap.

"Such a clever dog. Do you know, Nina, that I've taught her how to pray? Watch."

So saying, she put aside her book and stood.

"Mattie, up. Now, be a good girl and say your

prayers," she told the dog, and demonstrated by bringing her hands, palms together, to her lips.

The Aussie promptly stretched forward with her front paws, rump tilting up, and then dropped her fuzzy muzzle onto her extended legs.

I gave a delighted laugh as Mattie sat back up again, looking pleased with her doggy self.

"How clever...both of you," I told the nun. "I'll be sure to add that to her repertoire."

Then, changing topics, I asked, "Will Sister Mary Paul be making lunch for you again? If so, I'll set up the dining room...or will you be going out?"

"Don't worry, Nina," Mother Superior spoke up, setting aside her knitting. "The nice young man from the Piggly Wiggly stopped by a few minutes ago. We called up and ordered...what do they call those, Mary George?"

"Hoagies," the younger nun said with a smile. "As you can see, Nina, we're broadening our food horizons while we're here. Mr. Westcott told us that the supermarket deli makes an excellent sandwich, so we decided to give them a try."

"That's right," Sister Mary Julian bellowed. "And tonight, we're going to order in Chinese from a place called the Dancing Tiger!"

"Sounds great," I assured her. "Since you have everything under control, I'll stay out of your hair."

Leaving Mattie to hang with her nun friends, I headed upstairs. Time to let Harry earn his ridiculously cheap keep around here.

The hidden door was propped open, the better to get a little AC up into the tower until we found another solution. I called up the ladder/stairway, "Harry, are you there? I need to talk to you."

I heard a muffled response but couldn't make out the words. "Harry," I called again, "I'm coming up there. If you're not decent, you've got about ten seconds to rectify the situation."

I heard another semi-inaudible response, this time making out the words *talk to you*. Taking that as permission, I climbed up to the tower room landing.

Harry was on his hands and knees, halfway in— or maybe halfway out of?—the room's small closet, no doubt the reason his voice had been muffled. He scooched out the rest of the way and walked over to join me, swiping at the dust and cobwebs that clung to him.

"I thought you already cleaned everything," I told him, surprised at his condition. Forging on, I asked, "You wanted to talk about something?"

He hesitated, glancing about him as if he was afraid someone had crept up the ladder after me. My curiosity kicked up a notch. But all he did was shrug.

"You first. What did you want to ask me?"

"I need you to do something tomorrow...something that will require all your acting skills."

He cocked his head, reminding me of Mattie in her quizzical mode. Tone cautious, he said, "Go on."

"While I was out on the square earlier, I had a chat with Jack Hill. I'm still not convinced he doesn't know something about Bainbridge's murder. Plus there's the whole thing about this supposed repair quote he did for your aunt, but nothing he quoted needs fixing. I want to get to the bottom of this, for no other reason than I need to hire a handyman, and Mason recommended him."

"So what's that got to do with me?"

"I'm getting to that. I asked him to drop by tomorrow around two and do a walk-through of the place so he can put together a formal bid for me. The sisters will be gone at the convent, and I told Jack I was going to take Mattie to the groomer. I told him I'd leave a key stuck behind the screen door so he can let himself in."

I gave Harry a smug smile.

"I figure if he knows he's alone, he'll take the opportunity to search out whatever it is that he thinks is hidden here...and chances are he's going to take a look up in the tower room. So I need you to be my spy and watch what he does while I'm gone."

"Your spy?" Harry lifted a cobwebbed brow. "If you've forgotten, I'm a paying guest, which exempts me from playing cloak and dagger. You're going to have to find someone else."

I frowned, though realistically I'd expected a little pushback. Time to bring out the big guns and appeal to his not-so-insubstantial ego.

"I know, and I realize this is a huge favor, but it's important. I need to know if Jack is on the up-and-up before I trust him doing any work around here. And if there really is some sort of hidden treasure, I don't want him absconding with it."

I paused and gave him my best impression of Mattie pleading for an extra treat. "The truth is, I don't have anyone else to turn to."

Which technically was true. The sisters would be busy at the convent, and anyone else I could think of who I considered trustworthy would be in the middle of their workday.

He gave me a considering look. "Assuming I agree to this, what exactly do you want me to do?"

"Like I said, spy on him. I'll leave the details to you, but there are enough closets and niches in the house that would make good hiding places. Mostly, I want to see if he knows how to access the tower room, and if he goes up there for a look. I didn't mention anything to him about the hidden door, so unless he has specific knowledge about it, he won't be looking for it."

Then, when he still looked doubtful, I went in for the kill. "Seriously, you're the only one I know who has the skill set to do this."

He shrugged. "That's probably correct."

"So you'll do it?"

"On one condition."

Mental alarm bells went off. *Great. He's going to tell me he wants his house back.*

But surprisingly, what he said was, "I get to eat breakfast every morning with the rest of you, no questions asked."

"Done." Breakfast was a small price to pay. "We'll work out the final details tomorrow before Jack gets here." Then, recalling what he'd said when I'd first climbed up, I asked, "So what did you need to talk to me about?"

"It's more showing than telling, actually. And I can pretty well guarantee that you're not going to like it."

I could think of a dozen things right off the bat that the actor could tell or show me that I wouldn't like. Starting with *I used your mug again and broke it* and ending with *I'm staying permanently and you're going to have to evict me to get me out of the house.* At least the latter issue was supposedly off the table for the week, given the deal we'd struck. And since I didn't see any broken crockery lying around, my mug was probably safe. So I was prepared for anything else.

Or so I thought.

Turns out I wasn't prepared after all. He pointed at the open closet behind him and said, "I think I found a dead body here in the tower room."

TWENTY

"Wait! Dead body! What?"

I said a few more words, too, but those weren't suitable for print. Harry waited for me to wind down a bit and then asked, "Do you want to see it or not?"

"See a body? Are you kidding? No! Wait, yes!"

Though by now, rational thought was returning. From what I could see of the closet, it was far too small to hold a full-sized human corpse. Moreover, if there had been a body putrefying up there in the heat, I darned sure would have smelled it long ago. Plus, given the undisturbed layer of dust we'd found when we had opened up the place, Harry and I had been the first people to be in the tower room for a long while. And unless Harry's Great-Aunt Lathrop was built like a linebacker who could haul a dead guy up that ladder, no way had she done it.

I followed him over to the closet for a closer look. He'd already filled the single wood clothes rod with his shirts and jeans, and I saw that the space was wider behind the walls than I'd originally thought. But, no body…and nobody. I gave him a confused look.

"I was finishing hanging up all my clothes," he explained, "when I felt one of the planks here shift when I stepped on it. I realized someone had cut the boards to make a hiding spot. So, of course, I had to see if anything was inside. And that's when I found it. Take a look," he finished, and dropped to his knees.

I knelt as well, watching as he stuck a finger into what at first appeared to be a knothole in the wood grain but instead was actually a hole the diameter of a man's thumb. With a tug, he pulled up a one-by-two-foot section of the plank floor and set it aside, revealing an opening beneath. While he picked up a small flash-light that had been left near the closet door, I cautiously leaned forward for a look at the hole.

"I don't see any...*aahhhhh!*"

I broke off with a scream as Harry shined the flash-light beam inside the opening and I spied what was un-deniably bone. Human bone. I didn't need to recall my college anatomy class to know that the bone in ques-tion was a skull.

I dropped back so I was sitting on my heels now, feeling my heart pounding double-time in my chest. When I caught my breath again, I asked, "Is—is the rest of him in there?"

"Only the skull, as far as I could tell. So I guess tech-nically we're not talking about a whole dead body... just part of one."

"That's bad enough. I can't believe I've been living here for weeks with some dead guy's skull in my tower room, and I didn't even know about it."

Harry gave me the side-eye. "Well, how do you think I feel? I slept with it here last night."

"Yeah, good point." Then, giving him a suspicious look, I went on, "Wait. How long has it been here? It's not left over from when you were a kid here on sum-mer break, is it?"

He shook his head. "I'm pretty sure that fifteen-year-old me would have found a secret hiding place like that on day one. The hole had to have been cut in the last twenty or so years, after my last summer here and before Aunt Lathrop died."

We remained there silently staring at the hole in the closet for another minute. Then a thought occurred to me, and I reached for the flashlight. Steeling myself, I clicked on the beam again and leaned forward for another look.

"Hmm," I said after a little more study. Glancing back at Harry, I elaborated. "Something's kind of odd here. I mean, besides the fact there's a human skull sitting in the closet. I think we need a better look. Can you get me an old T-shirt or a hand towel or something?"

While he went to get the T-shirt/hand towel/something, I pulled out my phone from my pocket and took a few pictures. *In situ evidence*, I told myself, like when Deputy Mullins took those pictures of Mason's flatware box. Though I suspected the sheriff would be a bit more interested in my found skull than Mason's missing knife. Harry returned with a threadbare hand towel, which he gave to me. I dropped it over the skull; then, gritting my teeth, I carefully lifted the remains out of the hole and set them on the floor.

"Uh, you're not going to leave that thing there, are you?"

I rose and dusted my hands on the seat of my jeans. "No. I want to bring it out into the light."

I bent and picked it up again, trying to convince myself that as long as there was a piece of terry cloth between me and the skull, I wasn't technically touching it. I carried it over to the end table between the two chairs that were arranged next to one of the windows. I set the skull down there and gave a shudder that wasn't entirely feigned.

Then, with a stern eye on Harry, I said, "I did the hard part. Come over here now, and take the towel off."

Looking as uncomfortable as I felt, Harry came over as directed and gingerly removed the towel. Once again, we studied the skull in silence for a moment, before I said. "That's what I'm talking about. See how dark it is, like it's been stained with tea or something? And the lower jaw is missing, too. Maybe it's fake, and someone put it there for a joke."

Harry shook his head. "I've played in *Hamlet* enough times to know what a fake skull looks like. I'm pretty sure this one is real…and I have a feeling it's actually pretty old. Maybe from a Native American burial mound or something."

Which hadn't occurred to me until Harry made the suggestion.

"Oh, great. So you're saying this house is built on sacred land, and now that we've found the hidden skull, we're going to be haunted by a bunch of ticked-off spirits and end up fleeing into the night?"

He snorted. "More than likely, the skull was stolen from somewhere, or else someone bought it on the black market. Or maybe they just found it in their own backyard. But no matter where it came from, it's illegal to own any Native American remains. That's probably why whoever had it hid it up here."

Realization abruptly hit, and I gave a triumphant

nod. "Wait, that's it! That's why he wanted inside the house so badly. He wants his skull back."

"He? You mean Jack Hill?"

"It's got to be him. We know he's been in the house before while your great-aunt was still alive, doing those so-called repairs. At some point, he must have cut that hole in the closet floor and hidden the skull, planning to retrieve it when he was ready."

Harry considered my words for a moment before he shrugged.

"You might be right. He'd know my aunt wouldn't be climbing up to the tower room to check on things, not at her age. So if he needed a place to hide something valuable and highly illegal—something he needed access to once he had a buyer for it, but he couldn't risk keeping at his own place—what better hiding spot than that?"

By now, I was warming to my theory. Eagerly, I replied, "Exactly. The only problem was that Jack hadn't counted on your great-aunt dying unexpectedly before he could retrieve the skull again. And I screwed up his plan B by buying the house almost the same day it hit the market. He's probably been sweating bullets ever since, praying I never figured out about the secret door."

"And now you've given him the key to your house and plenty of time to look for his skull." Harry's enthusiasm, while not matching mine, had ramped up a bit. "Sure, I'll play spy for you. It'll be worth it to see his face when he finds his hiding spot is empty. And I'll video it all on my phone."

We grinned at each other for a few satisfied moments. Then I glanced back over at the skull and frowned again.

"So what do we do with it?" I asked, "You don't know any tribal elders we could give it to, do you?"

"Not offhand. Besides, we don't one hundred percent know for sure the guy—or, heck, woman—was Native. Our best bet is to give the skull to Connie. She can have an expert examine it, and they'll take care of proper burial, or giving it to a tribe for repatriation."

"Works for me. Let me get something to put our friend in, and we can drive him to the sheriff's office now."

Harry shook his head, his momentary enthusiasm flagging. "What's this *we*? It's your house. Why do I have to tag along on a skull-delivering errand? Besides, last time I talked to Connie, she arrested me."

"Not my problem. And don't forget, you're the one who found the blasted thing," I pointed out. "I'm pretty sure Sheriff Lamb will want a statement from you."

Then, when he still looked unconvinced, I added, "Unless you want me to put our friend back in the hole. We can pretend you never found him and leave him there until Jack comes poking around tomorrow afternoon. Of course, that'll mean you get to sleep with your bony friend in the room with you again tonight."

For emphasis, I did a little woo-wooing and finger wagging to pantomime ghosts fluttering about.

He raised his hands in surrender. "All right, I'm convinced. You go find a box, and I'll carry him downstairs."

I made a quick search for something suitable but not undignified in which to transport McCoy, as I'd unofficially dubbed the skull. (Okay, so you'd have to be a *Star Trek* fan to appreciate the reference.) I decided on a vintage-style hatbox I had tucked under my bed. I'd bought it a while back intending to store winter caps and gloves, until it had occurred to me that I'd probably need something a little more mothproof. And so it had been sitting empty in the interim.

Harry gave me a doubtful look when he saw the blue-and-silver-striped round box with glittery silver strings that did dual duty, keeping the lid attached and serving as a handle. He made no comment, however, as he stuck the skull, towel and all, into it and carried it down the ladder and to the foyer. In the meantime, I grabbed my keys and purse. Leaving Mattie to watch the place, I called a goodbye to the nuns and headed out the kitchen door in the direction of the garage where the Mini was parked.

Unfortunately, I'd forgotten about the bus. Despite Harry's claims to the contrary, the vehicle was taking up far more than its allotted space in the drive.

"You're going to have to move this hunk o' junk out of the way," I flatly told him. "I'm not going to risk a scraped fender trying to get past it."

"Fine. Hold our friend."

Handing off the hatbox to me, Harry popped open the bus door and climbed into the driver's seat. I wasn't overly surprised when he pulled down the sun visor for the keys. He'd removed anything of value from the vehicle already, and no one in their right mind would want to steal the battered behemoth. But rather than starting up when he turned the key in the ignition, the bus made a sluggish *rhwah-rhwah* sound before going silent.

He glanced around and up; then, flipping a rocker switch overhead, he gave me a sheepish look through the open door. "Dead battery. I kind of left the dome light on overnight."

"Great. And at the angle you're at, even if I can get the Mini partway out of the garage, my cables aren't long enough to reach from my battery to yours. I guess we're going to have to call someone to come out and jump it. So we might as well put McCoy somewhere safe for a while."

He didn't immediately reply, but pulled out his phone and scrolled through.

"Here's another idea," he said. "According to the news feed, today's press conference on Bainbridge's murder is starting in about fifteen minutes. We could walk over to the square, catch Connie afterwards, and give her the hatbox."

I sighed. I was getting a bit weary of tromping back and forth to the square in the heat of the day…especially with the media still lurking about. But better to unload the skull sooner rather than later.

"All right, let's do this. But I need to stop back inside for a minute first," I told him as he climbed out of the bus again. "You take our friend here, and I'll meet you on the front porch in five."

My five was actually closer to ten, but Harry was nowhere to be seen when I finally stepped out onto the porch. There was, however, yet another lost tourist hanging by my front gate. This guy was wearing baggy green cargo shorts and a tucked-in white T-shirt that matched his white socks and white running shoes. To further accessorize, he wore a black fanny pack spun around to the front, a backward oversized ball cap, and sunglasses.

And, I noticed with a reluctant grin, he was also dangling a blue-and-silver-striped hatbox from one hand.

"Great minds," I observed as I halted in front of him. I'd opted for a bit of a disguise myself—a floppy brimmed straw sunhat with a tied-on plaid scarf and a pair of oversized Audrey Hepburn–style sunglasses that I'd worn to a costume party once. Just in case Reporter Dave was near the square looking for interview subjects, I didn't want him recognizing me.

Harry grinned a little, too. "Looking good. All right, Ms. Golightly, we've got a press conference to catch and a skull to get rid of."

Oddly pleased that he'd gotten the *Breakfast at Tiffany's* reference, I slung my purse over my shoulder. We set off to the square in companionable silence.

Well, as companionable as we could get, given that he'd previously threatened me with a lawsuit. And given that he'd been arrested for murdering Gregory Bainbridge, and I was only ninety-nine percent sure he hadn't done it. And given that he'd drunk out of my personal Aussie dog mug without asking.

By the time we arrived at the square, Sheriff Lamb had already taken the microphone. I could hear her introductory remarks as I crossed the street and wended my way through the parked cars to the grassy area of the square. Though the crowd was far smaller than the past news conferences—maybe twenty people, including tourists, were gathered in front of the gazebo—I was glad to see that the Penguin Suit Murder hadn't entirely fallen off the media radar.

Playing the role of concerned Cymbeliner, I strolled with Harry toward the gazebo. The sheriff was now explaining that an unnamed suspect had been brought in for questioning the day before but had been released with no charges being filed.

"But that in no way means we're at a dead end in the investigation," she emphasized, her amplified voice sounding tinny but determined over the PA speakers. "We still have several persons of interest to follow up on, and our department is in process of fielding more than nine hundred tips that have come in since the afternoon of the murder."

I wondered if her tips included Mason's missing knife. I wondered, too, if Mason, Becca, and Jack were on that list of persons of interest. Thinking of Jack led to another problem, however. I leaned closer to Harry and murmured, "Should we tell the sheriff about our little sting operation we're planning with Jack, or wait until after you catch him in the act?"

He gave me a pitying look over the top of his sunglasses. "Do you really think she'd go for it if you told her first? Besides, finding whoever killed Bainbridge has got to be higher on Connie's priority list than a skull right now."

"Okay, it sounds like the press conference is winding down. Give me the hatbox. You can wait here if you want, but if she specifically asks to talk to you, I'm blowing your cover."

I waited until the sheriff and her crew had left the gazebo and followed after her, catching up as she neared her squad car. Whipping off my sunglasses so she could see my face, I said, "Sheriff Lamb, it's me, Nina Fleet. I've got something important for you."

The sheriff halted and turned. Unlike before, when

she'd always appeared crisp despite the early summer heat, the woman was looking pretty wilted. Doubtless this media frenzy on top of a tabloid-ready murder was taking a toll on the sheriff.

Still, she managed a polite smile. "I could use a hat like that today," she said with a nod toward my oversized chapeau. "I'm afraid I'm on my way to a meeting, Ms. Fleet. Maybe you can stop by my office later?"

"This really can't wait. Please, just take a look."

Raising the hatbox, I pulled off the lid and let the top dangle as I carefully drew aside the towel.

The sheriff leaned closer for a look. Her eyes abruptly widened as she saw the contents. She straightened and whipped her gaze back to mine.

"Where did you get this?"

"Actually, Harry Westcott found it."

"Why am I not surprised?" she muttered. "So where did Harry find it?"

"In the tower room of my house. To tell the truth, I didn't even realize there was a way up there until Harry showed me. We were cleaning up the room, and he discovered some of the closet floorboards were loose. When he pried them up, he found this hidden underneath."

"It would have been better, Ms. Fleet, if you'd left this where you found it and called us before you removed it."

The expected LEO chastisement. I nodded.

"I know, Sheriff, but you're so busy working on solving Mr. Bainbridge's murder, and frankly it was giving us the creeps, knowing it was there. But I took some pictures with my cell phone before we removed it from the hole. And I remember quite clearly that the dust on the floor was pretty thick when Harry and I first climbed up there. No footprints or anything, so it had to have been hidden for a while."

"No other bones or artifacts with it?" she wanted to know.

I shook my head. "Nothing else. Just the—"

She put a swift, silencing finger to her lips. Apparently, *skull* was a trigger word...at least, when the media were anywhere around. I tried again.

"Nothing else. Just this."

She sighed, and I had an idea of what she was thinking. One more problem on top of all the other problems she had.

"Wrap it back up again, and I'll take it to the station so I can send it off to an expert. But my guess is we're not looking at a crime scene...at least, not that sort of crime. This is probably a relic, and we'll want to track down the person who hid it in your house. We'll talk more once my expert gives me a report."

She took the hatbox from me, then gave me a keen look. "I'll want to talk to Harry, too, since he found the item in question. I don't suppose you know where he is right now, do you?"

Since he was about twenty feet behind her taking pictures of the dwindling press activity on the square—or, at least pretending to do so—I pointed over her shoulder. "He's the one dressed as Joe Tourist with the backward ball cap and fanny pack."

The sheriff looked like she wanted to say a few things that weren't on the official list of sheriff's department–approved public statements. All she said aloud, however, was, "Thanks, Ms. Fleet. I'll have a little chat with him. And someone will get back with you about this."

Indicating the hatbox, she tucked it under her arm and headed in Harry's direction. I busied myself with my own phone, watching surreptitiously while she did her chatting. Only after she'd made her way back to the squad car did I make my way over to where Harry was standing.

"Mission accomplished," I told him. "Did she yell at you too much?"

"Not at all," was his smug response. "Connie thanked me for being a responsible citizen in reporting my find. And now the skull is on his—or her—way to being examined by an expert. So now that's one less thing to worry about. Unless the skull mysteriously reappears in the closet tonight."

"It does, and you have permission to perform an exorcism, or whatever you need to do," I told him...kidding only a little. "Since we're finished here, I think I'll drop by to see Gemma and Daniel for a bit. Maybe you can head back to the house and make arrangements for someone to jump-start that hunk of junk for you."

"I take it that's not a hint. Fine, I'm out of here."

Leaving him to sulk his way home again, I crossed the street over to Peaches and Java. I purposely hadn't invited Harry to join me. Not because I didn't want his company—okay, that *was* one reason—but because I wanted to finish off my list that I'd started that morning.

Sister Mary George was near the top of the suspect list, second only to the mysterious Lana. And while I really didn't think a nun could have done something so heinous, I couldn't forget her juvenile conviction...that, and her obvious enmity when it came to Gregory Bainbridge. I couldn't quite bring myself to ask the nun outright if she'd done the deed, but maybe Gemma could relieve my mind, one way or the other.

TWENTY-ONE

THE COFFEE SHOP was busier than I'd expected at this hour, but things were definitely winding down. Gemma was working on a takeout order for a customer. She spotted me and gave me the *wait a sec* raised finger. I waited while she bade the customer a cheery goodbye. Then I ordered an iced latte—as much to counter the heat as to be polite. Once I had cup in hand, she gestured me over to a corner table to sit.

"What's with the hat?" was her first question. Not waiting for my reply, she jumped to another subject.

"It's crazy, but Greg Bainbridge has been a better neighbor to us dead than he ever was when he was alive. Seriously, our breakfast and lunch receipts have been double since the press came to town."

"I suspect a lot of shops in town are reaping the bounty," I agreed once I'd pulled off the offending hat and taken a big swig of the chilly coffee. "Maybe that's why they're expecting a crowd at the Rosary service on Friday night."

Since Gemma hadn't yet heard about that, I gave her what details I knew. "I'm tempted to go myself," I added. "I've never been inside a convent before, and there's something pretty intriguing about a vintage Tudor Revival."

"Sure, you'd enjoy a tour. But I think that's a hard pass for me and Daniel."

"Right, bells and smells," I replied with a smile, echoing the expression she'd used a few days earlier. Then, reminding myself why I'd stopped by, I sobered.

"So, speaking about the convent..."

I trailed off, trying to decide how best to broach the subject. As far as I knew, there wasn't an official protocol detailing ways to gently inquire of a friend if her relative by marriage might be a murderer. And so I opted for bluntness.

"Look, Gemma, I've got to talk to you about something that isn't easy. I suppose Daniel already told you about the sheriff arresting Harry for Bainbridge's murder yesterday, and then letting him go a few hours later?"

"Yeah, he did." Gemma paused and gave me a keen look. "And Jasmine mentioned that she saw that beat-up old bus of Harry's parked in your driveway this morning. Is that what you want to talk about?"

"Well, it's related."

Skirting around the Lana situation and totally leaving out the part about the skull, I told her how the sheriff had been enforcing the overnight parking regulation and that I'd let Harry move his bus into my driveway. That, and the fact that he had offered to show me the secret door to the tower room if I'd let him stay there until he made other arrangements.

"But don't worry," I added. "He's paying me for the week."

Gemma let out a laugh. "Well, he sure got you good, girl. If you'd have asked me, I could've showed you how to get up to that room. Remember, I told you I used to babysit for that boy when he was young. So is this what you're all worried about?"

"No. I mean, I'm not thrilled, but I've got something in writing. Besides, he gets along great with the nuns. I'm sure if I have any problem with him, they'll step in and roust him out of there, if need be. But that's not my question."

I hesitated, then forged on. "Gemma, do you think it's possible that one of the nuns might have been responsible for Bainbridge's murder?"

She stared at me for a long moment before finally giving her graying locks a disbelieving shake. "You're joking, right?"

Then, when I shook my own not-yet-gray-but-probably-would-be-after-all-this head, she snorted.

"Don't tell me, is this Harry's harebrained theory? It must be, because it's totally out in left field. Can you honestly picture any of those old nuns skulking around in an alley with a knife going after the man. Oh, wait…"

She gave me another look…this one harder.

"You're thinking it's Laverna, aren't you? What, because she got into trouble when she was a teenager?"

"It's not just that." Though hearing the words said out loud, I understood Gemma's upset. "I'm not supposed to say anything, so please don't repeat it, even to Daniel. You see, Laverna—Sister Mary George—told me yesterday that they'd all be heading to Atlanta in a few days for their new assignment. But only she and Mother Superior know that the sisters are going to be split up and sent to different convents after they get there."

"Split up? But those old ladies have been together most of their lives!"

"Exactly. And the thing is, Sister Mary George knew this was the plan even before they left the convent."

I set down my coffee and leaned closer.

"Gemma, I promise I'm not trying to insult you or your family. It's just that I can't stop thinking about how furious she was at Bainbridge for letting it happen…not for herself, but for the other nuns. I know she's a wonderful woman, and I truly admire her, but I'm afraid that maybe she ran into him that day in the alley and just snapped."

Gemma sank back in her chair, her expression momentarily dismayed. No doubt she was picturing the scene in her head, just as I'd done when I saw the nun going after that innocent apple with her paring knife. And Gemma would likely be thinking the same thing that I had…that even the best of us could go momentarily unhinged, given the right circumstances.

Then, seeming to rally, she straightened again.

"No, she didn't do it. Not just because she wouldn't do it, but because it doesn't make sense. For one thing, where would she have gotten the knife? And for another, even if she did have the knife, what are the chances she would have run across Greg in that alley the exact minute he happened to be there, just in time to kill him?"

I frowned and reached for my latte again as I considered her argument. The knife, I could build a case for. It might have come from the convent, or even from my own kitchen, since the drawers there still held a jumble of Mrs. Lathrop's silverware and serving pieces. And it would be easy enough to conceal the blade in the voluminous folds of her nun's habit.

But as for the timetable, Gemma had a point. The only reason the nuns had taken a break at that particular moment right before the murder was because Sister Mary Paul had gotten overheated. Even had Sister Mary George premeditated her plan to kill the developer, timing would have made all the difference. Sooner, and Gregory wouldn't have yet been in the alley. Later, and he would already have been across the square in his borrowed penguin costume, well out of stabbing range.

"You're right," I concluded, smiling as I allowed myself a small whoosh of relief. "The timing's off. Besides, whoever did it had to have been there right on the spot following Gregory around until he got into that penguin suit. And I'm sure Sheriff Lamb would have followed up if she couldn't account for which nuns were where, and when."

"Good. So that means you're going to drop this nonsense right now?"

"Consider it dropped," I agreed, feeling a bit chastened by her tone, which—not surprisingly, since I'd all but called her sister-in-law a killer—was still rather sharp. Hoping to clear the air, I changed the subject.

"Since the sisters are going to be with me at least through Sunday morning, can I take another look at the catering menu? I think it's time to shake up breakfast a little."

After a few minutes' companionable discussion, we agreed on egg puff pastries instead of quiche and fruit- and bacon-stuffed French toast instead of muffins, though we kept the usual peach cobbler. By now it

was almost closing time for the coffee shop, so I made
my goodbyes and pulled on the hat again, then headed
out across the square toward home.

I was only a block away from the house when I spied
it.

The *it* was a low-slung red convertible driven by
a brown-haired woman. Nothing particularly odd in
that. Except that, even at a distance, I could see what
appeared to be a brightly inked armband tattoo on this
driver's bare arm.

And, more importantly, she appeared to be steering
her little red car in my direction.

I froze there on the street corner as the speeding convertible rushed toward me. One voice in my head was
yelling, *Jump out of the way!* while a competing voice
was shouting, *Get out your phone and take a picture
of her license plate!* Meanwhile, a third voice—the one
I actually listened to—was busy reassuring me, *Don't
act crazy; she doesn't even know it's you, not with that
hat on.*

Sure enough, the driver didn't glance my way as she
abruptly rounded the corner without bothering to signal
and then sped on down the side street.

I stood there a moment staring after the car, trying to
decide if that really *had* been Lana behind the wheel. In
the end, I'd not had a close enough look at the woman's
face to say that for sure. Even the tattoo I thought I'd seen
could have been some sort of jewelry instead.

And then a disturbing thought hit me. Maybe she
had tracked down Harry to my place, where she'd over-
powered him and stuffed him into the small trunk of

that vehicle. Maybe now she was driving off with him for parts unknown…and for reasons better left unsaid.

What was it Gemma had said about harebrained theories? Still, I hurried that final block to the house.

Mattie greeted me at the door, not seeming the least concerned about my absence. Hanging my hat on the hall tree, I gave the pup a relieved hug and a scratch behind the ears as I called up the stairs, "Harry, are you here?"

He didn't answer, but I didn't panic. Not yet. The Aussie hadn't appeared agitated, which surely she would have been had the actor been sprawled somewhere with a knife in him. She wasn't pawing at the door to indicate something was wrong outside, either.

I peeked into the parlor to see the nuns gathered there for their usual afternoon Rosary, the murmur of repeated prayer drifting into the hallway. No Harry hiding within their ranks.

So the next step was trying to track him down by phone.

I'd actually saved his number from a couple of months back, when he'd been threatening me by phone about the house. I'd filed it under CRAZY MAN, so when I saw that name pop up I would know to avoid answering. I gave the number a try now, only for it to go to voicemail after a single ring.

"Okay, you can worry a little now," I said aloud. And then I heard the outside kitchen door open and close.

Mattie let loose with one of her patented hellhound howls and went bounding in that direction. I rushed after her, telling myself it wasn't a crazed murderer breaking in, that Harry likely had been outside checking on his bus. Sure enough, I reached the kitchen just in time to see the dog make a dramatic leap straight into Harry's arms.

"Oof!" was his response as he staggered, not so much at the weight but at the way he'd been thrown off balance. Regaining his footing, he juggled her like an oversized soccer ball and managed a "Good girl" before he set her down again.

"Where the hell have you been?" were the first reflexive words out of my mouth, even though the answer was pretty obvious.

Harry apparently agreed, for he raised a brow. "If I recall our last conversation on the square, you told me to get back here and find someone to jump-start the bus. Which I did, and which I'm in process of doing."

"Sorry, you're right. It's just that I had a little shock on the way home that I thought you should know about."

I gave him a quick rundown of what I'd seen. His skeptical look once I'd finished made me realize that, much like with Gemma and my suspicions about Sister Mary George, I probably was making too much of a minor incident.

That is, until I recalled Harry's story about the time at an Austin motel when he'd been accosted by Lana wearing little besides a knife tucked into a garter. What if she was the one who'd shoplifted that missing knife from Mason's store? Maybe she *was* driving around town in search of Harry's bus…and, ultimately, Harry.

Before I could offer up that theory, however, he replied, "The bus is pretty hard to see from the street, so unless she pulls into every driveway in town, there's a good chance she won't find me again…at least, not right away. Not that I don't appreciate your concern for my well-being."

"Actually, my concern is for the sisters. Last thing I want is some crazy woman hurting one of them while she's looking for you."

"Those nuns are tough. I'd be more concerned about Lana getting hurt."

I was trying to decide if he was serious or not about any of this when his cell phone abruptly rang. He glanced at the phone's screen and said, "It's the auto club guy. Got to take it."

Since the nuns would be occupied a while longer with their prayers, I spent the next hour doing what I'd dubbed *B&B biz*. First on the to-do list was advertising. And so I spent the hour scrolling through a few competitors' websites looking for ideas on business cards and fliers and cute little promotional items like soap and shampoo with my not-yet-designed logo printed on them, making notes and saving links to reference back to later.

Midway through the process, Mattie jumped up and started barking, which likely meant the auto club guy had arrived. At the end of the hour, I checked in with the sisters. They'd finished their prayers and were gathered around Sister Mary George, who was on her cell phone.

"Chinese food night," Mother Superior reminded me in a stage whisper, her expression uncharacteristically excited. "May we order something for you? Our treat, of course."

Still feeling the calories from my morning ice cream indulgence, I settled on an order of spring rolls. Then, leaving the nuns to their ordering, I went to check on Harry's progress.

I found him in the kitchen leaning against the counter drinking tea from a generic mug and looking rather pleased with himself.

"We got the bus running," he explained, "and I switched it so that it's backed in. That way, I could park closer to the edge of the driveway so you have more room. Plus, now it's harder to see the bus from the street."

"Good thinking," I agreed. Maybe he'd taken my possible sighting of Lana more seriously than he'd let on.

Then, glancing at his watch, he added, "Say, do you know if the sisters have called in that Chinese food order yet? I want to change my order from General Tso's Chicken to Moo Goo Gai Pan."

TWENTY-TWO

THE NEXT MORNING, the sisters were up even earlier than usual for their morning prayers. I'd barely had time to shower and pull on jeans and an oversized white cotton knit top before they had gathered in the dining room.

Jasmine arrived at seven with breakfast, accompanied again by her red-haired boyfriend. Once the pair had brought everything in and then headed back to the coffee shop on their bikes, Mother Superior took me aside.

"Nina, no need to go to all the trouble of setting a lovely table this morning. The mayor will be here at eight to drive us out to the convent. So we shall, as they say, be eating and running. But perhaps we can take some leftovers with us for our luncheon? I'm sure with all the cleaning and straightening that we'll have an appetite."

"Certainly, Reverend Mother. And I've got a soft-sided cooler you can use. Why don't I ice down some bottles of water and soda for you?"

While I took care of the drinks, the nuns made quick work of breakfast. In preparation for their day back at the convent, they were wearing their shorter gray work habits. Their excitement level was high as well. Anticipation at returning to their old home, I wondered with a smile, or maybe just a residual MSG high from last night's Chinese takeout feast?

Recalling my promise to Harry, I put aside a full plate for the two of us and then helped Sister Mary Christopher pack the rest of the food for travel. We were gathered on the front porch ready for action when Melissa Jane and her oversized gray SUV rolling up to the front gate at eight sharp.

"Morning, Reverend Mother... Sisters. Oh, and you, too, Nina," she greeted us from the open front passenger's side window as we marched down the walk toward her.

By the time we reached the vehicle, Melissa Jane—dressed today in a perky green-and-white-striped skirted suit—had climbed out and slid open the cargo door. I helped her load nuns and food safely inside. Then, as she closed the door, she reminded me, "The electricity and water are still on at the convent, but there's no phone service. Sister Mary George has a cell phone, so they have a way to call if they need anything before five when I pick them up again. But just in case I'm with a client, maybe you can keep your phone handy?"

"Of course," I assured her.

"Perfect. You have a great day, you hear?"

She paused as she opened the door and added, "Oh, and Nina...about that bus in your driveway. I don't know where you found it, but the town does have an ordinance about commercial vehicles being parked in residential neighborhoods longer than overnight. I'll look the other way for now, but as soon as someone complains, you're going to need to move it."

"Gotcha!" I agreed with an equally cheery nod.

I waved the group off and headed back inside, letting the fake cheery act drop. So much for the heap not being visible from the street. On the bright side, it was good of Melissa Jane to let me off the hook as far as the ordinance. But the fact that she'd noticed it meant that if Lana really was trolling the streets searching for Harry, she was bound to spy the telltale bus sooner or later.

For the moment, however, I was more concerned with our little sting operation with Jack later today. I let Mattie out and had my share of the saved breakfast. Harry still hadn't dragged himself downstairs by the time I finished, so I washed my plate and then went in search of him…which meant going upstairs and yelling up the ladder stairs.

"Harry! Rise and shine! Pat the pine! Daylight's burning," I called, drawing on the old chestnuts my dad had used to roust my siblings and me out of bed when we were kids. Then, in case that wasn't sufficient, I added, "I saved you some breakfast…cobbler and egg puffs."

That last seemed to work, for I heard some thumps and shuffling. Then Harry peered over the railing. I pretended not to notice that he was shirtless and showing off a nicely tanned chest and toned abs. With those sleepy blue eyes, he looked a bit too much like a rumpled Ralph Lauren model for comfort.

"I thought guests were exempted from being rousted out of bed at ungodly hours," he complained in a huskier-than-usual voice.

I shrugged. "It's after eight. You were up earlier than that yesterday. Besides, we need to work out how we're going to do our spy operation with Jack."

I could have reminded him of our agreement that

he was a renter and not a guest, but we both knew that was the case.

"Fine," he replied. "Give me fifteen minutes to take a shower, and I'll be downstairs."

He was downstairs in the agreed-upon quarter hour, wearing jeans and an orange-and-white Hawaiian-print shirt with the logo of a well-known surf shop discreetly embroidered on its pocket. He grabbed the plate I'd left on the stovetop warmer element. Not bothering with the dining room, he leaned against the kitchen island and began chowing down.

"We're going to have to get an easier system for calling up to the tower room," I told him. "Maybe I can find an old bell pull and install it for you."

"Sure," he mumbled through a mouthful of egg puff, "or you could try that newfangled thing known as the smartphone and just call me to say you want to come up. So, what's the plan for this afternoon? I'm assuming all you care about is if he goes looking in the tower room closet, right?"

I nodded. "Why don't we do a test run? You find yourself a hiding place up there, and I'll poke around in the closet and see if I if notice you spying on me."

A few minutes later, Harry had finished breakfast and gone back upstairs. I gave him a few minutes' head start while I hand-washed the remaining dishes, and then followed.

He'd closed the tower room door so that it faded seamlessly into the rest of the hall paneling, just as we'd leave it for Jack. I opened it and tugged the light cord. Once upstairs, I looked around.

Harry had pulled the curtains so the place was bathed

in dim light. Since the curtains were sheer, it was obvious he wasn't hiding behind them. Which meant he had to be in the closet, though of course Jack would have no reason to suspect that.

I opened the closet door, steeling myself in case Harry decided to prank me and jump out with a blood-curdling yell. He didn't, though I saw he'd rearranged the hanging clothes so that shirts were front and center, leaving the closet floor conveniently exposed. Trying to play it like Jack likely would, I parted the row of shirts down the middle and shoved them to either side, revealing the blank wall behind and a shoe-covered floor. I knelt and moved the shoes away from the removable section, glancing side to side as I did so. Still no Harry.

"So," I said aloud, and stuck a finger into the knot-hole, "I wonder if that creepy old skull I hid here is still where I left it. Let me check."

I pulled up the section of flooring, confirmed the space below was still empty, and settled the floorboards back into place. Then, moving shoes and hanging shirts back where they'd been, I backed out into the room again.

"Harry," I called, "I'm finished looking. Where are you?"

"Right here," came a muffled voice.

"Wait, what?"

I reached back inside the closet again and began shoving aside clothes. Nothing on the one side, but on the opposite I struck pay dirt.

"Pretty clever," I said in unfeigned admiration.

Harry had changed into an oversized flannel shirt and baggy jeans and then positioned himself sideways behind a section of hanging clothes. The apparel in question had been arranged to put both a shirt and long pants on a single hanger, resulting in what looked like a series of flattened scarecrows dangling from the clothes rod. Standing behind them, Harry blended right in.

He extricated himself and rejoined me in the room, holding out his cell phone. "I took a video of you. Let's see how it turned out."

Despite being in the closet, there was enough ambient light that I could make out a figure that obviously was me kneeling and opening the secret hiding place. And my voice was more than recognizable, too. While it might not stand up in a court of law, chances were any video would be sufficient to produce a confession.

"Perfect," I told him. "I'll set up the key behind the screen door and take off a little before two. Do you think an hour is enough time to give him?"

"An hour should be plenty. I'm guessing first thing he'll do is head for the closet. Once he sees the skull is missing, I'm betting he's right back out the door again."

Unspoken was a different scenario…the one with Jack discovering Harry hiding in the closet recording the incriminating video, and the resulting unpleasantness. But given that I hadn't spotted Harry, chances were the ice cream shop owner wouldn't either. Besides, Harry could take care of himself. Hadn't his bio said he had a black belt in some martial art or another?

I spent the remainder of the morning working on my B&B business plan. First on the list was arm-twisting Melissa Jane into adding me to the Chamber's website's list of links. And maybe I could convince some of the town's other B&B owners to do a little co-op advertising, too.

Busy as I was with this, it was well after one when I finally broke for a quick lunch—more egg puffs—and then rounded up Mattie.

"Key's set," I called up the ladder stairs to Harry, who'd been hanging in his room doing whatever it was that he did in his spare time. "It's almost two, so be listening for Jack."

I got a careless "Yeah, yeah, under control" drifting down from the tower room. Crossing virtual fingers that no one would screw up, I whistled for Mattie and went out the kitchen door. I loaded her into the Mini, and we squeezed out of the drive without incident.

"Let's go to the pet store," I told the pup, giving her a reassuring look in the rearview mirror before I steered us to the south side of town toward the mall.

The next hour passed with excruciating slowness. While I cruised the pet store aisle for a new doggy bandana to keep up the grooming ruse, I kept my phone handy so I didn't miss any communication from Harry. Good news: the screen remained blank with no frantic calls for help. Bad news: said blank screen didn't let me know what in the heck was going on.

By the time an hour passed, I was already in the Mini prepared to head back when a text from the actor popped up.

All clear.

"A little more detail would have been nice," I muttered to the Aussie, who gave a soft woof of agreement. Not that she objected to this unexpected afternoon out, particularly since it had resulted in a slider, meat and cheese only, on the way to the mall. That in addition to her new bright-red bandana.

K was my equally brief text back. Much as I wanted to call and pull more information out of the guy, I didn't want to risk it in case Jack was still in the house and might hear the ring.

Breaking only a couple of Cymbeline's speed-limit laws on the way back, I pulled into my drive about fifteen minutes later. No strange cars were parked in front, which meant Jack must have already left. And I found my door key propped between screen and front door, just like I'd instructed him to leave it. Even so, I let Mattie precede me into the house, in case her howling and jumping skills were needed.

I found Harry in the kitchen in the process of making tea. He'd changed out of the lumberjack shirt and pants and was back in the same Hawaiian shirt and jeans from that morning.

"Well?" I demanded.

Harry shrugged. "Nada. Zip. Zilch. Not only did Jack not dig through the closet looking for the secret hiding spot, he never even came up to the tower room. I could hear him moving around downstairs, opening doors and rattling things, but he never tried the panel. I think maybe you were wrong about him being the skull's owner."

"What do you mean, *you*? I thought *we* agreed it had to be Jack."

"Fine. *We* were wrong."

"Great," I muttered, and grabbed a bottle of water out of the fridge. "I can't believe we wasted a couple of hours on this. So we're back to square one. What do we do next?"

After a moment's silence, Harry replied, "You know, whoever put the skull up there could be long gone. Maybe they deliberately forgot about it…or maybe it was one of those *out of sight, out of mind* things. The skull might have lain around there forever if I hadn't twisted your arm into letting me stay up there."

"Well, that's a comforting thought," I said with a snort.

Though, in a way, it was. While I doubted any normal person could forget they had stashed a skull somewhere, I preferred that scenario to worrying someone might decide one day they wanted their skull back. But at least now I knew to turn a questioning eye on anyone who asked to go up there alone.

"All right, let's say we stick a fork in this one," I decided. "Good old McCoy is Sheriff Lamb's problem from here on out."

Barely had I made that decision when my cell phone rang. I took a look at the caller ID. No one's number I recognized, but since it was a local area code, I took the call. "This is Nina."

"Hi, uh, Nina," came a man's vaguely familiar voice. "This is Jack, uh, Jack Hill."

It's Jack, I mouthed in exaggerated fashion, and pointed at the phone. Aloud, I said, "Hi, how's it going? I just got back home. Obviously, it didn't take you that long."

"Don't worry, I gave the place a good looking over. But I wanted to report right back to you. About those things I told you that I let Mrs. Lathrop know needed repairing…"

He hesitated, and I waited for him to quote some absurd price for nonexistent work. Instead he said, "I guess she must have had someone else fix it after I gave her my price, because everything looks fine now. I mean, there are a few things that could be tweaked, but nothing big. So I don't need to write up a quote after all."

"That's great… I mean, for me," I replied.

Apparently, not only was the guy not an antiquities thief, but he was an honest contractor, too. Feeling guilty knowing I'd completely misjudged him, I went on, "But look, Jack, I do have some other projects I'm thinking about having done. Maybe I can drop by next week and talk about it."

"Sure," he replied, though he sounded rather less enthusiastic than I would have expected.

When he didn't say anything further, I prompted him, "So, is that all?"

"Not exactly." He paused again, and I could hear him breathing. Finally, he said, "While I was there, I noticed an old bus parked in your driveway. It belongs to Harry Westcott, doesn't it?"

So much for hidden from the street. I wasn't sure where this was going, but since Jack had established himself as trustworthy, I decided to take a leap of faith.

I glanced over at Harry, who was drinking his tea and looking lost in thought. Taking a few casual steps away from him, I lowered my voice. "Yes, it does. Why?"

"Look, Nina, none of this is my business. You don't know me, and I don't know you. But as a neighbor, I thought I should give you a heads-up. If you're letting Harry stay there at the house…well, you might want to rethink that."

Alarm bells began going off in my head. I took a few more steps away as I asked, "Why, what do you mean?"

"I'm not saying he's dangerous or anything. Well, not as far as I know. It's just that he's a little, well, off. I mean, the first day on the job, he told me—"

He broke off abruptly as I waited in dismay for what he was going to say, only to continue, "Sorry, Jill just walked in. Gotta go. But rethink letting him stay there, you hear?"

Since he was on a cell phone, there wasn't a click and dial tone that followed…just silence. Except for the frustrated voice in my head yelling, *Told you what?*

"Everything okay?"

This from Harry, who had roused from his reverie long enough to notice I wasn't talking anymore. Hoping I could manage half as good a poker face as his, I set my phone on the counter and nodded.

"Yeah, fine. Jack wanted to let me know that your aunt apparently had someone else fix those things he had told me needed fixing. She must have gotten a better price or something."

"Pretty long conversation just to say that."

"Oh, you know. He tossed in a sales pitch for why he'd be the best guy to do the work next time around."

"That's Jack for you." He finished off his tea in a final gulp and gave the mug a quick rinse under the faucet. "Well, I guess that's it. I've got things to do upstairs."

"Right, and I've got more paperwork."

I smiled, hoping that my sudden nervousness wasn't obvious. Just when I'd begun to lower my guard around

Harry, Jack made it seem that I'd been too quick to trust the man.

Of course, until about five minutes ago, Jack had been the one I hadn't trusted.

On the bright side, the sisters would be back in a couple of hours, I reminded myself in relief. Something told me he'd keep any "crazy" in check around them. But more importantly, I wouldn't have to spend the night alone with him.

THE NUNS RETURNED to the house a little after five, looking bedraggled but surprisingly cheerful after a day of prepping the convent for the Rosary service and reception.

"How did the cleanup go?" I asked Sister Mary George as they trooped inside.

"Surprisingly well," she replied. "It was a little more work getting things cleaned up to Reverend Mother's standards than we anticipated, but we managed. And it was good seeing the convent again, even for a few hours."

"And the leftover breakfast food was greatly appreciated," Reverend Mother chimed in, handing over the empty containers. "Though I am a bit embarrassed to admit that I'm more than ready to order in supper. Manual labor gives one an appetite. The sisters took a vote on the way back here, and we settled on Mexican cuisine tonight. Would you like us to call in an order for you, too?"

I glanced down at Mattie, who was dancing about her nun friends and accepting pats and ear scratches. "What do you think, girl? Mexican food tonight?"

When Mattie gave a woof of approval (she was always up for tacos), I smiled and nodded. "Sounds good. I'll take a chili relleno meal for me, and a single beef taco for my fuzzy friend here."

"Oh, and we should ask Mr. Westcott if he wants anything," Sister Mary Christopher decreed.

Since she was the one writing down orders, I merely nodded and indicated the plasticware I held. "I think I'll do a little washing up while we're waiting on supper."

Within an hour, the food arrived. As we began sorting through the orders, Reverend Mother said, "I almost forgot to tell you, Nina, but we will be staying overnight at the convent tomorrow after the Rosary and reception. Even though there will be a catering service, we'll still have some final cleanup to do."

"Sure," I replied, a bit puzzled, "but where will you sleep?"

"The diocese has not yet managed to arrange pickup for all the furnishings and boxes. We'll pull out a few linens and have a cozy place to sleep. Mayor Green has agreed to bring us back here on Saturday morning."

Holding up a foam takeout container, she added, "Sister Mary Julian, I believe you had the extra-cheesy quesadillas?"

The meal was cheerful but more than a little subdued. By eight o'clock the women had concluded their evening prayers and were headed upstairs. Harry had long since retired to the tower room. In fact, he'd been uncharacteristically quiet during the meal, attention focused on the grilled chicken dish he'd ordered.

I was glad he'd kept his distance. Even after doing my usual evening lockdown and retiring to my own room, I couldn't help feeling unsettled. I tried telling myself that Jack was probably just being melodramatic, but those reassurances didn't much help.

Finally, I gave up and went to bed a little before ten—early for me. Despite having Mattie curled up beside me, I slept fitfully, dreaming about buses and skulls and women with knives tucked in their garter belts. And so it was almost with a sense of relief that I jerked awake a little after midnight. Until I realized that what had awakened me was Mattie...and that she was standing on the foot of my bed, with ears at high alert and growling in the direction of the French doors.

TWENTY-THREE

"Shhh," I softly warned the pup as I slid out from under the covers. "We don't want to wake up the sisters."

At least, not until I knew what, if anything, was going on. It was probably nothing, but for the moment I preferred to keep things in stealth mode. Still, something obviously had set Mattie's Aussie senses tingling, which triggered my Nina senses, too.

I reached for my trusty golf club-slash-kneecapper. Times like these were when I missed having a significant other to put in charge of checking out late-night noises while I cowered under the covers. Not that I could remember Cam ever hauling his butt out of a warm bed to check for prowlers. But at least I'd had him as a potential human shield I could use if things ever went sideways.

On the other hand, right now I had Mattie, whose loyalty to me was unquestioned, unlike that of my only other option when it came to potential human shields. And until I knew more, I wasn't going to put it past Harry that he might actually be the target of Mattie's growls.

I patted my leg in a wordless *here, girl* command. Mattie obediently followed as I sidled over to the French doors. I was already dressed for late-night counter-prowling in a pair of dark-gray gym shorts and matching T-shirt that I had on as sleepwear. So not only were all vital lady parts modestly covered, but I could also blend in with the shadows.

Not that I was planning on rushing outside onto the porch for a look around. But maybe I'd take a peek past the curtains.

Holding my breath, I eased the curtain's edge over just enough so I could squint out into the darkness. The problem was, my view from that angle was limited. I could see only a portion of the porch, and a sliver of Mattie's side yard. Hoping my silhouette couldn't be seen from outside, I took a few quick steps to the other side of the door frame, and then lifted the curtain again.

Now my view encompassed part of the front property. Whatever light from the street that might have made its way over the fence and into the yard had been absorbed by the magnolia's sprawling canopy. Same problem with the moonlight, compounded by the fact that there was but a quarter of the moon showing. I gave an involuntary shiver as I clutched my putter more tightly.

And then a large dark shadow slid along the porch edge and disappeared near my front door.

I bit back a gasp and let the curtain drop. No bird or cat had cast that shadow. Definitely human shaped.

Mattie pawed at the curtain, and I could hear a growl building in her throat. Any moment, she would be letting loose with a sharp bark or ten that should serve to scare off any sensible intruder. But what if the prowler came back another evening? Time to nip this in the bud.

Swiftly, I padded over to the desk and picked up my phone. Time, too, to find out for sure if this was Harry outside…or someone else. I pulled up CRAZY MAN under contacts and pressed his number. If he were out there skulking, chances were he wouldn't have his cell phone on him. And so if he answered, that would likely put him in the clear. At least for this round.

Just as I feared that my call would go to voice mail, I heard a groggy voice answer. "This better be important."

"It is," I hissed, still mindful of the sleeping nuns, though I was pretty sure no one beyond the room could hear me. "I saw a shadow move past my French doors. I think there's someone prowling around outside."

I heard a muttered curse in a voice that sounded slightly more awake now. Then he replied, "So call the sheriff's department…or let the dog out. I'm not going out there with Lana still on the loose. For all I know, she saw the bus and she's looking for a way to get into the house and stab me."

I refrained from making chicken-clucking noises. "I'm not asking you to play hero. You've got that three-sixty view up there. All I want is for you to take a look out the window and tell me if you see someone. Remember, we've got a houseful of helpless old nuns here. I don't want them put at risk."

Not that I was too worried about their waking up and confronting an intruder after an exhausting day. When I'd gone to my room earlier, the sound of collective snoring had been quite audible drifting down the main stairway.

"All right, all right."

I could hear breathing and a couple of thuds. Then

it was silent for a moment, until he said in a low voice, "Looks pretty quiet."

"You sure there's no one near the front door? That's where I saw a shadow a minute ago."

"Yeah," he agreed, "but remember, there's a lot of roofline around the tower. Plus that big magnolia up front is blocking half the view. If someone was right up against the porch, I wouldn't be able to see them. Why don't you turn on a few outside lights? If someone's out there, that'll run them off."

"Okay. Stay on the phone while I do it, and tell me if you see anything."

Cell in one hand, I used the putter grip to flip the switch beside the French doors. Light spilled in a satisfying wave onto the porch and across Mattie's area.

"Nothing yet," I heard Harry say.

Moving swiftly, I made it to the front door and turned on that light. Then I cut back down the hallway to the rear door and lit up the brick patio in the back.

"Nothing. Wait…no, that was an owl. Nope, nothing," Harry said in turn, as I illuminated each zone.

Last was the light outside the kitchen, which I knew threw a wide enough beam to light much of the drive and the front of the garage.

"No, nothing—wait!" he said. And then I heard, "Son of a—! My bus is on fire!"

"Fire?" I echoed in confusion, forgetting for a moment to keep my voice down.

Then, snapping into reactive mode, I went on, "There's a fire extinguisher in the pantry. I'm going to grab that. I'll meet you outside. Try not to wake the sisters!"

Not waiting on a reply, I hung up the call and shoved my phone into the waistband of my shorts. Then, leaving the golf club propped against the counter, I rushed to the pantry.

A squat red cylinder with a black hose and nozzle sat on the floor beside a box of plastic garbage bags. The big ABC printed on its label indicated this particular fire extinguisher was good for anything burning... which, I prayed, included buses.

I grabbed the cylinder and hurried toward the kitchen's outside door. There I almost collided with Harry, who'd made it down both the tower room ladder and back stairway in a matter of seconds. I had just enough time to note that he was dressed much like me, in a white T-shirt and gray sweat pants, before he snatched the extinguisher from my hands.

"Don't let Mattie get out," I hissed at him as he started through the door and down the wooden steps. "If there's a fire, she might get hurt."

Blocking the anxious pup from following us, I slipped out the door after him. With the way he'd reparked the bus that afternoon, the passenger side was now facing the house. Harry was already shoving open the bifold entry door when I joined him.

"Is it bad? Should I call 911?" I croaked, panic swiftly constricting my throat.

"Not yet." He raised the extinguisher and freed the hose and nozzle. "Let me see if I can douse it myself first. If that doesn't work, then—"

He halted and abruptly lowered the red cannister.

Confused, I ducked around him for a closer look, and then frowned.

For what Harry had spied from the tower room wasn't an actual fire. Instead, it was the flickering flames from six pillar-style candles in cheap pink glass cylinders. They were arranged in a circle on the floorboard between the driver's seat and the steps leading in. Their lit wicks reflected in the glass holders and in the bus's windows, giving the impression of a full-blown conflagration. Within that small circle lay a picture held down by a heart-shaped pink crystal.

I gasped and took a step back. Rusty-colored drops of what looked suspiciously like blood were splattered on Harry's printed image.

Harry must have noticed that, too, for he grew suddenly still.

"Now that's some seriously creepy stuff," he muttered, except that he used another word for *stuff*. Setting down the fire extinguisher, he pulled out his cell phone and took a couple of pictures.

"Do you think Lana did this?" I wanted to know.

I hadn't yet shaken the suspicions about Harry that my call with Jack that afternoon had triggered. While he appeared legitimately disturbed by this little vignette, it occurred to me that maybe the actor had set up this scene himself, hoping to convince me that he was indeed being pursued by a stalker.

He slanted a look at me.

"Unless there's some voodoo queen running around Cymbeline, I'd say yes. Maybe if I show this to Connie, she'll start taking my stalking claim more seriously."

I leaned in for a better look. The candles appeared recently lit, since only a small amount of melted wax had pooled within the glass holders. That fact did seem to prove Harry's innocence in the stunt. In the time it would have taken him to set the scene, go back inside, and have a whole conversation with me, the candles would have been burned down more than they were.

"You want me to blow out the candles?" I asked when he made no other move toward the disturbing little display. "I know you want the sheriff to see this whole setup, but I'm sure you don't want to leave anything burning overnight."

"Yeah, go ahead. I'll email the photos to Connie. Maybe she can send someone over tomorrow to check for fingerprints and—"

"What in the world is going on here?"

The unexpected voice behind us made us both jump. We whipped about in unison to see an elderly woman with short-cropped gray hair wrapped chin to ankles in a pale-pink bathrobe standing on the kitchen door steps. If not for the oversized glasses that glinted beneath the exterior lights, I wouldn't have recognized Mother Superior.

Tugging her robe more tightly about her spare frame, she marched down the steps and took her own look at the bus. She gasped at the sight of the candles and made a swift sign of the cross. Then, turning back to us, she asked in a stern voice, "I trust, Mr. Westcott, that you are not responsible for this pagan display?"

"Are you freaking kidding me?"

This in an indignant tone; then, apparently remembering he was addressing a nun, he added, "I mean, certainly not, Reverend Mother. There's a very disturbed woman following me around, and I'm pretty sure she set up this whole crazy thing."

"That may be, but we still should dispose of this heresy at once," she proclaimed, and started forward.

"Wait, Reverend Mother." I held out a restraining hand. "I was going to blow out the candles for safety's sake, but we really should leave the display so that the sheriff can send a deputy out in the morning to take a look. Once someone comes out, I promise we'll throw everything in the trash."

The nun didn't look totally convinced; however, she nodded. "I concede your point, Nina. But let us make sure the other sisters don't accidentally see this. I know it would distress them."

"Of course."

I blew out the flames, and Harry closed the bus door on the scene. That done, the three of us walked back into the kitchen.

"Reverend Mother, I'm so sorry we disturbed you with this," I told her as we started for the foyer. "We tried to be as quiet as possible."

"Oh, it's not your fault. I couldn't sleep…not after the call from the diocese that I received this afternoon."

She halted and glanced my way, her glasses reflecting my shadowy image back at me.

"The official order has come from the archbishop. At breakfast I'll let the sisters know the bus will arrive here at noon on Saturday. We will pray the Rosary service for Mr. Bainbridge Friday night at the convent, as we've already scheduled. I'll ask Mayor Green to have us back here Saturday morning early enough for us to finish packing and be on our way at the appointed time."

Left unsaid was, *and then on to our individual final destinations.*

"I'm so sorry," I told her. "Would you like a cup of tea to help you sleep? Harry has this blend called rooibos that's supposed to be good for that."

The nun shook her gray head. "Thank you, my dear, but I'll content myself with prayer. Good night."

I waited until she'd mounted the stairs before turning to Harry.

"Well, this has *not* been the best night ever. I don't know about you, but Mattie and I are going to try to get some sleep. I've got to be up in"—I paused and glanced at my phone's clock—"about five hours so I'm ready when Jasmine brings breakfast."

"Such is the life of an innkeeper."

He gave me an innocent look and added, "Fortunately, I'll be sleeping in. Connie told me she's usually at her desk by eight, so no point in trying her office until then to make my report. But be a dear and save me a bit of breakfast, would you?"

With that, he strolled in the same direction as Mother Superior and disappeared up the stairs.

I muttered a few uncomplimentary things about the man's birth and then looked for Mattie. She was sitting beside the kitchen counter at the spot where her treat jar sat. Smiling despite myself, I walked over to where she waited.

"You were a big help tonight, girl. Here, you deserve a little reward."

I waited while she made quick work of the little crunchy bone-shaped treat and then led her from the kitchen. Tomorrow was going to be a long day, starting with breakfast and ending with the Rosary.

And since I was about to lose my current crop of

guests, it was time to start soliciting new ones. First thing in the morning, I'd stop by Becca Gleason's printing shop and see about getting the promo materials I'd designed printed up.

TWENTY-FOUR

BREAKFAST WAS A somber affair—at least for me. Not only was I feeling the aftereffects of my late-night wandering, but I was sadly anticipating the nuns' departure. Though they'd only been with me a few days, I'd grown more fond of them than I would have guessed. And I knew that once they learned that they'd all be sent in different directions upon arrival in Atlanta, it would break their hearts.

It definitely was breaking mine.

With all this on my mind, I was almost relieved when, once everyone had pretty well stuffed themselves, Mother Superior glanced my way and gave me a nod.

Taking the hint, I abruptly stood. Tone as cheerful as I could manage, I said, "I'll let you sisters finish your coffee while I start clearing and putting up the leftovers."

Juggling both the silverware caddy and the three-tiered cake plate, which still held a few egg puffs, I paused at the kitchen doorway long enough to slide the pocket door closed after me. Before it was completely shut, I heard Reverend Mother say, "Sisters, I've received important news from the archdiocese."

It was only a few minutes later that, through the open kitchen door, I glimpsed the nuns filing soberly out of the dining room and toward the main staircase. None of them was speaking, no doubt because there was nothing to be said. Mattie padded up the steps after them, her shaggy head drooping in doggy sympathy.

Drooping a little myself, I returned to the dining room to finish cleaning. I was surprised to see Mother Superior still seated there, staring into her half-empty coffee cup.

"Oh, I'm sorry," I exclaimed. "Let me come back later."

"No, no," the old woman protested when I started to slide the door shut again. "I needed a moment after telling them."

"How did everyone take the news?"

"They accepted it." She sighed and added, "I stayed up a while longer last night after we talked, praying for a miracle. I'd hoped for a message from the archbishop this morning saying he'd changed his mind. But my prayers were not answered. At least, not yet."

I could only give her a sympathetic shake of my head.

"If there's anything you need from me before you go, please don't hesitate to ask. I'll be heading over to the square in an hour or so. I can pick up anything you might want for the trip."

"Thank you, Nina, but we'll be fine."

At that, Mother Superior rose from her chair. As I watched her walk away, I noticed for the first time signs of the arthritis that Sister Mary George had mentioned—the stiff gait, the almost imperceptible intake of breath as unexpected pain shot through her. No doubt being expelled from their convent home had been a terrible blow to her in particular because of her role as the sisters' leader all these years.

"And it's all your fault, Bainbridge," I muttered.

I saw Harry coming down the stairs at the same time the old nun was headed up. They exchanged good-mornings, and then he strolled into the dining room where I waited.

"Any breakfast left?" he asked, looking far more refreshed with his extra couple hours of sleep than I felt.

I nodded in the direction of the kitchen. "It's already put away, but you can have some if you want to warm it up."

"I guess I can manage." Then, frowning, he lowered his voice—though there was no one around but us—and asked, "Did Mother Superior tell the other sisters yet?"

"You mean about them leaving tomorrow for Atlanta? Yes, she told them right before you came down."

"Oh yeah, right…good to know. Though, actually, I meant, did she tell them about the whole Lana thing from last night?"

Of course, that *would* be his main concern. "No, that whole love spell thing is still your little secret. Did you call Sheriff Lamb to report it yet?"

"Yeah, and she gave me the typical spiel. Don't touch anything, email her the pictures, and she'll send one of her deputies over to take a report."

"Then I trust you'll be sticking around the place until they show up. I've got an errand to run this morning."

It was a little after nine when I departed for the square, mock-ups of my promotional material tucked into a folder beneath my arm. No news vehicles were yet trolling the streets—a positive sign. I entered the print shop a few minutes later to the sound of banging.

An overalls-clad man perched on a tall stepladder

with his back to me. He was hammering away at what I recognized as a French cleat—an angled length of wood molding used to support a heavy shelf hung on the wall. Becca was behind the counter poking away at her computer keyboard. She caught sight of me and smiled.

"Sorry about the noise. We're adding some more display areas," she called to me. Turning to the man on the ladder, she yelled, "Hey, Dad, can you hold up a minute? We've got a customer."

Travis Gleason stopped hammering and turned in his daughter's direction. Spying me, he gave a polite nod. "Hello, Miz Nina. Sorry for all the ruckus."

"No worries, Mr. Gleason... Travis," I assured him as he set his hammer on the topmost ladder step and climbed on down. "I won't be too long."

"Please, take all the time you need," Becca said to me. While her father made his way to the chairs against the far wall that were reserved for clients, she asked, "So what do we have here?"

I spread my papers on the counter.

"These are just concepts, of course...promotional materials for my bed-and-breakfast."

"Sure, I can work with this." Becca gave an approving nod as she sorted through the pages. "It's a nice, clean design, and I love that peach tree logo you chose. Do you have some high-res photos of the B&B that you can send me? You know, shots of the rooms and anything pretty on the grounds."

We talked for a while longer, with Becca making layout suggestions that she guaranteed would add extra pop.

"If you can send me those photos ASAP," she told me, "I'll email you some mock-ups tonight."

"Sure, but no rush on tonight," I told her. "I'll be over at the convent with the sisters."

Then, when she gave me a quizzical look, I explained, "Greg Bainbridge's family asked them to hold a Rosary service for him this evening at seven. There's a reception to follow...you know, wine and cheese. Apparently they're expecting a pretty good crowd."

I heard a snort from the direction of the chairs. I looked over to see Travis shaking his grizzled head. "Guess all the invites went to out-of-towners, 'cause I sure didn't get one."

"Right, Dad, like you would have gone," Becca shot back, her friendly demeanor momentarily dissolving.

The old man shrugged. "Hey, if they're handing out free food, maybe I would. Maybe sneak out a couple of bottles of wine, too. The SOB owes me that much." To me, he said, "So you're gonna get a look at the convent?"

"That's mostly why I'm going," I admitted. "Plus there's going to be a lot of cleanup afterward, so I'll give the sisters a hand. They're already planning to stay the night. I imagine I'll be there pretty late myself."

"Well, be sure you fill up on that food for me," Travis urged.

Thankfully, Becca turned the conversation back to printing. We discussed a few more questions I had, and then I made my goodbyes to the pair. I thought about stopping by to see if Mason had found his missing knife yet, then figured I'd probably see him at the convent for the wake. So I headed home instead.

I arrived there in time to see a sheriff's department car pulling out of my driveway. Up near the garage,

Harry and the full contingent of nuns were gathered near the bus. The latter stood in a circle, heads bowed and praying. Harry stood to one side, looking uncomfortable. He spied me coming up the drive and gave me a pleading look, which I chose to ignore. Instead, I waited patiently until there was a heartfelt group "Amen" and the nuns broke formation to greet me.

"Isn't that something?" Sister Mary Christopher warbled. "I've heard of things like that before, but I've never seen it in real life."

"The devil's work," Sister Mary Paul muttered with a shake of her head.

"Shocking, shocking!" Sister Mary Julian bellowed in agreement. "The person who did this is in strong need of spiritual intersession."

"Which is why we prayed for her, and for Mr. Westcott, who is the target of her unholy attentions," Reverend Mother replied in a dry tone. "Now, Sisters, the excitement is over, so I suggest that we go inside. Since we have a long night ahead of us, and a good three-hour journey tomorrow, we should take the time to finish packing and then get some rest."

That reminder of their pending departure promptly let all of the excitement out of the surrounding air. Looking somber again, they let the elderly nun herd them toward the kitchen door.

I waited until the sisters were safely inside and then glanced Harry's way. "So what did the deputy say?"

"He took some pictures, dusted for prints. Then he suggested maybe leave the display where it is, in case Lana comes back to check on it."

I frowned. "Wait. We're supposed to leave her candles and such there in the bus hoping that she trespasses on my property again?"

"Pretty much. I think the idea is to catch her in the act. The deputy said they'd put out a BOLO"—I knew from the cop shows on television that meant *be on the lookout*—"and step up patrols in the area."

"Right, but what are the chances they'd spot her here on the grounds? The property has a wall around it, and at night half the lawn is in shadow. I'm not real comfortable leaving the place empty tonight while we head off to the convent."

"Then we stay here."

Which was the logical solution. Still, I stared at him for a moment. "But I told Mother Superior I'd be there tonight to help. And be honest…all you want is an excuse to not have to sit through Bainbridge's wake."

I waited for him to make a flip denial, but his expression was serious as he replied, "I admit I wasn't thrilled at the idea of going, but that's not the reason. Bottom line, this thing with Lana has got to stop. If we can catch her in the act tonight, maybe I can finally get a restraining order against her."

And then, as I considered his logic, he added, "Besides, this time it was candles. What if she stops by tonight with all of us gone and decides to light up the house instead?"

Visions of my beautiful Queen Anne burning flashed through my mind, and I couldn't help but gasp. By now I was pretty sure Harry hadn't staged these incidents, which meant this Lana was definitely fixated. Maybe, as he had suggested, even dangerous.

"You're right," I managed, nodding vigorously. "I'll

explain to Mother Superior that we have to stay here tonight. I'm sure she'll understand."

And of course, she did when I went to talk with her a few minutes later. Not that she quite approved of the plan.

"You must take special care, Nina. This woman obviously is not well, and confronting her might go badly. You really should let the authorities handle this."

"Don't worry, Mother Superior. If we see her on the property, I promise we'll call 911."

I left the nuns to their packing. Around noon I put out the morning's leftovers, along with the remaining fajita fixings from the previous night's meal. I deliberately took my own lunch in my room, wanting to give the sisters as much time together as I could. Thus, I spent the rest of the afternoon working on business plans and seasonal room rates and all the unglamorous details associated with running a bed-and-breakfast. It was almost five thirty when Melissa Jane arrived to do shuttle duty from my place to the convent.

"Please give my condolences to Mr. Bainbridge's family," I told Mother Superior as they were loading up in the SUV. "And remember, we'll have a final breakfast in the morning when you return."

I waved them off and then, trailed by Mattie, returned to the front porch. Harry lounged in the Adirondack chair like he was holding court.

"I checked the weather page," he said, holding up his phone. "Sunset is around eight thirty, so we should start keeping watch then."

"That's when I'll shut off all the lights except the front porch, so it looks like no one is home," I agreed.

"There's a good chance if she's in town that she might have heard about the service at the convent. She might think it's safe to come back again tonight."

I glanced around the property, considering. "Why don't you keep watch out of the tower room. I'll alternate between the front-door windows. Keep your phone handy, and whoever sees her first calls the other."

"Sounds like a plan. Uh, you don't happen to have a gun, do you?"

I grinned a little. "Why, because I'm from Texas? Actually, I had a little .357 revolver once, but I gave it away to a friend a few years back so I wouldn't be tempted to use it on good old cheating Cam. So these days my weapon of choice is that steel putter I left in the kitchen last night."

"Perfect. You know what they say about bringing a golf club to a knife fight," was his sardonic reply.

Mattie and I left him lounging on the porch and went back inside. But it was hard to concentrate on anything as we waited for the afternoon to fade into evening. I spent the next hour uploading data to a couple of B&B sites before throwing up figurative hands and spending the rest of the time binge-watching a nineties-era sitcom. Finally, just before sunset, I shut down all the lights inside and out except the small carriage lamp I normally left burning outside beside the front door.

That done, I went upstairs to the tower ladder and called, "Harry, it's half past eight. Are you ready?"

"Do I look ready?"

A black, featureless face abruptly peered over the railing. In the heartbeat it took me to realize it was

Harry wearing some sort of ski mask, I had already embarrassed myself with a reflexive little scream.

"Damn it, you could warn a body," I choked out. "You're supposed to be spying, not planning a bank robbery."

"Which is why I'm wearing this. Otherwise my face is going to be a big old beacon reflected in all those windows up here. I'll call you if I see anything."

"Fine." Still rankled over letting myself be spooked, I hurried downstairs again, Mattie following behind me, aware something was afoot.

I settled in the parlor on a hardback chair behind the heavy concealing drapes of the window looking out onto the porch. I adjusted the curtains so that they were open just enough to give me a view beyond. Then, phone in one hand, golf putter in the other, and Mattie at my feet, I began my watch.

About thirty minutes in, I found myself yawning and wondering what was going on at the convent. The reception should be well under way, maybe even winding down, though likely the family would stay longer than the guests. The cleanup would likely not take that long, assuming the catering people had stuck around to handle the food and drink. If they hadn't, the sisters probably would be packing up the leftovers for the family to take after the Saturday funeral.

Thinking about food reminded me that I'd not had supper tonight. At the usual hour, I'd been feeling too unsettled for an actual meal and had simply grabbed a yogurt from the fridge. But now, with boredom beginning to set in, I was feeling downright peckish. I was debating leaving my post for a quick run to the kitchen when I heard a growl that wasn't coming from my stomach.

Mattie rose from where she'd been sprawled beside my chair and poked her muzzle through the opening between the curtains. On full alert now myself, I squinted through the gap. Sure enough, a shadowy figure was moving up the driveway toward the house.

My phone, which I'd put on silent mode, began vibrating in my hand, Harry's number popping up.

"Someone's out there in the driveway," I answered in a whisper, not bothering with a hello. "Can you see them?"

"That's kind of why I called," came his snide whisper back. "I'm pretty sure it's her, and looks like she's headed right to the bus. I'm coming down."

He hung up before I could make a reply. Sticking my phone into my jeans pocket, I pulled Mattie back from her post.

"Good girl," I told her. "You wait here where it's safe. We'll take care of the crazy lady."

I met Harry at the foot of the stairs. He'd rolled up the ski mask so his face was exposed, basically leaving him wearing a knit cap. His expression was one of grim excitement, and I suspected he was thinking of this as a scene from a movie.

"We should go out the front door," I told him. "We can sneak around the house and catch her inside the bus. Once she's trapped, we can call the sheriff's department."

He nodded his agreement and followed me through the foyer to the front door. We slipped out, with me carefully holding and closing both the wood and screen

doors behind us so they didn't slam. Harry padded down
the steps and melted through the shadows around the
house like he was born to skulk. I followed close on
his heels, feeling equal parts nervous and idiotic as I
clutched my golf club.

The night air was warm and relatively silent save
for the sound of a passing car and a distant neighbor's
air-conditioner compressor kicking on. By the time
we rounded the corner of the house and had a view of
Harry's bus, the figure had pushed open the folding
door and climbed inside.

Sufficient moonlight streamed between house and
fence into the driveway to partially illuminate the area
around the bus. The intruder's shadowy shape inside
the vehicle was visible, though it was impossible to tell
who it was.

I heard an abrupt glassy clatter, followed by a tinkling crash as one of Lana's love candles rolled out of
the bus's open door and landed on the driveway. The
intruder had obviously tripped over the display and sent
the tall glass jar candles tumbling.

But if that was Lana inside, wouldn't she have known
the candles were there, blocking the way?

The same thought must have occurred to Harry, for
he halted and shot me a puzzled look. Leaning closer,
he whispered, "Probably some meth head looking for
something he can pawn. I'm going to run him off."

I nodded, though I wasn't aware of any meth heads
in the neighborhood. But no town was safe from petty
theft and vandalism, not even Cymbeline.

I followed him further down the drive so that we
were almost even now with the bus's front end. I raised

my putter, remembering Harry's comment about golf clubs and knives. I felt evenly matched in that scenario… but not so much if the other person had a gun. Though chances were, if this was just some local lowlife looking for something to steal, they wouldn't be armed.

Chances were.

I felt my heartbeat accelerate even more, while the golf club's leather grip grew damp in my suddenly sweaty palms.

"Hey, you in the bus! Come out where we can see you."

Harry's authoritative voice would have projected all the way to the cheap seats if we'd been in a theater. As it was, the unexpected sound made the shadowy figure swing about.

"We're armed, so don't try anything," Harry called. "Now step on out and keep your hands in the air."

Feeling rather like I was in a bad cop movie— thought the adrenaline rushing through me was all too real—I raised the putter higher. Not that I planned to come out swinging. If the intruder made a run for it, I'd step back and let him go. And I rather doubted that Harry, for all his movie-tough-guy attitude, would chase him down.

Then a reply came from the bus's open door. "All right, hold your horses. I'm coming out."

I recognized the speaker's voice, though in my current rattled state I couldn't quite place it. But when he climbed from the bus and stood in the moonlight, I immediately knew who it was.

TWENTY-FIVE

"Travis Gleason." I gasped in surprise as the old man slowly raised gnarled hands in imitation of every movie bad guy surrendering. He was wearing his usual putty-colored pants and a checkered shirt. But tonight he also had a thin blue cloth windbreaker zipped over the latter.

I lowered the putter and gave him a puzzled look.

"What in the world are you doing here poking around Harry's bus?" Then, realizing the actor might be in the dark as to the man's identity, I added, "Harry, this is Becca Gleason's dad…you know, she's the printer in town."

"And you're Daisy Lathrop's grand-nephew," Travis said with a nod, finishing the introductions before Harry could speak. "Harry Westcott, ain't it? I remember your daddy. Seems I saw you a time or two when you was a young'un, but I didn't know you was living here at the house now."

"He's staying on a temporary basis," I hurried to clarify. "But Travis, what are you doing here?"

"Right, what are you doing here?" Harry echoed, arms folded over his chest and expression suspicious. "It's not exactly neighborly to go poking around in someone's bus in the middle of the night."

The old man's expression turned sheepish. "I can

explain, but do you mind if I put my hands down now? Raising them up is aggravating my bursitis."

"Go ahead," was Harry's ungracious reply, not that I could blame him for being ticked. I wouldn't have been pleased if I'd found the guy searching through my Mini.

Travis lowered his hands and looked my way. "You folks was just kidding about being armed, wasn't you? You don't have a gun, do you, Miz Nina?"

Since he could see full well that I was toting a golf club and not a shotgun, I saw no reason to bluff my way through. "Well, I—"

"She might not have one," Harry crisply interrupted, "but that doesn't mean I don't."

"Now, son, no need to get riled up. I just want to be sure ain't no one is gonna do nothing foolish," the old man replied.

I could tell from his half smile, however, that he didn't believe the actor. I could see why. While Harry might be able to convince a film audience he was a gunslinger, in real life he obviously wasn't the type to be packing anything more dangerous than an extra teabag.

Travis went on, "Well, here's the thing. I wasn't expecting anyone to be here, but I thought I'd better double-check the bus, just in case. Miz Nina, you told me you was gonna be at that Rosary thing for Bainbridge tonight."

"I was, but we had a change of plans. We had a little incident the other night, and I thought it best that I hang around here. But what does that have to do with you?"

Though suddenly I had an unsettling certainty what—or rather, who—Travis was after.

He shrugged. "Let's just say that Miz Lathrop was

holding something for me all these years, and it's time for me to get it back. So why don't we all go inside now?"

"Mr. Gleason—Travis—I don't know what you're talking about," I lied. "How about I give Becca a call and have her pick you up?"

"Well, now, ma'am, I don't think we'll be doing that," he countered, and unzipped the pale-blue windbreaker he was wearing.

It wasn't cool enough even after dark to require a jacket. Not unless you had thinner blood than normal… or were trying to conceal something. Travis deliberately let the jacket fall open, and I immediately saw that his sartorial choice fit into the second category. For the moonlight was reflecting off a black, semiautomatic pistol shoved into the waistband of his baggy permanent-press pants.

Travis rested one gnarled hand on the butt of the weapon.

"I'm sorry, Miz Nina. You're a nice lady, and I hate to do this to you, but I ain't got no choice. Now, first off, I want you to toss that putter of yours across the driveway."

I did as he asked, and he nodded. "Now your phones. Set them on the ground, and then step back ten paces."

Once we'd complied, he bent and retrieved both cells. Harry twitched visibly as his phone disappeared into the man's pocket.

"Uh, Mr. Gleason, I really need that phone for work," he said. "I don't suppose you might consider returning it once you've gotten whatever you want from us?"

"Now, son, don't you fret," the old man reassured him. "I know these things are expensive, so I ain't gonna smash 'em up. I'll make sure I leave them somewhere you can find them again later. Now, let's go on inside."

"Sure, inside," I told Travis, not quite believing this was happening, "but we have to go in through the front door. All the other doors are locked."

And the foyer was also where I'd left Mattie. The Aussie would sense the danger and be on the old man the instant I opened the door. And surely in the confusion, Harry—or, more likely, I—could wrestle the gun away from Travis and put an end to this craziness.

But Travis M. Gleason wasn't anyone's fool. As we climbed the front porch steps, he said, "Now, Miz Nina, I know you've got that big dog of yours waiting inside. I don't want to have to shoot her, but if she comes charging at me, I will. So here's what we're gonna do. You head inside first and go lock her in a closet or bathroom. Understand?"

I allowed myself a few mental cuss words. Now that there was no element of surprise left, no way would I risk Mattie's safety by letting her play attack dog. Gleason's eyes visible beneath the glowing porch light held a hard look of determination. I had no doubt he'd shoot her if she attacked, and I'd never forgive myself if she was hurt.

"And while you're locking her up," he added, "you might be tempted to take a little detour and make a phone call on your landline, but don't bother. I cut the lines first thing when I got here. Oh, and your Internet cable, too."

Which meant no email summoning for help. *One of the disadvantages of being home-invaded by a profes-*

sional handyman, I thought in dismay. *They know where the bodies—and the phone lines—are.*

Convinced now that the only way out of this situation would be by complying, I eased open the front door. Mattie burst out barking as she came bounding toward me. I managed to grab her, and with a bit of wrangling led the protesting canine to the powder bath off the hall.

"Good girl, good girl," I reassured her as I shut her in. "Take my word on this one. Sit and stay, and I'll let you back out as soon as I can."

Trying not to picture the damage the dog might do to my bathroom door if she really wanted out, I rushed back to the front porch. Harry entered, followed by the gun-toting Travis. Neither man looked particularly pleased. And I could hear Mattie woofing from her bathroom prison, letting us know she was pretty ticked, too.

"Go ahead and turn on a couple of lights," Travis directed. "No point in us falling over things in the dark."

"So where are we going, Travis?" I asked as I flipped the light switch. "The parlor is always comfortable."

"Now, Miz Nina, you know this ain't no social call. We're going upstairs."

As we made our way up the steps, I recalled how Travis had been surprised and then concerned when I'd mentioned I was making the tower room habitable again. At the time, I'd chalked it up to his being overly cautious. Obviously, he'd had another reason he'd wanted to keep me out of there.

Still, if the relic was what he sought, why was he going through all the skullduggery—pun definitely intended— to recover it? I'd already offered him work in the tower room. That would have given him a perfect opportunity to retrieve the skull without anyone being the wiser (had Harry and I not already removed it, of course). And yet, for some reason, the old man had felt compelled to threaten us at gunpoint to recover it.

I wasn't looking forward to seeing the old man's reaction when he found out he'd taken this criminal chance for nothing.

After a slow climb punctuated by gasping and coughing on Travis's part, we reached the second-floor landing. I turned on the hall light. "Where to next?"

"We're headed to the tower room."

"I don't think there's much up there that you'd be interested in. Harry and I already cleaned the place up and rearranged all the furniture. We didn't find any bags of money or anything."

The old man gave a grim little smile. "It's not treasure I'm looking for. It's an insurance policy."

We halted at the wall panel that opened to the tower room. Since there wasn't any point in pretending we didn't know how to access it, Harry twisted the piece of trim. The hidden door popped open, and he reached inside to pull the light chain. "All yours, Mr. Gleason."

There was an awkward pause as the old man examined the ladderlike steps leading upward. I could guess what he was thinking. At his age, and with his breathing problems, he'd be hard-pressed to make the ascent. And even if he could manage that feat, he couldn't climb while also holding on to his pistol.

But Travis apparently had a plan B.

"All right, folks," he told us. "This next part is going to take a bit of cooperation. I've treated you fair so far, so I'm expecting the same outta you. Young fella," he addressed Harry, "I'm going to need you to go up there and find that insurance policy I told you about, and bring it back down to me."

"Right," Harry replied. "So you're talking about an envelope full of papers or something?"

Travis gave his head a disgusted shake.

"That was a figure of speech, son. Now here's what you do. There's a closet up there in that tower room. Open it and get down on your knees. You're looking for a knothole in the wood that goes all the way through. Stick your finger in it, and a section of floorboards will come up, like a lid."

He paused and reached into his windbreaker pocket, pulling out a folded cloth. "Now, what you find inside, I want you to put it in this bag and bring it back to me. All this should take you maybe a minute. Once you do that, I'll walk out of this house, and you won't ever see me again."

"Got it," Harry agreed. "But how will I know if I'm bringing you the right thing?"

"You'll know."

Taking the bag, Harry started the climb. Travis, meanwhile, gestured me back into the hallway. "Sit down if you like, Miz Nina," he told me.

I shook my head. "I'm fine. Like you said, it shouldn't take more than a minute."

And then Harry's voice drifted down to us. "It's going to take more than a minute. I forgot I piled a bunch of boxes and stuff in the closet. I've got to clear it all out so I can get to the floorboards."

"Well, then quit yakking and get to work," Travis called back up to him. "We don't got all night."

In the meantime, I changed my mind about sitting and settled onto the floor, stretching out my legs. Obviously, Harry was bluffing to gain time. At some point, however, he'd have to quit stalling and tell Travis the hole was empty. From there, it was on Travis.

But for now, I needed to know the why of the situation.

"None of this was necessary, you know," I told him. "You could have retrieved your mysterious insurance policy when you did the handyman work for me, and I wouldn't have been wiser. Heck, the other day you could have told me you'd stored something there back when Mrs. Lathrop was alive, and I would have told you to come get it. So why the gun?"

"I told you, Miz Nina, we have a situation. I'm leaving town tonight, just as soon as I get my, um, thing. There wasn't time to do this the nice way."

An old retired guy fleeing town in the middle of the night. There had to be more to the story than just a pilfered skull.

"But what about your daughter?" I persisted. "Does Becca know about this?"

"She'll find out once she gets the letter I'm mailing her." He heaved a sigh. "She's the reason I'm going. I—I couldn't bear to stay here and see the disappointment in her face when it all comes out."

"So what in the heck did you do, Travis?" I demanded, though an uncomfortable suspicion was taking hold. "Tell me. Maybe it's not as bad as you think."

"Got it," Harry called before the old man could answer me. "I'm headed back down."

Since there wasn't an *it* for him to get anymore, that

announcement took me by surprise. I scrambled to my feet. Harry obviously had something up his thespian sleeve.

He made his way swiftly down the ladder stairs, holding Travis's cloth bag, which he'd closed with a single knot. To my shock, I could see a decidedly skull-shaped lump beneath the cloth.

The old man sagged in obvious relief as he reached for his prize.

"Here you go," Harry told him. "But you might want to wait until you're alone before you open it. You know," he finished, with an exaggerated nod of his head in my direction.

The translation being, *Don't want to upset the lady with something so gruesome.*

Being decidedly old-school, Travis immediately agreed.

"It's not something you really should see, Miz Nina," he assured me. To Harry, he said, "Thank you, young fellow. Now, how about we head downstairs again, so I can leave you nice folks in peace."

The descent was faster than the climb, likely because Travis's spirits were lighter. What his connection with the relic was, or why he had to have it now, I wasn't certain. But I didn't want to be around when he opened the bag and found whatever Harry had stuck in there instead of the skull.

No one spoke until we reached the partially lit foyer. At that point, Travis tucked the gun back into his waist-band and zipped up his windbreaker again, then gave us a crooked smile.

"Well, folks, this is it. I'm sorry for disturbing your

night, but maybe we can part friends. Hope your B&B makes a go of it, Miz Nina."

"About our phones?" Harry reminded him as the old man reached for the front doorknob.

Travis nodded. "I'll leave them down the street on the curb. This is a nice little town, so I don't think anyone will steal them before you have a chance to pick them up."

"We appreciate that. Good luck, Travis," I told him, surprised to find myself meaning it.

I was standing in front of the closed powder bath door, hand casually on the knob. With the pistol no longer in play, I was debating setting Mattie free to stop him from leaving when a car screeched to a halt in the driveway.

Travis shot me an accusing look. "You didn't tell me you was expecting visitors."

"I'm not," I protested, equally surprised. "Harry?"

But before he could reply, the front door flung open. Backlit like vengeful angels in the high beams of an unfamiliar blue sedan backing out of the drive were Mother Superior and Sister Mary George.

And that's when I twisted the knob beneath my hand and yanked open the powder room door.

With a bloodcurdling bay, Mattie burst from her prison. Startled, the old man looked up in time to see forty pounds of black, white, and gray Australian shepherd launch in his direction. She hit him midchest, knocking the breath from him in an exaggerated *oomph*.

Unlike Harry, Travis didn't have the strength or reflexes to play goalie to a canine soccer ball. And so he fell over backward, hitting the wooden floor with an audible thud. The cloth bag he held went tumbling as well.

Harry swooped in and retrieved the pistol from Travis's waistband; then, after a moment's seeming indecision, he stuck it on the top shelf of a nearby bookshelf for safekeeping. Mattie, meanwhile, remained crouched atop Travis's chest, her nose almost touching his.

The two sisters surveyed the scene with typical nun-like aplomb.

"Nina," Mother Superior coolly addressed me, the foyer light glinting off her oversized glasses, "is something wrong?"

At a momentary loss to explain what was going on, I stared from Travis to the nuns. When I could summon my voice again, what burst from me was, "Whose car was that? How in the world did you get back here?"

"Uber," was Mother Superior's succinct reply as she closed the door behind them.

Sister Mary George nodded and pulled her cell phone from her habit. "I have the app."

"But you were all supposed to stay at the convent tonight. What made you decide to come back?"

"Reverend Mother was concerned after the situation with that young woman threatening Harry," the younger nun explained. "She tried calling earlier and got an out-of-service message, so she insisted on checking on you."

"Travis cut the phone and Internet lines," I explained. "Plus he took our cell phones. So Reverend Mother was right. We definitely needed a little divine assistance tonight."

The older nun gave a crisp nod. "I will not stoop to saying *I told you so.* And now, I believe Mary George should call 911."

TWENTY-SIX

WHILE SISTER MARY GEORGE made the call, I rushed to the kitchen for one of Mattie's leashes and then coaxed the Aussie off her prey. Clipping the leash to her collar, I tied her to the stairway's newel post so that she could watch the human activity but not interfere. Then, more than a bit concerned, I went back to check on Travis's condition.

Mother Superior was already kneeling beside him, examining him for injuries. In a plaintive voice, the old man muttered, "My skull, my skull."

For a few frightening moments, I feared he'd done worse than a simple bump on the head. Visions of lawsuits flashed through my mind, and I prayed my B&B insurance policy covered criminals injured in the commission of their crimes.

"I asked the dispatcher to send an ambulance, too, just in case," Sister Mary George assured us as she tucked away her phone. "Someone his age, you can't be too careful."

Harry, however, was faster on the uptake than I.

"Your skull? You mean this?" he asked, retrieving the bag Travis had dropped when Mattie bowled him over.

"Yes, yes," the man choked out, struggling free of the nun and dragging himself into a seated position against the foyer wall. "Let me have it!"

Mother Superior gave a little head shake that I interpreted to mean he wasn't going to suffer any further injury. She took the hand Sister Mary George proffered and stood.

Feeling more than a bit responsible for his situation, I remained beside Travis while Harry shook the bag containing the ersatz skull. I heard something inside shifting about, the telltale sound signaling obvious irreparable damage to the piece. With a flourish, Harry poured the bag's contents onto the floor beside the old man, who frantically picked up one broken piece and then another.

Of course, the shards didn't belong to anyone's skull, let alone the one Travis had once hidden in the tower room closet. The giveaway, had it not already been blatantly obvious, was the yellow glaze on each broken piece.

"Candy dish," Harry confirmed as I recalled where I'd seen that bright color before. "It was the only thing I could find on short notice up there that was about the right size and weight."

"So where's my skull?" Travis demanded with a cough. "You had to of seen it, or you wouldn't know what you were supposed to find."

"Harry found it the other day," I explained. "Don't worry, the skull is safe with the Cymbeline sheriff's department now. I'm sure they'd appreciate any information you can give them to help establish its provenance. Though I'm pretty sure you won't get it back."

"It don't matter anymore," the old man muttered, letting the pottery shard he held drop to his lap. "That was my insurance policy. I coulda sold it for enough to move to Tahiti…but it's too late now to cash it in."

As he spoke, I could hear the faint sound of emergency vehicle sirens growing louder. Mattie gave a sympathetic howl in return.

Leaving Harry to keep an eye on Travis, I scrambled to my feet and went to the front door. As I opened it, I could see red and blue lights flashing at my gate before two sheriff's department vehicles followed by an EMT truck slid into the driveway.

The lights remained flashing while paramedics wrestled a gurney from the emergency vehicle's rear doors. Deputies Mullins and Jackson piled out of one car, followed by Sheriff Lamb from the second. The trio didn't wait on the EMTs but rushed up the front steps. I pointed them in Travis's direction.

Deputy Jackson squatted beside the man and gave him a quick once-over, though by then the paramedics were rolling the stretcher filled with portable equipment through the front door.

While they checked out Travis, Harry directed Mullins to the pistol he'd confiscated and I gave Sheriff Lamb a brief rundown of the night's events.

"That explains a few things." She glanced over at Travis, who was hooked up to various machines. "Does he need to be transported?" she asked the female EMT.

The paramedic nodded. "We'll run him by the ER to make sure he's okay. Just a precaution because of his age."

Lamb waited while they lowered the gurney and moved the old man onto it. But when they raised the gurney again, she put out a restraining hand. "My deputy will need to go along for the ride."

And, then to my surprise, she pulled a set of handcuffs from her belt.

I stared from her to Travis, who looked very old and beaten. "Is all this really necessary? I mean, he might be in trouble about the skull, but what happened tonight was pretty much a misunderstanding. I know Mr. Gleason didn't have any intention of hurting us. I don't want to press charges…and Harry doesn't, either."

I looked over at the actor, who nodded. "What she said."

The sheriff shook her head. "I'm afraid it's not up to you. There's more going on with Mr. Gleason than what happened here tonight."

My earlier suspicion returned, full blown. And so I was dismayed but not overly surprised when the sheriff fastened a cuff on one of his wrists and then clamped the other to the gurney railing.

"Travis Gleason, you're under arrest for the murder of Gregory Bainbridge."

"BELIEVE IT OR NOT, the skull is what set everything into motion," I explained.

It was eight o'clock Saturday morning, and the sisters, Harry, and I were sharing a final breakfast from Peaches and Java. Four of us—me, Harry, Mother Superior, and Sister Mary George—looked more than a bit bedraggled following the evening's excitement.

It had been a long night. After giving our statements to Sheriff Lamb, we'd stayed up late comparing notes and theories. Fortunately, Harry had convinced the sheriff to return our cell phones that Travis had taken before the EMTs rolled the old man out, since we were minus landline and Internet service. Around midnight the sheriff gave me a call—a courtesy heads-up to let me know that Travis had confessed to Bainbridge's murder.

Mother Superior and Sister Mary George had stayed the night at the house. As for the other sisters, they had heard nothing about the arrest until Melissa Jane picked them up for the ride back to the B&B. Being the mayor, she'd already had the scoop on Travis Gleason.

"I'd stick around to chat," Melissa Jane had excitedly told me as she idled at the curb waiting for the nuns to exit her SUV, "but we have a news conference at nine am sharp to announce that the Penguin Suit Murder is officially solved!"

Still, she'd taken a moment to whisper a few bits of what probably was confidential information regarding Travis's confession. And I had eagerly listened.

Now, I unabashedly shared that gossip.

"The mayor told me that Travis said he'd found the skull a few years ago while he was doing handyman work at the convent. He was reconstructing a dilapidated well house, and he literally dug it up while he was putting in a new foundation."

"I remember that," Sister Mary Christopher exclaimed, earning nods from the rest of the sisters. "We were worried that the goats might wander into that shack and get hurt, so we had it fixed. But I never heard anything about a skull!"

"Travis knew if he reported his find, the sheriff's department would investigate. If it was a recent death, they'd declare the area a crime scene. If it turned out the skull was older, maybe Native American, the state would send in people to do a dig. But either way, he'd lose the skull."

"But why keep it?" Sister Mary George asked with a frown. "I mean, there's such a thing as having respect for ancestors, even if they aren't your own."

"He told us it was his insurance policy."

This from Harry, who was wearing the same T-shirt and sweat pants as the night before.

Downing a fortifying swallow of tea, he went on, "I had a little chat with Connie last night after the rest of you went to bed. She was pretty tight-lipped about the murder, but she did tell me that Gleason's original idea was to use the skull against Gregory Bainbridge. You know, revenge for cheating him and the others out of their homes when he built Southbridge."

I rolled my eyes. "What, he was going to go all *Poltergeist* and claim Bainbridge was building on sacred Native burial grounds?"

"Close. Bainbridge had been waiting years for the convent lease to expire so he could break ground on the golf community. Gleason told him that if he tried to move forward, he'd tell the state where he'd found the skull and get them to shut Bainbridge down. Because it turns out there are all sorts of prehistoric sites in Georgia. We're talking a couple of thousand years old…some twice that. Apparently, Gleason had an expert confirm the skull was a true relic, which probably means there's an old burial mound on the convent property."

"You're kidding." I hadn't heard this part of the story. "You mean I was carrying around the head of someone who'd died back around the time of Christ? That's unbelievable."

Harry shrugged. "That's pretty much what Bainbridge told him. He figured Gleason was scamming him, and without the skull as proof, he refused to be intimidated. And just to be a bigger jerk about it, Bainbridge was in the process of buying the building on the square where Gleason's daughter has her printing shop. He said if Gleason tried to blackmail him with the skull, he'd evict Becca."

"Shameful," Sister Mary Julian bellowed.

Sister Mary Thomas nodded. "It is. But I still don't understand how Mr. Bainbridge ended up in the penguin suit."

"That's the easy part," I assured her, recalling how I'd offered the same explanation to Sheriff Lamb. "The day before you sisters checked in, Bainbridge stopped by for a visit. He told me that he was so unpopular with everyone in town that he'd started wearing disguises. According to the statement from Travis, he caught Bainbridge taking a shortcut through the Taste-Tee-Freeze, and he watched Bainbridge put on the costume. Travis followed him out into the alley, and that's when things went…well, bad."

Harry added, "That was when Jill locked me in the walk-in freezer."

"You mean Jill Hill?" I asked in surprise. "I thought she was the one who let you out. Are you saying she's the one who trapped you in there in the first place?"

He nodded. "She finally admitted all this to Connie. The day Bainbridge was murdered, she'd been pushing Jack harder than usual. You know, deliberately flirting with me, and then making fun of him for taking it. He finally snapped, and she was afraid he was going to do something drastic. So when she saw me come back into the shop, instead of giving me a heads-up like any rational person would do, she decided to hide me in the freezer until her husband cooled down."

"Uh, she does realize you could have died in there, doesn't she?" I asked, unsure whether to be amused or appalled.

Harry shrugged. "Who knows. But that's not the worst of it. You want to know why Connie dragged me in for some one-on-one questioning the other day? Turns out she got an anonymous tip that someone had seen me arguing with Bainbridge right before the murder."

"Don't tell me. Jill again?"

He nodded. "Turns out she'd made the whole thing up because she was afraid that Jack stabbed Bainbridge, thinking he was me. She was trying to divert suspicion off him by throwing me under the bus."

Conversation petered out after that, until Mother Superior finally pushed back from the table.

"Sisters, the bus from the archdiocese will arrive at noon. We should go upstairs to finish our packing. Nina, perhaps we can prevail upon you a final time to wrap the leftovers for us?"

"Of course, Reverend Mother."

While they returned upstairs, I squared away the remaining food, then grabbed my cell and called my phone and Internet provider, invoking Melissa Jane's name to get a promise of a repair guy by Sunday. Of Harry, I saw no sign.

The one positive note was a text that popped up mid-morning from Mason Denman.

Hey Nina. Got ur # from Jack. Wanted u 2 know I found that knife in a Roseville vase. Tourists!

A second message followed. BTW heard about Travis Gleason. Come by the shop next week and tell all!

It was ten minutes to noon when the nuns came downstairs again, dragging their rolling bags behind them. All six wore composed expressions, although more than one of the women sported suspiciously red eyes. They assembled at the front door, lined up like the first time I'd met them from shortest to tallest. Harry and Matilda rounded out the somber gathering.

"I've had a call from the driver," Mother Superior said. "His ETA is approximately two minutes. I suggest that we walk to the front gate and wait there."

I gave Sister Mary George the breakfast leftovers, then handed a reusable grocery bag that I'd filled with half a dozen bottles of chilled water to Sister Mary Christopher. "And here's something to drink."

Both women smiled their thanks, Mary Christopher's lips trembling noticeably. By the time we reached the front gate, a big three-row van was pulling up along the curb. Harry helped the driver load the luggage while the sisters gathered around me for a final goodbye.

"You were the best first guests I could ever have," I told them as we exchanged hugs. "Please, let me know when you're settled somewhere."

"We will, we will," the nuns agreed as, the farewells made, they began loading into the van. Sister Mary

Thomas paused long enough to give Mattie a final hug, not caring when the pup left a scattering of gray-and-white fur on the woman's black habit.

"Thank you again, Nina," Sister Mary George said as we exchanged a final embrace before she took her seat in the van. "It has been a pleasure to know you."

That left Mother Superior standing alone on the curb. The old woman smiled, glasses flashing in the sunlight.

"Thank you for all you've done for us, my child. I'll pray for you and for the success of your business. I believe we promised you five stars on TripAdvisor."

She held out her hand, and we solemnly shook before Harry helped her into the van. And then the vehicle was pulling away, Mary Christopher and Mary Thomas waving frantically from the back window while Harry and I waved back and Mattie yipped her farewells.

"Well, that's that," I told Harry as they turned a corner and vanished from our sight. "My first official B&B guests have come and gone.

"And no," I lied as we started back up the walk, Mattie trotting ahead, "I'm not crying."

"Correction. You're not crying yet."

Since that was all too true, I didn't bother replying. I'd already cleaned the kitchen, so I decided to tackle the guest rooms next. I wasn't much surprised to find that the sisters had stripped the beds and neatly folded the used sheets. As for the bathrooms, the glass and tile literally gleamed. All I'd have to do was bring in new towels and linens and the place would be ready for more guests.

With Mattie supervising, I hauled everything down to the laundry room and started a wash. That accomplished, I headed to the kitchen for some bottled water and all but barreled into Harry. An overstuffed duffle bag hung over one shoulder, while both arms juggled a stack of lidded boxes.

"Mind getting the door?" he asked.

"Sure." Then, curious, I told Mattie to stay and followed him outside.

"What's going on?" I asked as he opened the bus's back door and loaded duffle and boxes inside. "You look like you're packing to leave."

"I am."

"But you paid for a full week."

He set the last box inside and straightened, then gave me a triumphant grin.

"So give me a credit on my account. I got a call from my agent right after breakfast. You know that pilot I shot last year in Mexico? She called to tell me that it just sold to one of the cable networks. Filming for Season One of *John Cover, Undercover* starts in Baja in one week. Once I'm finished packing, I'm heading west."

"That's fantastic news. I promise I'll watch the show. I'm really happy for you, Harry."

"Thanks. And that solves the problem of my stalker, too. I'll be halfway to California before Lana knows I left town."

Lana. I'd almost forgotten about her. "So, do you think she's still waiting on the love spell to work?"

"Actually, that why Connie called me last night. While the EMTs were loading Travis into the ambulance, the deputies spotted a woman matching Lana's description lurking around the front gate. She took off before anyone could question her, but at least now she's on the sheriff department's radar."

He gave an exaggerated shiver, as if shaking off the woman's presence. "No time to chat. There's still more to load."

I followed him back inside. I really *was* happy for Harry. Starring in an actual series on television—even on a minor network—was huge. And if the series took off, surely he could afford to buy his own place...hopefully far from Cymbeline.

So why was I swept by sudden regret at the realization that Harry was leaving town?

"Snap out of it," I scolded myself. What I needed was to start advertising for new B&B guests in earnest. Though something told me I might need a new printing company, since I suspected Becca Gleason would be closing shop for a while.

I was leaning against the kitchen counter scrolling through names of local printing services on my cell phone when Harry came strolling back in.

"Well, I guess this is goodbye," he said, giving the Aussie a scratch behind the ears. "I made a last sweep of the tower room. You'll never know I was there."

Smiling, he added, "Do you want the *parting is such sweet sorrow* farewell? Or maybe you're in the mood for *So long, farewell, auf Wiedersehen, good night*, from *The Sound of Music*. Or we can do a little Casablanca. *Here's looking at you, kid.*"

"How about we stick with a good old-fashioned handshake?" I suggested, smiling a little, too.

"Works for me." He stuck out his hand, and we

shook. "Thanks for your hospitality, Nina Fleet. This has been an…interesting stay."

"Interesting," I agreed; then, realizing the handshake had gone on for longer than was strictly necessary, I disengaged my fingers from his grasp. "So, have a safe trip."

I followed him outside, relieved that no press hordes were hanging about the front gate. Hopefully, that meant my name had been kept out of the morning's news conference…would stay out of it, too.

And, hopefully, that also meant the whole penguin theme of the past couple of weeks had officially run its course.

Somewhat to my surprise, the bus started up the first time. Harry had settled in his seat and started to close the door when a thought occurred to me.

"Hey, Harry," I called over the bus's rumble. "I guess you've changed your mind about the lawsuit over the house?"

He quirked a brow.

"Why would you think that? I'll need a place to stay next time I'm back in town. Now that I've got a decent gig, I can afford to pay my lawyer again," he finished, and then slid the bifold door shut.

Great, I thought as I watched him pull out. I had a sneaking suspicion that I wasn't going to be rid of Harry permanently after all. On the bright side, that earlier twinge of regret at his departure had been neatly choked out by the cloud of diesel fumes he'd left behind.

I walked back into the kitchen, where Mattie was waiting patiently for my return. "It's just you and me

again, girl," I told her. "But don't worry, we'll find ourselves some new guests soon."

I grabbed a water from the fridge and started for my
room, Mattie at my heels. I was halfway through the
hall when my cell phone rang.

Ha, what did you forget? I thought, prepared to see
the name CRAZY MAN pop up on my caller ID. He'd
driven maybe a mile and then realized he'd left something behind. And he'd probably expect me to fetch it
and run it out to the gate for him.

But it wasn't Harry. The number showing was local,
however, and so I answered it. "Hello, this is Nina."

"Nina, it's me!" a woman's excited voice said. "Sister Mary George. Can you switch over to Facetime?"

She referred to a phone app that allowed two-way
viewing during a call. I hurriedly made the switch, and
the nun's smiling face popped up on my screen.

"Sister Mary George, it's wonderful to hear from
you," I exclaimed, adding, "But a bit unexpected." Then,
frowning, I asked, "Wait, did the bus break down or
something?"

"Nothing like that." She moved her phone so I could
see a familiar group of women crowding in next to her.

"Hi, Nina!" the nuns called, smiling and waving, before the phone refocused on Sister Mary George's face.

"All right, I'm confused," I said with a laugh.
"What's going on?"

"Oh, Nina, it's such wonderful news. We had just
pulled onto the highway when Reverend Mother got
a call from the archbishop. There's a convent in East
Texas that is part of our order, and the sisters there have
a cheese-making operation similar to ours. But, quite

frankly, while they are spiritually strong, they're not good businesswomen."

"Really?" I asked, feeling a frisson of excitement on the nuns' behalf.

Sister Mary George's videoed smile broadened. "Not only that, but it's a far larger convent with only a handful of sisters to care for it, and their Mother Superior has been forced to retire because of poor health. Because of that, arrangements were made between our two dioceses, and…oh, Nina, all of us have been asked to join them. We're going to Texas to make cheese again!"

"Sister Mary George, that is fabulous. I am so happy for all of you," I exclaimed, tears of happiness welling in my eyes.

She gave a trilling laugh. "We're so excited. And, do you know, this will be the first time any of us has been on an airplane. We have reservations on a flight first thing Monday morning."

"We be cowgirls now!" I heard Sister Mary Paul exclaim in the background, while the other nuns gave a hearty cheer.

I laughed, too. "Talk about divine intervention. I know all of you will be happy there. And next time I visit my family in Dallas, I'll have to make a special trip to see all of you."

"That would be wonderful. Okay, I've got to go now, but we'll be praying for you. I'll call you again after we're settled. Goodbye!"

She pulled back the phone long enough for me to see the other nuns waving again. Even Reverend Mother was grinning broadly, looking a good decade younger than she had that morning. A final chorus of goodbyes rang out, and then Sister Mary George hung up.

Smiling, I looked at Mattie, who'd been listening to the exchange with cocked ears.

"Hey, pup, it's good news, I promise. I'm just crying because I'm happy," I told her, swiping away the tears. "Things are working out for everyone. Harry has his cable TV series, and now the sisters have a new home together. And since these things come in threes, I guess that means we're due for a little success of our own."

As if on cue, my phone chimed as a text message popped up.

Help! it read. My name is Joyce & I'm a friend of Melissa Jane. She told me about yr B&B. I need 2 arrange a last minute bachelorette weekend 4 my BFF & 6 friends. Pls send info.

I looked up from the text and gave Mattie a thoughtful frown. "All right, now that was *too* coincidental. But you know what they say about gift horses. Or is it divine intervention? So what do you think, girl? Are we up to handling a bunch of bridesmaids?"

The Aussie gave herself a shake—which might have been a *yes* or might have been a *no*—and then trotted off in the direction of the bedroom. I followed after her, texting as I went.

Hello Joyce. We would love to assist you with your event. Send me your email address and I will forward you a brochure telling you all about Fleet House. All best, Nina Fleet.

* * * * *

ACKNOWLEDGMENTS

Few books are possible without the support of numerous wonderful folks. Thanks as always to my agent, Josh, and his assistant, Jon, for all their hard work on my behalf. And thanks to Jenny and the other editors at Crooked Lane, who care deeply about putting out a perfect book. Woofs to my own beloved Aussie pups who are now over the bridge: Matilda, who could solve any puzzle, and Oliver, who was the best boy ever. And finally, hugs and kisses for my husband, Gerry, who has always been my number-one fan.